Pride Publishing books by Samantha Cayto

Single Books
One Night in a Dungeon
Man Candy

Alien Slave Masters
The Captain's Pet
The Rebellious Pet
The Untamed Pet
The Captive Pet
The Inconvenient Pet
The Undercover Pet

Alien Blood Wars
Blood Dance
Dangerous Dance
Slave Dance
Star Dance
Mating Dance
Healing Dance
Smoke Dance

Anthologies
His Rules: Safeword
Right Here, Right Now: Never the Groom

Alien Blood Wars

SMOKE DANCE

SAMANTHA CAYTO

Smoke Dance
ISBN # 978-1-83943-833-2
©Copyright Samantha Cayto 2020
Cover Art by Cherith Vaughan ©Copyright January 2020
Interior text design by Claire Siemaszkiewicz
Pride Publishing

This is a work of fiction. All characters, places and events are from the author's imagination and should not be confused with fact. Any resemblance to persons, living or dead, events or places is purely coincidental.

All rights reserved. No part of this publication may be reproduced in any material form, whether by printing, photocopying, scanning or otherwise without the written permission of the publisher, Pride Publishing.

Applications should be addressed in the first instance, in writing, to Pride Publishing. Unauthorised or restricted acts in relation to this publication may result in civil proceedings and/or criminal prosecution.

The author and illustrator have asserted their respective rights under the Copyright Designs and Patents Acts 1988 (as amended) to be identified as the author of this book and illustrator of the artwork.

Published in 2020 by Pride Publishing, United Kingdom.

No part of this book may be reproduced, scanned, or distributed in any printed or electronic form without permission. Please do not participate in or encourage piracy of copyrighted materials in violation of the authors' rights. Purchase only authorised copies.

Pride Publishing is an imprint of Totally Entwined Group Limited.

If you purchased this book without a cover you should be aware that this book is stolen property. It was reported as "unsold and destroyed" to the publisher and neither the author nor the publisher has received any payment for this "stripped book".

SMOKE DANCE

Chapter One

Damien pulled out his double batch of cinnamon rolls and placed the tray on one of the cooling racks on the kitchen counter — right next to the first double batch. He'd learned pretty quickly that when cooking for the Stelalux family, you had to re-define the meaning of 'extra'. He'd never seen any group of men put away so much food in one sitting — or twenty sittings, for that matter. They had an endless capacity to pack away the calories without ever gaining an ounce of fat. It was as if they'd mastered a way to convert sugar into seriously jacked muscles. Working for them was a gay boy's wet dream, for sure.

But that wasn't why he came to the family's personal apartment building most mornings after working all night in the club's kitchen. It had nothing to do with watching drool-worthy men devour his meals with hearty appreciation. He had plenty of that at the club, where the members showed no end of delight at his cooking — and at him, as well. There had never been a time when he hadn't had to politely fend off all kinds of offers. Most of them were thinly veiled attempts at seduction, even though they came wrapped up in job offers to become a personal chef. Many of the members were gorgeous, and they were all rich. But he turned them down. He wasn't going to leave Lux's kitchen any time soon.

It was all about gratitude and his endless need to show his appreciation for what this family had done for him. Emil Stelalux had quite simply saved his life. Damien owed him, big time. The kindly chef had brought him in literally from the cold and had taught him how to make a real living, instead of surviving on his knees in an alley—or, worse somehow, letting a strange man use his body just to have a safe, warm place to sleep for the night and access to soap and water. Being a street rat had seemed his only choice at the time. Emil had shown him otherwise.

So, yeah, putting in the extra hours to prepare breakfast for the family was the least he could do. Knowing that the men and the boys that they'd let into their lives loved sweets, he always baked something to go along with the mountain of eggs and meat that they also craved. This morning he'd prepped veggies and grated cheese for omelets and had a few pounds-worth of apple-smoked bacon to go with it. In a few minutes, the inhabitants of the apartments would wander downstairs looking for food. He was ready for them.

Damien was in the process of pouring himself another cup of coffee when a voice startled him.

"Good morning, Mr. Damien."

Jesus, how does she always manage to sneak up on me?

Sucking on the side of his finger where he'd sloshed coffee, he turned to greet the girl. "Hi, Annika." He plastered a grin on his face, even as he busied himself with sipping his drink.

The girl's gaze homed in on his hand. There was something really freaky about the way she looked at everything intensely — and knowingly, as if she were the master of the universe. Or the mistress more like, since there was nothing she didn't notice. Her bright blue eyes, so different from the others of her family, flicked up at his. He felt an almost irresistible urge to squirm.

"Did you hurt yourself?" As she asked the question, she walked into the kitchen area. She was dressed in a long, white lace nightgown, looking like some Victorian miss. Her bare feet made no sound, even when they hit the tiled floor. The way she walked with such easy grace made it seem as if she were almost floating. The mop of white fluff masquerading as a dog pranced beside her, as always. Its nails click-clacked, breaking the eeriness of its mistress' approach.

Damien cleared his throat to hide his unease. "Um, no. Not really," he amended, because he couldn't quite bring himself to lie to her. It was so freaking weird. She reminded him of his granny, like she would rap his knuckles or something if he dared try to answer with anything but the truth. And this was true, even though she was a tween.

She appeared satisfied with that answer. Her gaze slid from him to the rolls. Her eyes lit up, morphing her into just another kid. "Those smell delicious. May I have one, please?"

He was on surer footing now, serving up his food. "Of course. Why don't you sit and I'll plate one for you." He turned back to the kitchen's island and put his mug down to do just that. "And you want a glass of milk, right? Chocolate, I presume?"

"Yes, please." Annika practically skipped out of the kitchen area and over to one of the high chairs ringing the counter. She hopped up on one with that same ease of movement. The dog, Babette, sat its fluffy butt down by her food dish and looked up at Damien with wet, hopeful eyes. He shook his head at it.

Not a chance, sweetheart. You're the kid's domain.

Damien picked a fat roll from the first batch, because he'd already iced those. Then he pulled out the bottle of chocolate milk and poured a tall glass for her. He handed it all over without a qualm, knowing that her father allowed her to eat anything she wanted at any time. To say that the child was indulged was the understatement of the year. The entire family treated her like a little princess, acting as if the world revolved around her. It wasn't surprising, really. In a family dripping with the heaviest amount of testosterone outside of something like a Navy SEAL team, she was an obvious anomaly. The Stelalux men orbited her like massive dark planets around a blinding sun.

It wasn't merely that the foreign family with their hard-to-place accents and their military bearing was heavy on the Y chromosome. They were all gay, as well. Whatever genetics were involved in sexual orientation, it had completely blown the statistical modeling when scrambling to form the Stelalux men. Forget about arguing over two percent versus ten percent. From what he'd seen, the family was one hundred percent gay and perfectly at ease with the situation. It was one more thing he admired about them. With the whole surrogacy thing still gaining traction, he couldn't imagine what Harry and his husband had gone through to bring their son, Demi, into their lives. At least the boy looked like his parents. Annika was a whole other matter. It seemed impossible that she was related to her Stelalux father by blood. He suspected she was the product of a more typical hetero relationship of Will's dead partner. Either that, or said partner had been the sperm donor.

Not that he'd dare to ask or anything. Regardless, she was astoundingly beautiful, angelic even.

Annika grinned widely at him with icing-sprinkled lips. "This is scrumptious, Mr. Damien. Thank you ever so much."

Jesus, she talked like some character out of a Dickens novel. It left him tongue-tied, feeling the inadequacy of his truncated education. "You're welcome," he murmured, before retreating to the relative safety of his mug of coffee.

He pretended to be busy in the awkward silence that followed. Well, it was awkward for him. He wasn't certain this obviously brilliant and undeniably unusual child ever felt uncomfortable in any situation. She exuded a confidence that few adults could pull off, as if wherever she was and whatever she was doing, it was right and proper because it was *her*.

Then his eye caught the time and he knew that others would be joining them soon. He needed to get the bacon started. No one had asked, let alone demanded, that he add making the family breakfast and some other occasional meals in their new personal quarters to his list of duties. He did it because he liked doing so. Keeping the Lux Club members well-fed was rewarding enough, he supposed. It certainly allowed him to test the range of his skills. There was something almost anonymous about it, though. He rarely got to see them enjoying their food. It had always been the family's appreciation that he'd used to judge himself. Since renovating the adjacent building into a large residential space, they no longer came into his kitchen—well, Emil's kitchen really—so he'd lost that contact. This was his way of maintaining it.

He'd just slid the first tray under the broiler when the sound of footsteps making their way down the staircase leading to the upper floors caught his attention. Damien froze for a second before straightening and grabbing a super-sized mug from the cabinet. He recognized who it was, although how, he couldn't say. There was nothing in particular about the tread of Annika's father that distinguished him from his family members, yet Damien always knew when it was him, nevertheless.

His heartbeat ticked up a notch, which kind of irritated him. He'd sworn off becoming attached to men once he'd come off the streets. He wanted to focus on his profession in order to ensure his future security—*no more dependence on someone forged by sex. Sure, a random from a club for a quick fuck or blow job was fine, but nothing serious. Not yet.* Maybe when he was thirty, he'd start thinking of finding the right man and settling down. But this almost-school-boy crush on the guy was too ridiculous.

Strike the 'almost'.

As he turned to greet the man, coffee in hand, his heart actually skipped a beat. For a moment, he feared he would drop the mug. He saved himself from that ungodly embarrassment by grabbing it with his other hand so that when he held it out, it was as if he were presenting an offering to some cranky deity.

There *was* something god-like about Willem Stelalux. Although he wasn't as tall or wide as his kinsmen, he was definitely bigger than the average man. He dwarfed Damien, that was for sure, and at five-nine, he'd never thought of himself as short. As usual, Will looked as if he'd just rolled out of bed, his black hair falling in tangles past his ears. His fitted T-shirt outlined his impressively broad shoulders and muscled arms, although he was on the leaner side. He didn't have Emil's MMA fighter look—or even the others' *I must break you* vibe—but still, you wouldn't want to get on the guy's wrong side.

He was also different from the rest of the family in the way that you couldn't tell how well-off he was. He didn't share the family's obsession with designer labels. Will's jeans were simply a worn pair of Levi's, not unlike Damien's own denims. Damien didn't think it was a matter of Will being the poor relation, either. Annika was always dressed in obviously expensive clothing. Will was merely more chill in his own choices, Damien supposed.

Will accepted the coffee and smiled. It was the kind of look that would sell a gazillion of anything if plastered onto a billboard. The man was that gorgeous. His daughter's good looks were no great mystery, once you'd met her father, assuming he really was the bio dad. All the Stelalux men were perfect examples of masculine beauty, but Will especially so—at least by Damien's estimation.

"Thanks. Is that bacon I smell?" The man's voice held the same undefined lilt to his perfect English as the others', except it had the power to send a shiver down Damien's spine.

For half a second, his practically adolescent brain basked in Will's attention before he shot over to the oven to catch the bacon so it wouldn't burn. "Thanks for the reminder," he said as he turned the slices over.

"Good morning, Father Willem. You really must try one of these cinnamon rolls."

The way the girl addressed her father was another oddity that Damien didn't dare ask about. It was as if she were addressing a priest or something. It didn't seem like a Stelalux custom, either, given how Demi addressed both his fathers far more informally. Maybe it was a Dutch thing. That's where they'd been living until very recently…in Holland.

Damien shoved the tray back under the broiler and straightened. He nearly jumped back when he realized that Will had come into the kitchen. Only the need to keep a sharp eye on the bacon kept him rooted to the spot as the man sauntered in close to help himself to a roll. He consumed half of it in one bite. Then his eyelids drooped for a moment in obvious appreciation, the look doing funny things to Damien's stomach.

Will washed down his mouthful with some coffee before saying, "Delicious…as always." He gazed at Damien much as his daughter had. His eyes were the same beautiful violet as the other men in his family.

Damien could have stared at the man for hours. Only the presence of the child and the sudden yip of the dog brought him out of the trance he was falling into. He turned back to the stove, but not before seeing Will bite off all except a tiny piece of the rest of the roll. He tossed that bit over to the dog. The fur ball jumped and caught it handily. Damien grinned as he pulled the tray out again. He finished the bacon with a sprinkling of sugar. That wasn't something he'd learned from Emil. He'd seen it on an episode of the sixties' television show *Gomer Pyle*, of all places. It was a big hit with everyone, lending a hint of sweetness to the smoky meat.

He busied himself with the second batch, trying to focus on his job and not on how Will had stayed in the kitchen. The man was leaning against the counter, nursing his coffee as if he had all of the time in the world. It was unnerving, especially because it seemed as if the man's attention was on him.

"Anyone ready for an omelet?" he asked, in an effort to distance himself from the distraction that was Will.

"Thank you, yes," came Will's reply. He shifted his gaze over to his daughter. "What would you like in yours, honey?"

"Everything, if you please."

The answer didn't surprise Damien. Annika's appetite was huge, when you considered that she was a slender child. He supposed she was entering puberty. That stage increased appetites, based on his experience. He wondered idly how the Stelalux men—the owners of a sex club filled with barely legal go-go boys, who were also themselves in relationships with very young men—were going to handle this girl coming into her own sexual awakening. Not well was the safe bet. They were so protective of her that he could only assume they'd form an impenetrable wall for any boy or girl to get past.

None of it was his business anyway. He was there to make breakfast and he had two hungry customers already. The heat from the burner he turned on, added to the emotional warmth created by his distracting guest being in the kitchen, made him uncomfortable. As unprofessional as it was, he took off his whites, carefully folding the jacket and placing it on a shelf. He tossed the cap on top of that and returned to the stove. He thought he felt eyes on him but tried not to think about that. Omelets were easy, so long as you concentrated on your task.

"Is that a new tattoo, Mr. Damien?"

Glancing at his arm, he was reminded that while the image had passed the peeling stage, the skin around it was still shiny. "Yes, it is," he replied as he whisked eggs. He was surprised that the girl knew him well-enough to realize that he'd added ink to his body. That led to the more disturbing thought that maybe the kid was developing a crush on *him*. And wouldn't that ratchet the awkwardness level to somewhere around thirteen, because even an eleven wouldn't do it justice?

"Why do you paint pictures on your body and stick things through your skin?"

Such a direct question caught him off-guard. He hesitated a moment before ladling egg into the omelet pan, wondering what kind of answer he could give that didn't include *'When your family calls you an unnatural freak for years, you develop a perverse desire to make them even crazier.'* Something more like *'It's a fun way of expressing myself'* would do as well and was mostly also true.

Will came to his rescue before he could respond. "Annika, remember please what I've said about personal boundaries and what constitutes rude questions."

Damien was about to say it was fine, that he didn't mind the question—because he really didn't—before it dawned on him that he shouldn't interfere with Will's parenting. He might indulge his daughter more than most, but obviously he'd set some limits. He must be good at it, too, given how generally sweet Annika was.

If she ever had meltdowns, Damien had never been privy to one.

"I beg your pardon, Mr. Damien. I meant no offense."

The apology was so almost tragically formal that Damien changed his mind about the interference. Maybe this was a cultural thing, but really, asking about his ink and piercings hardly ranked as deeply personal or offensive. It was nothing like *'Are you a top or a bottom?'*, which is what his granny had once asked with a twist of accusation on her lips. He'd answered with *'I love the idea of a big cock up my ass'* to perversely piss her off — or piss her off *more* — without really knowing what he wanted. He'd only been a few years older than Annika was, his sexuality had been a raw topic and a bit confusing and, God, all he'd wanted was some understanding. None had been given. Just the fleeting thought of those words coming out of a child's mouth made him wince inside, even though he knew whatever Annika might ask would be out of honest curiosity and perhaps some questioning of her own sexuality.

He slid her omelet onto a plate and added a few strips of bacon. Then he turned to serve it to her, along with utensils and a napkin, a reassuring smile on his face. "No worries. I wasn't bothered by the question." He shrugged. "It's just my style."

As she picked up her fork, she flashed him a grin. "It's very pretty." She daintily worked a piece of omelet into her mouth.

Damien looked at the rather fierce red dragon he'd chosen for his arm and wondered how a child could describe the image as that. He glanced quite involuntarily at her father. The man looked back at him from over the rim of his mug and shrugged. The scene that the three of them presented—hanging in the kitchen on a Sunday morning as Damien cooked and they all chatted—suddenly felt too intimate, as if they were a family or something.

Okay, weird. Damien forced his focus back to the food, dealing with the bacon, starting Will's omelet. This was what he was here to do, feed the family. While he knew that he'd become more of a friend than simply an employee to Emil and perhaps the others, he needed to remember his place.

"I assume you want the works, too?" he asked Will without looking at him.

"Yes, please."

That smooth voice slid right under Damien's skin and made him wonder how much of a good idea coming to help the family in their private space was.

Willem knew he was being just shy of rude leaning against the counter and watching the human cook for him. He simply couldn't bring himself to move. This had been happening more and more since he and Annika had come to stay in Boston. At first, Emil's helper, as Will had thought of the boy, had been merely one of the many humans hovering around the family. Bit by bit, however, Damien had entered Will's field of vision and consciousness with greater force and attraction. Now Will found himself acutely aware any time the guy was in the room—even the freaking building, for that matter. His senses had become that attuned to him.

He'd caught the human's scent while still upstairs. He'd become like a shark, able to detect the presence of minute amounts of the man's unique and delectable smell, even within a highly diluted environment. With each step closer to the first floor, the heady aroma had clung to him, invaded his nostrils and lured him down to the kitchen with a disturbing urgency. This close, the sweet smell took almost his entire attention. It eased his nerves in a surprising way — as did the steady warmth of the boy bridging the few feet between them and giving Will a feeling of comfort that he'd never felt before on this damnable planet, not even when he'd been wrapped in Luuk's arms. The notion bothered him if he dwelled on it, a betrayal of sorts of his dead lover and Annika's father. So too was the way his dick hardened at the mere sight of Damien.

Not that anyone knew this. He was careful to bank his desire, keep his expression open and friendly and not hungry. He'd taken to wearing long, loose shirts to cover his embarrassing reaction. Forget his shipmates... He didn't want his daughter to see. She wasn't a child anymore, and while she hadn't asked him for the particulars as yet, he suspected she already understood the way of their species, as well as that of humans, in the making of young. She seemed to know an awful lot that he hadn't told her. It was thanks to the Internet, in part, he suspected, and Doc MacPhee had spent quite a bit of time with her. That was all to the good. Annika needed females at this stage of her development. Him, not so much.

It was another constant struggle of his, raising a Queen. Back home, he would have already been relegated to a background role in his daughter's life. She would be surrounded by female relatives who would become her court in time. He was never meant to be in the position of seeing her to adulthood. Yet, here he was, against all reason. No, that wasn't entirely true. As Harry would remind him, their species had always found a way to keep going. Given how long they'd been on Earth, coupling with humans, exchanging blood, it had only been a matter of time before the need imbedded deep within their genes would find a way to create a true hive. Lucky him to be the one picked.

It should have been Alex.

Maybe it would be still his captain's destiny to father a girl-child, but Will had been first. And the rapidity with which Annika was maturing guaranteed that she would be the uber-Queen of this world. All others would be lesser. The weight of his responsibility threatened to crush him on a daily basis. Except right now, standing against the counter in the kitchen, sipping coffee while Damien expertly whipped up an omelet, Will felt a little lighter—not so oppressed and rather optimistic about what the future would bring.

A puny whine caught his attention. The ridiculous tiny creature Annika had insisted on getting, her pet, stood on its hind paws, pleading for something to eat. He ignored it this time. Despite his occasional lapse, the deal was that Annika took care of the thing, not Will. The idea of having lesser-evolved creatures live with one for personal amusement wasn't something his species did. Even humans hadn't done it for very long—not in this pampered way, at least. He could see no benefit in doing so, except that it obviously made Annika happy. It was nearly impossible to deny her anything, let alone something that brought her such joy.

"Hey, Babette. Here, girl." Damien slid Will's omelet onto a plate while he held a scrap of bacon up with his other. The dog pranced and yipped in orgasmic enthusiasm until the cook dropped the food. Annika's pet caught the pieces mid-air with an impressive jump of her short legs.

Annika giggled. "Such a naughty thing for you to do, Mr. Damien."

The boy flashed her a grin while he finished filling Will's breakfast order. "I can't help it. Whenever she begs, I tell myself I'm not going to give in, but then I do. She's so cute, and a chef always loves it when his food is appreciated." Damien shrugged, then he held the plate out to Will. "Here you go, sir."

Will could have taken what was offered without ever touching the human. He'd intended to. At the last second, however, he gave into the urge to allow their fingers to collide, briefly and almost impersonally. And yet, a spark shot through him, leaving his whole hand tingling. For a long, drawn-out second, he felt the simple contact providing a strong bodily connection. He could hear a quickening of Damien's heartbeat that matched his own. The guy's pulse thrummed at the base of his neck. Their gazes met in that blink of time and held for what seemed like much longer. Within those greenish eyes, Will could swear he saw a spark of interest.

"Thank you." Will forced the simple pleasantry past his lips and took a step back.

It would be madness to start something with the human. His love for Luuk would wreck any new entanglement. Plus, what with Annika's rapid maturation and the ongoing threat from Dracul's former followers—if not the male himself—the last thing Will needed was to become involved with a human. And this one didn't even know who and what Will really was. There wasn't the time to carefully plan an evolving love affair that could lead to that big, messy reveal. It had taken three years of careful cultivation with Luuk before Will had believed he could bring the man fully into his confidence.

Needing to put physical distance between himself and temptation, Will moved around the dining counter to sit next to his daughter. It helped, as well, that others chose to come down for breakfast at that moment. Alex arrived at the front of the group, his arm wrapped around Quinn, holding him tight. The boy still had his usual well-fucked look that lasted through most of breakfast every day. They were both so obviously happy that it made Will smile to see it. Alex deserved this, after so much time alone on this planet.

Next came Val. His unhurried pace down the staircase was overshadowed by his husband's antics. Mackie had a hard time controlling his enhanced abilities. Val's blood made him stronger and faster than any human. Will could see that the boy loved the change and chafed under the need to rein himself in. Normally Val made sure of it, especially when Damien was around. Not this morning, though. The not-quite-human hopped up on the railing and slid all the way to the bottom. He stuck a landing that would have earned him a gold medal at the Olympics and bounced over to the kitchen.

"Ooh, cinnamon buns," the boy practically squealed. He snatched one and stuffed it nearly whole into his mouth. He made moaning sounds that put Will in mind of other appetites being sated.

He seemingly wasn't the only one to have those thoughts pop into his mind.

Val sauntered over and smacked his husband on the ass. "Bring it down a notch, baby. Annika's going to think eating is hurting you." He did eat a bun in one bite before adding, "Don't you dare take another one until you've had an omelet."

Mackie shot him a mulish look before letting a second treat go. "Yes, Sir."

Will didn't get this relationship of theirs, where Mackie willingly played the role of a slave. From what he'd seen, humans had struggled for most of their history in which some tried to enslave and control others while their quarry fought to remain free. It had taken thousands of years for them to nearly eradicate the practice from their world. And yet, there were those such as Mackie who willingly put the control of their lives with another. At least Val could be trusted to not abuse his power.

The others trickled down, mostly in pairs, although Demi was without his man, Duncan, this morning. Only one other came alone—Alun, a former slave from Dracul's castle. He slinked in, bringing up the rear of the group, making himself as unnoticeable as possible. Will assumed he'd learned do to that with terrible punishment as the teacher. He kept his gaze on the floor, with his long, loose hair hiding most of his face. His hybrid son, Merlin, wasn't with him, which was also typical. The boy spent much of his time upstairs in their suite of rooms, mostly because he was anti-social, but also because he could be disruptive. Alun would hang back and fix plates for them both, after everyone else had been served, then take them upstairs. Harry and Lucien had taken the laboring oar in getting the hybrid to some normalcy—and good luck to them—although he couldn't be trusted yet to play nice in front of someone like Damien. Will figured the boy had been hopelessly ruined by his upbringing in the castle of horrors. The only good sign was that Merlin did respond to Annika's authority. Will had refused to allow her to be used as a curb on the kid's behavior all the time, however, and so far, Alex had conceded to his wishes.

He couldn't help returning his gaze to Damien, who got two pans going to make his omelets even faster. As he steadily ate his own meal, Will watched with admiration as the man served first Alex and Quinn, then Mackie and Val and all the others with admirable speed and dexterity. He only felt slightly guilty about focusing his attention on the human. The kitchen was an open area, after all. He wasn't lurking in a dark corner somewhere, drooling at the thought of sucking the guy's blood. Although, truth be told, it had been a while. His body was getting sluggish, a sure sign that feeding was needed. He would have to raid the family's frozen stash. It wasn't as satisfying as taking a vein directly, but since Luuk's illness and death, it had been his only source of blood.

His gaze homed in on Damien's neck again when he turned to hand a plate to Alun. There it was, the faint and steady pulse. The taste would be amazing, he had no doubt—warm and salty, with a hint of sweetness that was unique to humans. At least, he'd always thought so. His gums itched as his fangs clamored to descend. He had to swallow back a sudden mouthful of saliva. Shit, he was taking the fantasy too far this morning.

Knock it off, asshole. He's not for you. Remember?

A sharp sound took his attention as Mackie dropped his plate on the counter and slammed his hand over his mouth.

Damien whirled around. "What's wrong? Is there something bad in your eggs?"

Mackie shook his head in denial, then mewled behind his hand before turning and racing toward the bathroom. With a muttered curse, Val left his own meal and hurried after him.

Annika watched them go before tuning to Will. "Oh dear, I do hope Mackie isn't sick."

Will exchanged a look with Alex. There wasn't much that he could say, not in front of Damien. He wasn't even sure what he should explain to his daughter, given her in-between-stage development. A good part of him longed to keep her young and innocent as much as possible. It wasn't any of his business, either. Not really.

"He's fine, I'm sure. Finish your breakfast and we'll take Babette for a walk."

Her face lit up at the suggestion. "Oh, she'll love that." She plowed back into her breakfast, so heartbreakingly young and enthusiastic that he fervently wished he could keep her like that forever.

Chapter Two

The cinnamon roll didn't taste quite as good on the way back up. Mackie hugged the toilet bowl of the downstairs bathroom as if it were his lover and retched until his stomach felt like he'd been kicked. God, he hated throwing up more than anything else in the world. He knew it was some peoples' kink but couldn't imagine why. To him, this early morning technicolor yawn was pure torture. He slumped against the wall when it finally ended, too exhausted to even flush. Thankfully, if mortifyingly, Val had followed him in and was there to lend a helping hand.

"Thanks," he muttered, closing his eyes and begging the gremlins plaguing his stomach to leave him in peace. "No offense to Damien, but I think I ate something bad." Although, as he said it, he wasn't sure it was food poisoning. He'd been feeling 'off' for a few days now.

"I don't think so, baby."

Mackie opened his eyelids to slits. Val crouched down in front of him, his beautiful violet eyes filled with concern and sympathy. So many people judged the man by his size and stern expression. They didn't see the side of him that Mackie did. It was on display here and now. The look Val gave him was like a tight, comforting hug. Mackie always felt perfectly safe…and loved.

Mackie tried for a smile. "You think it's like a stomach virus or something?"

Val shook his head even as he stood once more and grabbed a small towel from the rack. He ran the cloth under the faucet, then wrung it out. "No," he said, kneeling now and gently rinsing Mackie's face. The delicious coolness of the towel eased the hotness of his cheeks.

Val's lips thinned in a grimace. "My blood would fight off any of those human illnesses."

When he didn't say anything more, Mackie grabbed his wrist. "What is it, then?" Even as he asked, he already knew the answer. In truth, he'd probably known for days.

"You're breeding." Val's words were loaded with a harshness that Mackie couldn't identify.

His stomach lurched, and he twisted lightning fast to heave up what amounted to no more than bile into the toilet. Val was right with him, making sure that Mackie's hair stayed away from his face, then rubbing slow circles on his back while he trembled.

"I'll be right back," Val said quietly, reassuringly.

Mackie took in deep, slow breaths to convince his stomach that it had done enough partying for the day. Val was back quickly and produced a bottle of water. Mackie took a small sip to swirl around his mouth and spit before Val helped him sit again. He shook his head slowly when Val held the bottle to his lips once more.

Neither of them said anything for long seconds, the only sound in the small room being Mackie's uneasy breathing.

"You think I'm pregnant already?" he finally asked, trying not to sound as freaked out as he was feeling.

Val's expression turned extra grim. "I'm sorry, baby, but yeah, I do. I, uh…recognize the signs."

Of course Val would. Mackie didn't dwell on it much, but he did know that long ago, Val had loved and lost another human boy and his son in the bargain. It was why Val had fought his love for Mackie for so long. The big, bad warrior couldn't bear the idea of losing another lover and child. Yet, he'd come around in the end, needing to love Mackie as much as Mackie needed to love him. Their marriage was rock-solid, and the alien blood that his husband fed him made Mackie feel wonderful.

He'd known the price he would eventually pay for it—the changing of his body into something capable of nurturing and bearing life without completely transforming him into a woman. In the abstract, it hadn't sounded like a bad bargain. He got to live a lot longer and all of it with his husband. Pregnancy and childbirth wouldn't be so bad. Women did it all the time, and with modern medicine and Harry on hand, it could be done safely.

Now that the theoretical had become concrete, he found himself scared out of his mind. "I'm not ready," he confessed in a voice laced with the insecurity he always hid.

Val cupped his cheek and stared down at him. "I won't let anything happen to you."

You won't let me die like Robbie did, you mean. He didn't voice his fear, because he knew how painful Val's past losses were to him. There was, however, a feeling of resentment that tried to rise up in him, much as his breakfast had. It wasn't fair, yet he couldn't help wishing that they'd been more careful about all this. He'd trusted that Val had known what he was talking about.

"You said it would take years for me to change enough for this." Shit, he hated the whininess in his voice. He'd moved on from being a brat.

Val squeezed the plastic bottle in his hand so hard that water spewed out and over it. He ignored it and kept right on staring Mackie in the eye. "Yeah, I did, baby. Obviously, I was wrong. I'll ask Harry, but maybe it has something to do with the drug in your system."

Ah yes. Mackie often forgot about how Dracul's synthesized drug had been slipped by a club member into Mackie's drink. It would have killed him if Val hadn't thought to feed him his blood. It had saved his life and fast-tracked the effects on Mackie's body. Really, they should have realized that it wouldn't stop with increasing his speed and strength. He was as much at fault as anyone for not considering the ramifications. Plus, only he could perceive the changes to his body. That weird sensation deep in his gut was something he shouldn't have ignored.

"Hanging with Annika might be a factor, as well," Val mused.

"Really? I would have thought having the Queen around might have stopped my transition. You don't need to manufacture a female when you've got the real deal." He thought his logic was sound.

Val was already shaking his head, indicating another 'no' before Mackie had finished his thought. "The

Queen's pheromones have a strong impact on hive fertility. She's already in the process of bringing us all together with her in the epicenter. I didn't think I'd ever experience that sense of belonging again."

Val went quiet for a few seconds, his gaze unfocused, an almost wistful look on his face. Then he snapped his attention back to Mackie. "Baby, you know you don't, um…have to go through with this. Harry can take care of it for you."

It took Mackie a moment to understand what Val was saying. When he did, his hand instinctively cupped his still-flat abdomen in a protective gesture. "What are you saying? It's *our* baby. *Our* son. Or maybe it will be a girl, like Annika."

Val was shaking his head again. "Right now, it's only—"

"Our baby," Mackie repeated. "We took vows, Val. And maybe we didn't specifically make promises about children, but I understood that was what I was signing up for. I'm your husband, and giving you children is part of my job."

Val raised his eyebrows. "Your job is running the go-go boys, Mackie. Our BDSM contract doesn't run to my getting to knock you up any time I want."

Mackie pouted. "Poor choice of words on my part. What I meant is that it's my pleasure, my way of showing you my love and devotion. So, we're ahead of schedule? It just caught me off guard, that's all. I want to have this baby," he added, with as much conviction in his tone as he could manage. He swallowed down his fear and doubts, much as he did the bile threatening to escape once more.

"Okay, baby. Don't upset yourself," Val soothed. "It's your choice. Totally. Only, it's going to get rough. If" —

he coughed as if something was stuck in his throat—"if Robbie's experience was anything to go by," he choked out. "You're going to be sick for the next few months. I'm pretty sure Lucien had it just as bad. Hopefully he can give you some tips about what helps. In the meantime," he added, tossing the bottle into the sink, "I know that I can help by feeding you."

So saying, the alien whom Mackie loved and had married without hesitation, let his fangs descend. It was exactly like any vampire movie he'd ever seen, with the gleaming pointed teeth dominating the guy's mouth. The sight of them always made Mackie shudder, and goosebumps popped up over his arms. But it was all positive, a sign of arousal and not fear. His dick came to life and a sweetly torturous thirst claimed his throat. He leaned forward, even as Val scored the inside of his wrist and brought it to Mackie's lips.

The first sip always broke what little control he had. Within a second, he'd fastened his mouth around Val's flesh. He tugged in rhythmic pulls that came naturally to him now, taking the life-giving blood. It slid down his throat, soothing, yet never quite satisfying the burning need there. His stomach quieted almost immediately, and soon he went limp against the wall with his eyes closed. He felt relaxed and energized at the same time.

Too soon, Val tugged free. Mackie couldn't hold back the whimpering protest. Sometimes he wondered if Val didn't control the feeding, would he take and take until there was nothing left for his husband to give? The thought always disturbed him, but he reminded himself that he was Val's slave twenty-four seven. He didn't need to worry about anything. Val was in control. His husband would take care of him. All Mackie had to do was obey.

Oh, and incubate and give birth to a human alien hybrid. *Piece of cake.* Speaking of which... He opened his eyes and said, "I think I'm okay now to eat breakfast."

"No way, baby." Val's tone brooked no argument. He scooped Mackie into his arms effortlessly as he stood. "Let's get you lying on the couch then ask Lucien for advice. Privately, of course, given that Damien is still out there. My guess is that he's going to recommend some ginger ale and saltines until we're sure your stomach has truly settled."

Mackie wrapped his arm around Val's neck and rested his head on his husband's broad shoulder. "I feel fine now."

"Good. Let's make sure it stays that way."

Mackie knew better than to argue the point. And truly, if Val pampered him through the entire pregnancy, would that be so bad? Except something he hadn't considered before suddenly occurred to him.

"Wait," he said before they returned to the kitchen. "How am I going to hide this from the other boys, you know, the ones who don't know, like Damien? They've all seen me naked, so I can't pretend to be a transgender man."

"Sorry, baby. You're going to have to make like Earth women did way back when pregnancy was treated as too private to be seen by others and go into confinement as it advances. No one outside the family will be able to see you, once you start to show."

"Oh, shit, I never thought of that." He was going to have to be essentially locked away for months. Kind of like that brat Merlin. God, if he had only that kid for company… And he and Val couldn't even play, not in any way that Mackie craved, while he was pregnant. "This is going to suck!"

Val stopped out of earshot of the human in the kitchen and glanced down at him. "You can always…"

"Don't say it. I'm going through with this. I'll deal." With the boredom, he meant. But no small part of his brain was trying to raise the threat level to Defcon One over the enormity of what was happening to him.

He snuggled closer to his husband for comfort and strength, rubbing the tag he wore around his neck with thumb and forefinger for extra grounding. It marked him as Val's, and nothing made him feel better than that reminder. He would get through this difficult journey. He'd survived living on the streets and attacks by Dracul's minions. This was nothing compared to that, because in the end he'd have a child to love — and Val's child at that. Besides, with Val looking out for him, he was damn near invincible.

* * * *

From her perch at the counter, Annika watched the warrior, Val, secure his human husband on the big sectional couch in the middle of the large living room. Most everyone was focused on the boy after his obvious distressful time in the bathroom, hovering around and offering him comfort. Mackie was going to have a baby. She'd known for a few days now and was surprised that no one else seemed to have realized it. She pretended ignorance of the fact, as well as other things she knew sometimes, to help her hive adjust to her ascending dominance. Nevertheless, she acquired new perceptions every day. There was a nascent drone burrowed inside Mackie's body, and the idea that she would soon have another hive member pleased her immensely.

She enjoyed seeing her hive acting in concert to help one of its members. It was how it should be. It was really quite interesting the way the humans' behavior approximated her own species. And she did think of herself in those terms. If her human father had contributed to her being, she felt nothing of it. To her way of thinking, the humans were the aliens, not her or the others of her kind. Earth might be a new home for them, but it was exactly that. And it would change for the better. She was the beginning of the process and felt the weight of that obligation more heavily each day.

Babette whined and pawed at her foot. Annika grinned at her pet, delighted as always at its devotion. She broke off a tiny piece of bacon from her plate and said, "Sit pretty." The dog complied immediately, sitting back on her hind legs while lifting up the front ones. How could Annika resist such beseechment?

"Good girl." She dropped the food right into her pet's yawning mouth.

The human who'd provided such a sumptuous meal passed by on his way to the living room area. He held a bottle of some drink and a plate of plain crackers. Annika watched him bring his offering to Mackie. From where he stood with his legs braced and still drinking his coffee, her father tracked the human's movements, as well. It was always thus, since they'd first arrived. Her father wanted Damien with the same ferocity as Babette wanted bacon. Annika found it confusing—not the desire, but rather her father's reticence in the matter. It was not in their nature to be anything other than forthright. Why did he hold himself back?

It was time to ask, she decided on the spot. Some matters should not wait. As Queen, she had a duty to make sure everything within the hive was harmonious. It would be easy to play the little girl and let everyone dote on her, and it had been fun these last few weeks. But there were troubles from the outside that had to be dealt with and the hive could only do so if it were strong.

Hopping off the stool, she went straight to her father. Babette trotted by her side without prompting. Dogs, unlike humans, understood hierarchy and instinctively knew authority. *Such uncomplicated creatures.* As focused as he was on Damien, Willem nevertheless shifted his gaze and his attention to Annika before she even reached him. She was his primary concern, which was exactly as it should be.

Their relationship was changing rapidly, however. He'd always been a solid, loving presence in her life. She'd spent many happy hours wrapped in his arms — protected, educated and entertained by him. She loved him in a way that she would never feel for anyone else. But as much as he'd been both mother and father to her, the time had come for their roles to switch. She was his Queen, and that meant control was shifting to her. Sometimes the enormity of it scared her. It wasn't possible to show it, but she thought perhaps Willem understood it anyway. He was there, solid and steadfast, ready to help her in any way he could.

And she could still hug him and take comfort from his strength and love. When she did so now, wrapping her arms around his waist and pressing her face against his chest, he didn't hesitate to hold her tight and run his hand down the back of her head like he'd always done.

"Mackie is frightened about his condition and Val worries about him," she said quietly, very aware that Damien didn't know who and what they were. It was tedious to hide themselves from the humans. That would change soon, though.

"Yes," Willem replied, equally softly. If he was surprised by her knowledge, he didn't show it. "It's a scary time."

"Were you frightened?" she asked, because it occurred to her for the first time that her existence might have been worrisome to her father.

"A little, but more astonished, really. I hadn't expected it to play out quite the way it did."

Annika could imagine that was true. She knew he fretted over whether he was doing right in raising her. He had nothing in the way of knowledge and experience, after all. "You've done very well," she said, because encouragement was always important. "I'm ever so grateful," she added, because appreciation cost her nothing in her standing and power. Or, if it did, there was no one to tell her that she was doing things the wrong way. She was the Queen. She could make up her own rules, couldn't she?

Willem kissed the top of her head, a familiar gesture of affection. It made her smile and cuddle closer. "Raising you is my greatest honor and pleasure."

"Your job is almost done."

"I'm in no hurry for it to be. Can you not stay my little girl a while longer?"

She smiled at the almost-teasing question and pulled back enough to raise her face to look at him. "Well, I'm happy to have you baby me, if that's what you mean. Cuddles and stories at bedtime are most welcome."

He tapped her nose with his fingertip. "That's good to hear. I haven't used up my full allotment of fatherly instincts yet."

"You could always have another child," she reminded him. "I wouldn't mind a sister, in fact." She slid her gaze over to Damien, who was walking back to the kitchen area.

Willem made a sound deep in the back of his throat that she couldn't quite decipher. His normally strong, steady and comforting heartbeat skipped as the human passed, shooting a quick grin in their direction.

"Mr. Damien is ever so nice, don't you think, Father Willem?" She whispered the questions so that the human couldn't hear.

He made that weird noise again before dropping another kiss on her head and gently disengaging their bodies. "I think, with your permission, I shall go see if I can help Val by checking on the club. He's obviously occupied still with Mackie and someone needs to do a security sweep to make sure there is no trouble."

Annika frowned. "Are you avoiding my question?"

"I am. I'll await your chastisement later when I'm done working." He didn't seem the least perturbed by the idea.

"You promised we'd take Babette for a walk," she reminded him.

"And so we shall, after I help out Val."

Annika wanted to stamp her foot in frustration. Instead, she said, "Very well," and switched her attention over to Babette. Her dog, at least, could always be counted on to do her bidding instantly.

With a furtive bow of his head, her father turned on his heel and left—but not before shooting one last look in Damien's direction.

Honestly, males can be so stupid sometimes.

* * * *

Val forced himself back to his usual routine by mid-morning. Mackie was in good hands, with Quinn and the other boys dancing attendance. He was, in fact, taking a nap on the couch—or at least Val had left him doing so. With the feeding and the human comfort of food and drink, Mackie's stomach had settled enough for him to rest. He'd been more like his old self very quickly. Of course, Val knew that everything was temporary. The next few months were going to be rough on his human husband. The thought of it made Val want to cut his own balls off.

I did this to him. Goddamn, he should have started using condoms. It was supposed to have taken years for Mackie's transformation to finish, not mere months. Except Val knew better than to make assumptions. Everything about his life with Mackie had defied expectations. Maybe none of this had been predictable, but complacency was always a bad thing.

If he dies... No, Val couldn't let himself think in those terms. Mackie was not Robbie, and this was the twenty-first century. Harry knew what he was doing, too. This time, it would be different. He had to believe that, otherwise he'd go mad. And with Dracul potentially still lurking out in the world, ready to pounce, Alex needed Val operating on all cylinders, not curled up in a terrified ball in the corner. He did, however, regret giving up smoking at Mackie's request. If ever he needed a hit of nicotine, it was now.

Will had done a great job making the rounds at the club for him. That was, until Damien had come back from the family's quarters. At that point, Will had done his usual puppy-eyed longing for a few seconds before excusing himself and heading in the exact opposite direction. *Christ, what is the guy waiting for?* Even Val, who barely knew the kid, could see that Damien was equally interested. And it wasn't as if Annika needed her father's constant attention and monitoring. She was practically growing right before their eyes. In the not too distant future, she'd be a fully mature, if inexperienced Queen.

Of course, maybe that was problem with Will making a play for Damien. The human spent so much time with them as it was that he wouldn't miss how Annika was having the growing spurt to end all growing spurts when it finally happened. Val knew the guy was loyal to their family in general and Emil in particular, but could he be trusted with their secret? Val didn't know. And it wasn't really his problem anyway, except fuck, how long had it been since Will had been laid? Probably since his lover had died, and all that pent-up sexual frustration wasn't good for their kind.

Val found Emil with Alex in Alex's office. They were both watching something on the big flat screen on the wall.

"What's doing?" he asked as he entered and joined them. "Oh fuck me," he said when he saw the screen. "Is it election time again?"

"It is if you count an election that's more than a year away," Alex replied.

Emil tsked. "It gets longer and longer every cycle. It's as if having found democracy, humans can't resist exercising it endlessly."

Val plopped onto the couch and made a rude noise. "Stupid humans. If they could only recognize the value of having queens."

"They have from time to time," Alex reminded him.

Val repeated the noise. "I mean intuitively recognize their natural leader—and for her to rule with selfless devotion to her people."

"It's not in their DNA," Emil reminded him. "They've done very well to have evolved to this system."

"And yet, they seem intent on fucking it up. Who is this asshat anyway?"

A bland man who was rather on the young side, with perfectly coiffed hair and an earnest look on his face, was droning on about forgotten morals or some such crap.

It was Alex who answered. "He's one of the Massachusetts delegates to the House of Representatives. He's just announced that he's running for President."

Val tipped his head back and folded his arms. "Well, I didn't vote for him."

"Ha ha, as if we can vote at all in this country. Quinn, on the other hand, is quite excited at the prospect of voting in the national elections for the first time. It's adorable."

"You think everything he does is adorable," Val countered.

Alex shot him a sharp look. "As do you, when it comes to Mackie."

"Huh! That's not how I'd have described him this morning as he hugged the porcelain god."

Emil landed a hand on his shoulder. "He's going to be fine."

"Indeed," Alex intoned. "We shall make sure of it."

Shit. He should have known he couldn't hide his fear from his shipmates. They knew him too well. Val sighed and stared at his feet. "Yeah, I know. It's just..."

"Robbie," Emil said quietly.

Val nodded. "But more than that. What if that crap our kind manufactured and that human shithead doped Mackie with is still in his system? And what if it fucks with the whole pregnancy? Harry still can't say if there was any lasting damage. And we're got one eye out for you-know-who, and that keeps me up at night."

"We understand your worries, Val," Alex replied. "Rest assured we are here to help you both. We will all see Mackie through this event unscathed."

"Thank you, sir. I'll feel better when the others arrive."

"It will only be three more—Christos, Antoniu and Claudiu. Tony and Claude are bringing their lovers and a hybrid each."

Val raised his eyebrows. "They've been surprisingly busy."

"Indeed."

"And the others?" Even with many of Dracul's men decimated, it didn't pay for them to fight with less than a full complement.

Alex shook his head, a resigned look on his face. "A thousand years locked in a deadly fight has taken a toll. I can't ask more of them than they are willing to give. It's a miracle I've kept my authority this long. They want peace and quiet, and I can't say I blame them."

"*I* can." Val was disgusted that they all weren't coming when called. As far as he was concerned, they owed what lives they had on this miserable ball of dirt to Alex. Fighting for him one last time was a fair trade. He couldn't say more, however, because the door opened and in came Damien, carrying a tray. "Hi, guys. I brought you lunch."

Emil's sous chef was getting to be as good as his boss. The meal he delivered smelled delicious, even before Val saw the pulled pork sandwiches.

"Thank you, Damien." Alex flashed a smile. "Please put it on the coffee table. We'll serve ourselves. This private service almost makes up for the tedious paperwork we need to catch up on."

"Happy to do it, bossman."

The man who would be President continued to blather on in the background. Val caught something about how the guy loved all his constituents and would serve them equally. But yes, in answer to someone's question, he continued to hold the belief that the bible was the inerrant word of God, that marriage was the union of one man and one woman and that he hoped his LGBTQI brothers and sisters would see the light and come in from the destructive lifestyle that they'd chosen. *Blah, blah, blah. Holy God indeed.* Val hated the sanctimonious asshole.

Damien glanced at the screen. "Oh that guy. Man, what a cocksucker he is."

"Yes," Alex agreed. "He does seem to hold very disagreeable positions."

Damien snorted. "Nah, I mean he's a real cocksucker, in the literal sense of the word. When he's not giving his stump speech next to his sweet, little wife, he likes to hang out in the skeeviest of gay bars and suck randos' cocks. He's on his knees so much that I'm surprised he doesn't have holes in his pants." He chuckled again. "Hypocrite."

"I'll say." Emil shook his head. "I hope he's caught out in his lies before his candidacy goes much further. You've had enough deceitful Presidents in this country."

Val reached for a sandwich, only half-paying attention to what was going on. His mind kept wandering back to Mackie, worrying. He couldn't help it. No matter what anyone said, he wasn't going to rest easy until Mackie was safely delivered of their son — unless, of course, he carried a daughter. And wasn't that an even scarier thought? The idea of raising even a worker daughter, let alone a queen, scared him shitless.

But then all thought of that possibility fled and he forgot the sandwich in his hand. Because as the cameras panned out to show the crowd of supporters and volunteers for the asshat's campaign, a horribly familiar face came into focus. The guy was dressed in an expensive-looking suit, with carefully styled short hair and wrap-around sunglasses that hid his eyes. Val knew him in an instant, regardless.

"Fuck!" He uttered the swear and rose out of his seat without caring that Damien was in the room. "Alex, it's Bran."

Alex and Emil both shot to their feet as well, their mouths moving with all kinds of profanity.

Damien looked back at the screen once more. "What? Is that someone you know?"

It was Alex who said it for all of them in his usual understated way. "Regrettably, yes."

Chapter Three

"Here you go, Mackie, homemade chicken soup courtesy of Emil." Damien placed the bed tray carefully across Mackie's lap.

The guy was propped up against a mound of pillows in one corner of the large sectional sofa in the family's living room. His boys—Quinn, Demi and Brenin—surrounded him, munching on more hearty food and watching crappy reality TV. They'd been at it since morning, when Val had carried his husband out of the bathroom and had placed him on the couch with tender care.

Damien could acknowledge to himself, if no one else, that he felt a sting of envy seeing how much this guy was loved. And, to his shame, that sting turned into a massively painful bite as he catered to these pampered boys who could afford to lie around when one of them was sick and laze the day away. Only Jase was working, as usual. That kid never quit.

He hated the sentiment and tried hard to both hide it and tamp it down. Every one of these boys, other than

Demi, had lived as he himself once had—on the street, by his wits and sometimes using his body as currency. They were the extraordinarily lucky ones, having found love and protection. He had too, he had to acknowledge. Emil had given him a chance and the break of a lifetime by teaching him a valuable skill that he—*bonus*—absolutely loved. Yeah, he was one lucky son-of-a-bitch and he'd better remember that.

Mackie smiled. "Thanks, Damien. It smells delicious. I'm really fine, you know." He pulled a face. "Val's being super overprotective, as is his want." He shrugged. "What's a slave to do but obey?"

Damien didn't get the BDSM thing. The club he worked in catered to that lifestyle for the ultra-rich, and at first, it had kind of wigged him out. Emil had made it clear that it was all about consent, so if any member made him uncomfortable, he should tell him right away. Damien didn't doubt he was safe. The Stelalux men were walking wet dreams, if you spent your nights with visions of giants dancing in your head—which he did. That brought his mind back to thoughts of Will, something he'd managed to banish for oh, about five minutes.

He glanced around but Will was nowhere to be seen. He was probably with the other men down in the basement. That interview with Congressman I-love-you-but-you're-defective on TV had caused quite a scene. He was used to the men being pretty chill and circumspect when he was around. The word 'furtive' came to mind, although he didn't think they were doing anything illegal. They just closed ranks an awful lot. Yet, they'd let him see some genuine emotion this morning—and not in a good way. It had lasted only a few seconds before Alex had dismissed him with his usual calm and gentlemanly manner. Then Damien had spied them all trooping through the always-locked door that led to the bowels of the club's building. The sight of it gave Damien's imagination all kinds of fodder.

"Park your butt and join us, Damien," Demi said around a mouthful of sandwich. "You are never going to believe what kind of dress this bride just picked out." He made a gagging face.

"Thanks, but I have to get back to the kitchen. The Sunday brunch crowd is surprisingly large today and with Emil, um…otherwise occupied, I can't leave poor Jase to deal with it on his own. The new help Emil hired are good and eager…but inexperienced. They need a lot of supervision."

"Oh, yeah, I forgot."

Damien could swear tension entered the room, each boy going a little bit more on alert, as if they were worried about something bad happening. He couldn't help poking at the situation. It seemed to him that the men confided in their boys.

"Yeah, everyone's in the basement for some reason." He chuckled. "Do they, like, have someone chained up down there?"

He'd meant it as an absurd suggestion, his overactive imagination stirring the pot. The tension rose, however, and every boy almost froze mid-bite, with a glass raised to his lips—or in Mackie's case, a spoon. They looked everywhere except at him for a few long seconds.

Then Quinn said, "No, of course not!" He laughed, a forced sound. "That's just silly. Harry has his lab there, and you know how our men like to hang with each other. It's their version of watching reality TV. Right, guys?" Everyone nodded now and murmured in agreement. "We don't take it personally when they want to get away from us."

They still weren't looking at Damien until Demi finally did. He gave him a tight smile. "Thanks for lunch, Damien. When there's a lull in the food service, you and Jase should come and hang out."

"Thanks, but I have to do dinner prep after that. I'll tell Jase, though."

Mackie frowned. "You work too hard, Damien. When was the last time you went home to get some sleep?"

He shrugged. "Work equals paycheck, you know? Money is what makes the world go 'round." After a few years of having nothing, not even a home, he now had an apartment all to himself. It was small and in an old building in Chinatown, but it was his. He had enough clothing to go a week or more without doing laundry and he was never, ever hungry. Emil's generosity with food meant his grocery bill was small. Alex's employment benefits gave him health insurance, so he never had to worry about being sick and not getting the help he needed. Best of all, he had savings. His bank account had a nice, growing balance. Knowing that he had that to fall back on if something horrible happened allowed him to sleep at night.

There was no doubt about it. He was a lucky bastard. The only thing missing was a man who could rock his world in bed and love him, too. Except that wasn't part of his immediate plans, and now he was back to thinking of Will. Jesus, that wasn't going to earn him his wages.

"Have fun, guys. If you need anything, you know the kitchen's extension."

He left with the boys' goodbyes ringing in his ears, which was nice, except he couldn't shake the other thought that had been stuck in his head.

Just what the hell is going on in that basement?

* * * *

Val slammed Petru up against the wall, his hand around the guy's throat. Will, Alex, Emil, Malcolm and even Harry stood outside the tiny cell. It wasn't big enough for all of them to enter, and besides, they were rather superfluous. Really, they served as human exclamation points to Val's admonition to Petru of *'Don't fucking lie to me, asshole'*.

To his credit, Dracul's former lieutenant didn't shit his pants, not that he was wearing any. The guy had the whole sangfroid routine down pat. He merely gazed at Val with a calm expression, his hands hanging by his sides, not making any effort to defend himself from the immovable force that pinned him to the wall.

"I can only repeat," he said in that unctuous voice that had always driven Will crazy, like oil being poured into his ears, "that I have no idea what Dracul's idiot pup is up to. If he's ingratiated himself with some rising politician, it's his own plan. Dracul had decided decades ago that whispering into world leader's ears was a wasted strategy.

"He thought dictators and fascism were going out of style." He huffed out a laugh. "More fool he. Humans are forever power-mad. They only pretend to evolve."

Coming from someone who'd spent centuries trying to take over this planet, the observation was laughable. Not that anyone listening to him was…laughing, that is. Seeing Bran so openly participating in a presidential election gave them all a case of *'holy fuck'*. Mackie's morning sickness had nothing on the way Will's stomach churned with dread as to what the guy was planning. Obviously, he didn't mind being found out, which was either a mark of extreme stupidity—and really, when dealing with Dracul's sons, that couldn't be ruled out — or a sign of confidence that he was untouchable by any of them.

Alex spoke. "You must know something about the little fuck that would prove useful. We know him only as a physical adversary."

"Of course." Petru gestured toward Val with a slight tip of his head in a silent request.

"Val," Alex barked.

Ever-obedient to his captain, Val let go of Petru and took a half-step back, ready to re-engage in a moment of need. Will had to admire Petru's balls. He didn't appear the least bit intimidated. Will himself would never go against Alex's right-hand man. Even with Mackie softening the edges, Val remained the most volatile of them all. Thank their previous Queen and her lucky stars that the man had chosen to be on the right side of things.

Petru cleared his throat almost delicately before speaking. "Both boys were constant sources of disappointment to Dracul, naturally. He tried to mold them into his own image, but half their genetics were of weak stock, so it didn't quite take."

Will pictured the wan Welshman Dafydd, who was becoming less like a ghost, thanks to the attention of his human lover. He figured anyone who'd survived centuries of Dracul's torture could hardly be described as anything other than strong. He said nothing, however, knowing his place in the hive. His skills ran toward to the technical, like piloting and stealth. He could slip in and out of any location without detection, becoming one with the night, in particular. If need be, he could hold his own in a fight — and then some. Val was the front man this time and Emil was next on deck. Will hung silently back, listening to this totally useless information, being the punctation in the melodrama of Petru's ramblings, as intended.

"Frankly, I always thought he underestimated Bran's cunning," Petru continued. "Cadoc was the flashier of the two, but Bran took in everything and squirreled it away for later use. I wouldn't go so far as to say he was clever, but he's certainly proved to be a survivor. I would have thought, though, that he'd slink away and live a quietly decadent life. I'm surprised he's showing this much ambition."

"He could be following Dracul's orders," Harry interjected. "This may be proof that the devil still lives."

Good old Harry, casting their enemy in allegorical terms. Personally, Will had always thought of Dracul as a traitorous fucker—or asshole, depending on his mood. Either way, it was the betrayal of Alex in particular and the hive in general that Will couldn't forgive. His family had been in the Queen's hive, closely related to her and her predecessors. He felt the pull of her orbit perhaps more strongly than any of them. Maybe that's why he'd produced Annika. In hindsight, he should have expected that eventuality.

"He *does* live!" Petru exclaimed, real emotion showing in him for the first time. "And, no," he added more calmly, "I doubt very much that he's following Dracul's orders. They fled early when you raided the castle. Of that, I'm sure. There is only one of their number who would have stuck with Dracul once you'd left him for dead."

The guy's voice and expression changed in some nameless way. In any other person, it would have read as sadness or longing. Will found it hard to believe that Petru was capable of that type of feeling, except that he knew what it was about. Petru had been clear that he was trustworthy in joining their cause because the nameless someone was a human boy, someone Petru wanted to get back very badly. *Someone he loves?* It was impossible to accept that Petru could achieve that kind of devotion to a species he'd always decried as inferior and good for—*What had he said? Oh, yeah, fucking and killing. Charming.* So no... Will figured it was more about having his toy stolen from him than anything else.

"It may be as he says," Alex opined. "Bran might simply be parroting his father's previous schemes to get close to power."

"Risky, though, don't you think?" Emil asked. "It gets our attention and yet it's a long shot that this... What did you call him, Val?"

"Asshat."

"Yeah, *that* makes it all the way to the White House. There's like a million candidates already. I mean, the asshat has pretty hair and straight white teeth and all, but does he really have a shot at holding the most powerful position in the human world? If and when he fails, what has Bran accomplished, except issue us an engraved invitation to turn him into dust?"

Will had no opinion about any of this, either. He hadn't seen said asshat making his announcement, nor had he bothered following US politics more than was necessary to stay a well-informed inhabitant of Earth. He'd settled in the Netherlands deliberately. It was a small, mostly quiet country. He liked the slow pace of his life and how no one around him tried to make a big splash in the world. Of course, trouble had come to the country more than once, including in recent years. Nowhere on this miserable planet was safe and harmonious.

But America was a big, noisy country with battling factions, even without Dracul's son stirring the pot. He would have preferred to stay away from it for the rest of his life, except he went where Alex needed him. And Annika couldn't remain outside the fray. It wasn't in her nature. She had the duty to lead and manage, even if meant doing so with another species. To do otherwise would destroy her, eventually. As her father, his destiny was to follow her and serve in whatever way she needed.

"It brings us back to Bran being not as bright as he should be," Alex said. "Either that or he has an agenda that is so clever we can't see it yet."

Val made his thoughts clear on that possibility. "Like hell! With Bran, I'm going with what you see is even less than what you get. What's our next move, boss?" he added, looking at Alex.

"Research the asshat and see if there's anything useful in plain sight. Other than that, we need to figure out a way to get close to him and Bran."

Val grimaced. "It won't be easy. On a quick search, I've already learned that the guy is getting around-the-clock protection because of death threats. Although little names him in particular, my bet is that Bran is head of the security team."

"That's a start. See what more you can dig out. We'll meet again tonight in my office after dinner."

"What do we tell our boys?" Emil asked.

"The truth. They need to be on alert as much as possible. Keeping them in the dark has never worked for us before anyway," Alex added with a flash of rueful grin. He grew somber again. "And Dafydd has to be warned that his other son is here. We can't blindside him if this ends in a predictable fashion."

Alex turned his attention back to Petru. "You think long and hard, too. You lived with the man since his birth. You must know something about him that's useful."

"Of course, I'll put my thinking cap on. I can tell you one thing, although what use it would be, I couldn't say." When they remained there staring at him, he continued. "He, ah, likes girls."

They all stood mute at that pronouncement.

Once again, Petru didn't need any kind of response. "He used the slaves in the castle, of course, but sparingly. Once a year or so, he'd drag in some female he'd find God knows where, shower her with his unwanted attention, which of course, eventually killed her. Dracul wasn't much pleased with the whole thing. It was messy and required the disposal of a body from his very home. Still, he could be an indulgent father when the mood struck him." Petru shrugged. "Again, not sure what use that information is."

"I'm not sure, either," Alex bit out. "Except I didn't think I could possibly hate him more. Live and learn." He signaled Val to come out of the cell.

"Wait," Petru said before the door shut in his face. "When can I see Her again?"

Will knew—they all did—whom he meant. Rage rose within him at the very mention, however obliquely, of his daughter. Queen she may be, but she was also his little girl, and he wouldn't let anyone harm her. The idea of her breathing the same air as this fucker was intolerable to Will. A growl pushed past his lips, earning him a glance from everyone.

Alex spoke before Will could. "Is there a reason in particular why you want to see the Queen?"

"You need to ask?" Petru scoffed. "It's been so long." He licked his lips in an unexpected tell of his nervousness. "I'd almost forgotten what it was like to be in Her orbit. So…soothing."

Will did understand. They all did. It had been a slow realization for him, but in recent months, he'd detected a change in his own mood when he was with Annika. She was coming into her maturity and there was a sense of relief that their lives weren't going to be an endless survival on this miserable planet. There was real hope of a new life.

Alex made no promises. "We'll see. Do some serious thinking. We can't go after Dracul while this new threat grows right under our noses."

With that, Val shut the cell door and locked it. They filed out of the room.

Harry spoke before they reached the stairs. "I wonder if Petru hasn't already handed us the key to solving our new problem. The Queen," he added when they stopped and looked at him. "Maybe it's as simple as having Annika speak with Bran. She could possibly bring him to heel with just an order. She has a very positive effect on Merlin. I can tell how hard he tries to stay mad and rebellious, but when she's in the room, he becomes almost docile, certainly more obedient. It's quite a relief, I must say, as someone who is trying to civilize him."

"No!" The word was out of Will's mouth before he could stop it, not that he would have. He spoke to Alex. "With respect, Captain, she is too young. Her power is at its infancy and she is a child, regardless. Although technically Merlin and Bran are biologically and socially similar, Merlin is a mere child, while Bran is fully grown. We can't assume he will be as malleable as that boy. We can't risk her life like that."

As far as he was concerned, there was no question about what to do. Obeying the Queen was embedded in every nucleus of every cell in their bodies. It was in their very nature, with no choice about it. And sure, that was why Petru had been completely coopted to their side, his hatred for Dracul being beside the point. His conversion could be trusted because it was genetic, not deliberate. There was a very real hope that Dracul could be defeated in the same way. In theory, it should work, although his mind had become so twisted with his power that it might be enough to override even the most basic drive of their species.

Time would tell, and the thought of his precious daughter getting anywhere near that monster kept Will up at night. He was going to have to trust Alex to broach the plan carefully. Protecting the Queen was another part of their makeup, so that helped ease his terror. But Bran was different. He was a hybrid. There could be no expectation that a Queen would mean anything to him. He hadn't been raised in a hive, after all, and his watered-down DNA could just as easily dismiss Annika as the ordinary little human girl that she appeared to be. Demi and Merlin were too small a pool of subjects to be a predictable outcome for another of their kind.

Will swallowed hard when Alex didn't respond right away. "I'm sorry, sir. She's my daughter. Nothing matters more to me than keeping her safe."

Alex reached out and, for an instant, Will braced himself for a blow. Instead, his captain put his hand on Will's shoulder and gave it a reassuring squeeze.

"I promise you, Willem, that nothing will be done to risk her life. I know it's a lovely thought that our Queen could control Bran, but he is a hybrid, as you say, and unpredictable. We won't risk it unless he's contained, as Petru is. We take no chances," he emphasized before letting go. We've taken down better adversaries than this. We're not going to start running scared now and hiding behind the Queen's skirts."

He glanced at Harry. "Someone still needs to tell Dafydd what's happening. We mustn't lose sight of the fact that Bran is his son. His death, however necessary it may be, will still cut deeply, I'm sure. Besides, Dafydd might know something about his son that will help us."

Harry nodded. "I've already called Ric so he can be here when I break the news to Dafydd. He's had an amazingly good effect on the boy."

"And I'll bring Trey up to speed," Emil said, then snapped his fingers. "I better get back to the kitchen. I left poor Damien in charge of the brunch crowd. The new staff need constant supervision."

The mention of the human took Will's thoughts in another direction, a welcome distraction from what they'd been discussing. Not that his longing for the human was any better than the worry about dealing with Bran. It was merely different. And picturing taking hold of Damien was far more satisfying that doing the same with Bran. They would both end with a fucking, except one was euphemistic and the other far more pleasurable. Too bad the figurative one was the only thing Will could count on. The very real fucking he wanted to give Damien would have to remain an untouchable fantasy.

They were all safer that way.

* * * *

Mackie flopped back onto his pillow and breathed noisily through his mouth. "Thanks, Lucien. I'm sorry it's so disgusting." He hadn't managed to digest much of Emil's delicious chicken noodle soup, apparently.

On his way to empty the barf bucket into the toilet, Lucien tsked loudly. "Nonsense. It doesn't bother me.

I'm married to a doctor, remember?" he added on his return to Mackie's bedside. "I've seen and smelled far worse, in particular from my time carrying Demi. I was much the same as you are now."

"How come no one mentioned this part when I got the whole 'drink my blood and live forever' talk?"

Lucien bent over him and placed a cool cloth on his forehead. "Well, for one thing, the information came from a man who has never been in this condition. Our husbands are unreliable sources about what it's really like. Seeing it and experiencing it are two entirely different things."

Mackie closed his eyes and focused on the comfort of the wet cloth. "I've talked to you about it, and somehow vomiting your guts inside out never came up, either."

"I believe I mentioned morning sickness was the toughest part of pregnancy," he replied with a hint of defensiveness.

"Yeah, I focused on the morning part and figured it wouldn't be this bad."

"I believe it's variable by person, much as it is with women. I'm sorry if I misled you about the enormity of what you were agreeing to."

Mackie rolled to his side and opened his eyes. "No, I'm sorry. I'm being a brat. I made the decision to continue to take Val's blood and to fuck without protection. It's a commitment to my husband and I don't regret it. I'm scared though," he admitted. "It feels as if I'm going to puke the kid right out."

Lucien smiled. "That's not going to happen. I promise you that the only risk is getting dehydrated. That's where regular feedings will help. In fact, I've texted Val to come see you."

"Oh no, Lucien! Val's busy with this whole Bran thing. I can wait."

"Bullshit." The firm rebuke was uttered by Val as he strode into their bedroom. "Nothing matters more than you."

His husband didn't hesitate to come right to the bed, scoring his wrist with his fangs at the same time. He shoved it against Mackie's lips as he sat down beside him. Regardless of how guilty Mackie might have felt at taking the man away from important stuff, he latched on to Val like a striking viper. The warm blood sliding down his throat soothed his stomach within seconds. The experience in the bathroom that morning hadn't been a fluke. Chicken soup had nothing on Val's blood when it came to healing powers. He moaned like a greedy pig.

Val landed his free hand on Mackie's head. "Good boy, that's it. Take what you need." He turned to Lucien. "Thanks for watching him."

Lucien moved away. "You're quite welcome. With Dafydd more than capable of looking after Idris these days, I have a lot of free time. I'm happy to help Mackie through this difficult point in his pregnancy. It's certainly more appealing than babysitting Merlin." He pulled a face. "If you'd like, I can get a blood bag from storage and—"

"No," Val cut him off firmly. "My blood is best. Harry says so. I won't allow Mackie to have less than everything he needs unless absolutely necessary. Thank you," he added.

"Then I'll leave you to it."

Mackie closed his eyes before Lucien had fully left the room. His lids were heavy, as was typical with feedings. And it was such a relief for his stomach to be settled that he relaxed completely. The next thing he knew, he was blinking his eyes open again, his mouth no longer latched onto Val's wrist. Even though the lighting in the room was the same, he felt as if he'd slept for a while. Val hadn't moved from his side, though. He sat on the edge of the bed with his elbows resting on his knees, his gaze fixed on the floor.

Mackie stretched and rolled onto his back. "How long have I been out?"

Val turned his head to scrutinize him. "About an hour. How do you feel?"

Mackie took stock of himself. "Lethargic but not nauseated. Not yet anyway."

"I'm here for you if need another feeding."

"What about this problem of Bran popping up all of a sudden?"

"There's nothing to be done about it yet. He's out in the open, which is alarming in its novelty, but at least we can see what he's doing, in some sense." He shrugged. "I did a bunch of research on the politician he's working for and gave it to Alex, for all the good it is. Bran has laid down a pretty decent paper trail with his new persona. Good enough for a government security clearance, at any rate.

"He's calling himself Bran Nyx, which makes sense, because Dracul always used the surname Stelanyx when there was a need." He grunted out what could possibly be mistaken for a laugh. "You know it's the opposite of the name Alex chose for us, Stelalux—'star night' versus 'star light'?"

"Oh, I hadn't really considered where my new last name came from."

"It's kind of cheesy, I know, and a bit of a mouthful. We should have chosen Smith when we emigrated here."

Mackie scoffed. "That would be boring."

"We'd blend in better."

Now Mackie snorted. "You guys couldn't possibly blend in anywhere, regardless of the name you use."

Val smiled, although it didn't quite reach his eyes. "You might have a point there." His expression turned grim. "Anyway, I've done what research I can. It's up to Alex to decide what our next move is going to be. Unless and until he needs me, I'm sticking to your side."

Mackie suppressed a sigh. He loved his man to pieces but months of being tied to his hip was going to drive them both mad. Plus, they had jobs to do. Even if Mackie couldn't work, it didn't mean Val should be kept from his duties.

"Don't they need you in the club?"

Val shook his head. "MacLerie's got it covered. He's more than effective at keeping the members in check. And Will's been hanging out there when Annika doesn't need him. We have three more shipmates coming in the next couple of weeks, as well. They'll help out wherever needed. That's what drones do."

"I thought their one and only job was to inseminate the queen?"

Val gave him the side-eye. "That's true for bees. We're not that. Our social structures are similar, but hardly exactly analogous. For one thing, all of our females are fertile, not just the queens. For another, we have more males than females, so all of us are productive members of the hive. We don't merely contribute sperm to future generations."

Mackie wrinkled his nose. "I have had a hard time picturing all of you lined up waiting for your turn to, um, *service* someone like Annika," he confessed. He was endlessly fascinated by his husband's species yet always sensed that Val didn't like discussing it. It was too painful, Mackie imagined, given that they could never go back to their home planet. Still, he didn't want to lose an opportunity to learn more when Val was in a talkative mood. And given that Mackie would be bringing a half-alien child into the world, ancestry and customs would be important to pass along.

Val winced. "That is not an image I want in my head, thanks very much." He sighed, a very un-Val-like sound that concerned Mackie. Val had more self-confidence than any creature on Earth. "If this were an ordinary hive, I wouldn't exactly be lined up. I spent one time, when I'd matured, with the lesser queen who directly ruled my family—like Demi's night with Duncan. It would be up to each queen, of course, whether she'd do a repeat with a particular drone or not, but all males would have at least that one experience. It's one of the ways we keep hive cohesion.

"Jesus, though, I can't begin to imagine that each of us will…" He swore. "With Annika?" He shook his head. "I guess I've spent too long living with humans. I can't think of her as anything other than a little girl. A niece, for lack of a better word," Val said. "No, I think those of us who landed here will have to forego that and leave it up to some of the hybrids to, as you say, 'service' her when she and they are grown."

Mackie put his hand on his husband's thigh, loving how the steel quality of his muscles reminded him of Val's power. "I'm glad to hear that, because if you sleep with her—or anyone—I will cut off your balls." He smiled sweetly into Val's startled face.

His husband did what Mackie had hoped and chuckled. "Okay, baby, I consider myself warned, and frankly, I'm happy to have our marriage vows as a good excuse." Leaning over, he kissed Mackie sweetly, carefully, pulling away far too soon. "I meant what I said at our wedding, 'forsaking all others'. I'm your husband, Mackie. I'll always be yours and take care of you."

Mackie loved the certainty in Val's tone. When he reached over to return the kiss, however, Val didn't permit more than a brief peck. As Mackie considered how he might increase the passion level, Val spoke again. Apparently he was in an unusually talkative mood. Listening was an important role for a spouse, so Mackie reined in his desires and paid attention.

"Servicing a queen hasn't been on my radar, but I am starting to wonder what the hell I'm going to be good for. With the others joining us and more on the way, we have plenty of muscle to run the club. I'm superfluous in the bouncer role these days."

Mackie squeezed the fingers on the hand resting on his man's thigh. "That's nonsense. The club would fall apart without you."

"Maybe." He looked thoughtful. "I used to know my place better when there were endless human wars to join. I'm not sure this civilian life suits me. Bran isn't making himself a very appealing target. Maybe he's really into politics these days and not world domination."

"What's the chance of that, given who raised him?" Mackie asked, stating the obvious.

"Fair point. I can look forward to turning him into dust in the near future. It's what I'm good at, after all."

Mackie worried his lower lip. He didn't like the way Val was second-guessing his worth. In the past when the guy had gone all moody, it had been simply a matter of scheduling a little play time. Nothing lifted both their spirits more than a good scene. Except that was off the table for the duration of this pregnancy. How was Val going to cope without the outlet?

Staying cooped up in their room wasn't going to help. Mackie had only come up when his nausea had returned. "Let's go downstairs."

"Are you sure you're feeling up to it?" When he nodded, Val scooped him into his arms without another word.

"I keep telling you that I don't need to be carried," Mackie admonished, although he was always thrilled to be in his husband's arms.

"And I keep telling you that you don't get a choice in this."

"Fine, but when we get to the living room, I'm going to want to watch crappy TV, so you'd better make yourself scarce." Val's expression turned stony. "I'm serious. There's no need for you to make yourself crazy waiting for me to get back on the vomitron."

"I happen to like crappy TV, as you put it. And I love you, so this is really a waste of your breath."

"Fine." Mackie shut his mouth, knowing that arguing with Val was pointless.

Mackie needed to be more subtle in his efforts. Maybe Annika was already there. She usually was, playing with her adorable dog. He'd invite her to join them and let her pick what they watched. He was betting on *Frozen*. The little Queen really loved Elsa and could watch that movie ten times in a row without getting tired of it. He supposed the girl could really empathize with the isolated ice queen.

Mackie liked the movie too, although not quite so much. He identified with Olaf, naturally. He could suffer through a marathon for the rest of the afternoon. And it would likely mean that Will would eventually join them, because he rarely strayed from his daughter's side for long. Then Will might crack under the strain of the endless *Let it Go* loop and ask Val to play pool or something. They could amuse themselves while still keeping an eye on Mackie and Annika.

Yeah, that was a plan—so long as Mackie could convince his stomach to go along with it.

* * * *

Val escaped to the roof of the club, something he hadn't done in a long time—not since he'd given in to his heart's desire and bound himself and his life to his play partner and brat, Mackie. From the moment Alex had relocated them to Boston, this had been his sanctuary. He loved hanging out here in the relative cool of the night, especially. Earth was too hot, always had been for their kind. Putting up with the sun during the day was a chore. Yet, staying inside in modern air conditioning had its limits as well. He liked fresh air, not that there was much to be had in any modern city. *Fucking industrial revolution.* Up here, he could stand in the relative peace, smoke a cigarette, drink some whiskey even. It was a rare respite from his club duties and the never-ending war with Dracul.

Except that right now there was no solace to be found. Dealing with Mackie's pregnancy without showing his husband his own abject terror was grinding on his nerves. Keeping his emotions in check wasn't his forte. Neither was standing around with his thumb up his ass, but that's what it felt like he was doing. He had only one way to ease Mackie's suffering and that effort was only a temporary reprieve at best. Plus, Val was the cause of it all. Guilt ate at him. And no matter what Mackie said, the boy had to blame him, as well, not that he so much as looked askance at Val while cycling through the vomiting, endless fatigue and desperate feedings. Normally Mackie wore his feelings on his sleeve. Right now, Val couldn't get a read on him at all, other than a fierce determination to see this pregnancy through, no matter what.

Val strode to the edge and stared out at the skyline. It was hardly the prettiest view of the old city, but it suited him well enough. Christ, he wanted to light up, but he wouldn't do that to Mackie. Not only had Val vowed to give up *'the disgusting habit'*, as Mackie called it, but he wasn't going to risk causing a lingering smell on himself that might make Mackie feel even more sick. It was a stupid indulgence anyway, one that he'd adopted long ago to fit in better with his human comrades during times of war. Because his kind was immune to such troubles as cancer, it hadn't hurt him to continue, even as humans had wised up and quit. It hadn't been important enough to keep the habit in the face of Mackie's dislike, however. As he stood there craving a hit of nicotine, it surprised him that he had become somewhat addicted to the stuff.

He paced to work off his nervous energy. It wasn't helping, though. He felt as if he were going to jump out of his skin. Being so irritable and restless was also not going to help Mackie. So, without much thought, Val ran to the side of the roof and vaulted over the next building — and he didn't stop there. This was familiar. It had been a while, but exploring Boston by its roof tops had been an activity he'd enjoyed many times in the past.

Playing with Mackie had taken up all of his free time recently, making this kind of nighttime goofing off something he'd put aside. He'd almost forgotten the exhilaration of giving his strength and speed full throttle. It was late and dark and he was up high. He could speed and leap past the streets and neighborhoods with little worry that he would be seen.

There was no plan inside his head, no path he chose. He simply improvised in the route he took, leaping over HVAC units and across yawning alleyways. The times the space between buildings was almost too wide were the most fun. It tested his muscles and eyesight to span the chasm without falling, not that he'd be hurt if he did. Like a cat, he knew how to land on his feet. The air was blessedly cool for the end of summer. He took in great lungfuls and poured on the speed.

He stopped at some point to catch his breath and stand on the ledge of an unknown building. His journey had mostly taken him in circles and he hadn't strayed too far from the club's neighborhood. He was not so jammed inside his own head to take undue risks. The tonier the areas of Boston, the more likely for very tall buildings to be where people lived. It wouldn't take much for someone to look out of their window, even in the middle of the night, and see some weird-ass guy prancing across roofs. Yeah, Alex would really hate it if Val made the morning news or if video of him hit the Internet.

Street sounds reached his ears and male voices laughing in particular caught his attention. It was the pitch of them...something edgy and nasty. He'd heard it before in the club when members had had too much to drink and were having it on with someone. Normally he wouldn't care, unless it involved teasing one of the boys. That was his job, to keep them safe from the excesses of men who thought they could do whatever they wanted. This was what the current situation sounded like to him. A few men were having a great time at someone else's expense.

Val's hackles went up in an instant, especially when he heard a sort of whimpering underneath. Leaning down the side of the roof, he saw a group of what appeared to be young men surrounding a pile of something. *No, someone.* As a guy moved aside, Val could clearly see now that an old man, a street dweller, was huddled against a wall, cringing from the taunting.

Val didn't hesitate. He vaulted over the edge and dropped the four stories into the alley. One or two of the young toughs heard him and spun around. Their eyes went wide.

"Where the fuck did *you* come from?" one of them asked.

Val didn't bother to answer. He merely walked slowly, sauntered almost, toward them. He wanted them all to get a good look at him as he approached.

"What the fuck, dude?" another one sneered. "We found him first. Whatever he's got on him is *ours*."

Rolling a drunk? How charming. It was clear now from the way the boys were dressed that they were not much better off than the old man. But they were young and fit and if they needed booze or cigarettes or a few coins for the same, then they were capable of working. In fact…

Grabbing his junk with one hand, Val said, "If you boys need some extra cash, drop to your knees and suck me off. I'm good for a few rounds, so you each stand to make some money. I'd certainly pay you the same amount as this poor guy might have on him."

Their reactions were text-book perfect. One rushed him with his hands balled into fists. Val backhanded him with little effort, sending him careening into the wall. One of his friends was right behind him, although a hair smarter. He'd pulled out a switchblade as he made his attack. The knife caught the light from the streetlamp. Val smiled and let the guy get very close before turning sideways, grabbing his wrist and twisting. His would-be assailant howled as his bones snapped. Val flung him into the third and fourth tough, like bringing down tenpins.

He actually laughed, which caught him by surprise. It had been a while since he'd felt that kind of joy, and only really when he was with Mackie. He hadn't realized how much he'd missed a good fight, where right and wrong were clearly delineated.

Alas, it ended far too soon. The boys picked themselves up and scrambled like cartoon villains in their haste to get away. He could practically see the smoke rising from their fast-moving feet. They disappeared around the corner. He followed them to make sure they were really leaving, watching until they were no longer visible from the mouth of the alley.

He turned to the old man and reached out to help him up. The guy recoiled at first, then took Val's offered hands and stood. He peered at him through his rheumy eyes. "Which branch?"

"Sorry?"

"Of the military…did you serve in?" the man clarified. He didn't wait for an answer before turning away and picking up his stuff. His attackers had upset his grocery cart and apparently had pawed through his meager belongings.

"Oh, none." That was technically not true but, really, he couldn't name the human armed forces that Alex had seconded him to.

The man eyed him suspiciously. "Bullshit. I know professional training when I see it. I'm thinking special forces for sure. Green Beret maybe—or SEAL."

Val grinned. "Afraid not. Are you okay? Did those assholes hurt you?"

"Nah. Punks." The man spat on the ground. "As if I have anything to steal." He repacked his possessions with great care and grabbed hold of the cart handle.

"You know, most people would at least break both their legs dropping four stories like that."

Oh shit! With the immediate thrill over, Val hadn't thought through what his antics might mean to whoever saw him. "I'm afraid you're mistaken, sir. I came out of…" Oops, there weren't any doors in this particular alley, so he just shut his mouth and tried to look innocent.

The old man chuckled. "That's okay. You keep your secrets, kid. I'm grateful for the help. I was a marine once, but that was a long time ago. I can't take on four punks the way I used to."

"I have a military friend, an ex-marine," Val said, thinking of Logan. And yes, somewhere along the way the woman had changed from one of Emil's strays to a friend. She was certainly a comrade. "Her name's Logan."

The old man's eyes narrowed then he grinned, displaying about five teeth in his whole mouth. "I might know her. I guess you're all right. So long." He pushed his cart toward the sidewalk.

"Be careful," Val called out, knowing there was no way to do that when one lived on the streets.

Feeling surprisingly calm and centered for the first time in days, he ran and jumped up to a roof and began his journey back to Mackie.

Chapter Four

Will settled into one of the side chairs in the conference room. The space was much bigger than Alex's office, and being in the family building, it was far from prying eyes and ears. It was relentlessly corporate, all leather and dark wood. A projection screen had descended from the ceiling at one end. The family members, minus the boys and Annika, had gathered around the rectangular table, as if a board meeting were about to start. There was even coffee and pastries, courtesy of Emil. The one anomaly was the veteran, Logan, the lone woman. She sat not in one of the comfy chairs that made your ass think it was on top of a cloud, but on the wide windowsill at the opposite end of the room. She had her knees tucked up under her chin and she watched everyone like a hawk.

Alex had asked her to come, so Will assumed she was expected to be of some help as they evaluated how to tackle the problem that was Bran. Will knew from experience that she was a fierce and trusted warrior. This situation seemed to call for more subtly than brute force. Again, what did he know? He remained committed to being the good soldier, following orders. He'd let someone else figure out the strategy.

"Val," Alex said from where he sat near Logan at the head of the table, "please begin."

A mosaic of pictures popped up on the screen. "Here's what we have for images of Bran," Val said. "They're all tied to the asshat's campaign. There are a few photoshopped pictures that Bran obviously used to lay a paper trail for himself. He's created an interesting persona that uses enough truth about his life to make it all plausible. You have to dig really deep before you realize it's an illusion."

"How old is the oldest real image of him?" MacLerie asked.

"About a month after we struck the castle in Wales. He must have come over here directly and started hatching his plan. And who knows what that was originally, but somehow—probably through Cadoc's boy-whore enterprise—Bran latched on to Congressman Do-What-I-Say-Not-What-I-Do Asshat."

"You think he's using this politician's gay activities to blackmail him into a job?" Harry asked. He was too mature to use Val's nickname.

Val shrugged. "It's our working theory." He changed the onscreen image to show an aerial view of some large compound with a dominant multi-story building surrounded by a few smaller ones. "This is Hope Hills, a gay-conversion camp. I kid you not."

From her perch, Logan made a rude noise. Val grinned. "Yeah, that." He clicked onto the next slide, showing a website touting the benefits of attending the away-camp for young adults who wanted to rid themselves of their confused sexuality and find God's grace again.

Will rolled his eyes and grabbed a donut covered in chocolate icing. "And why are we looking at this bullshit?" The light when on. "Oh, is the asshat involved with it?" He bit into half the pastry and had to hold back a moan. Emil had made a point of saying that Damien had made these. The boy was both sexy and talented. Will was so screwed.

Alex answered him. "Mr. and Mrs. Asshat are, actually. It's their passion as well as their mission to help those poor lost souls who have been seduced by the 'gay lifestyle'. Conversion therapy is illegal in Massachusetts for children, but this 'camp' is geared toward the newly emancipated."

"Wow," Will said around his mouthful. "This guy is balls-to-the-wall in his hypocrisy."

"Yes," Alex agreed. "You have to admire the level of his assholery, to some degree. And before you ask, the reason this camp is relevant is because it's also tied to the campaign. They have a small office front on Boylston Street, but the real guts of the campaign are located here, apparently. It's in Worcester County, his constituency, and the congressman and his wife have their primary residence right on the campus."

"And that's where Bran is, we presume?" Emil chimed in.

"Exactly," Val confirmed. He ran through more slides showing various aspects of the conversion camp, some of it obviously from a website, the others more aerial shots. "We can't see much from any of this. To really understand what's going on and possibly what Bran is up to, we'd need to get inside this camp."

"I could jump into the new chopper Alex bought and do surveillance," Will offered. It was a self-serving suggestion, given how itchy he was to get his hands on those controls. Flying helicopters was a new skillset of his. Waiting for humans to develop flight capabilities had been agony—and not much of a challenge once they'd done it. Choppers were a different animal and far more fun.

Alex dashed his hopes. "We've already considered that option, Will, but we don't want to tip our hand too soon or too obviously. Bran would notice that kind of activity, given how remote the camp is."

Damn. He said nothing more. Trying to get Alex to change his mind purely to amuse Will was not acceptable hive behavior. The needs of the many outweighed the needs of the few—or the one. *Not an original idea, Mr. Spock.*

Val continued. "We could have someone volunteer for the campaign to snoop around, but I really think the answer lies here. There seems to be a lot going on, and hopefully, both Bran and the candidate let down their guard in this relaxed setting. More usefully, there are a lot of people there, making it easier for someone to blend in, not get noticed as paying attention to matters that they shouldn't. Still, an obvious first effort would involve someone working for the campaign in Boston."

Alex twirled his chair to speak directly to Logan. "We'd thought you might be able to help, work your way into the campaign? The congressman makes veterans' issues a central part of his platform. And we don't think Bran would recognize you. You've changed since Wales."

Indeed she had, with her hair grown out and having put on some weight, she looked less waif-like and much healthier. But she was shaking her head as Alex spoke.

"I'd like to help, except the idea of working in an office makes my skin crawl. Sorry. I can't do that. I'm happy to break into the camp, though. Say the word and I'll do a B and E, no problem."

Alex smiled. "I appreciate the offer and I understand about not wanting to play eager volunteer in their small office. If we simply break into the camp, however, we run the substantial risk of alerting Bran. It has the same problems as doing aerial surveillance."

"Surely he already knows we're on to him," Will interjected. "He's practically waving a flare at us."

Alex rubbed his finger along his lip. "He does seem to be taunting us. Or perhaps this is merely his way of showing he's not afraid to make his mark in this world in a blatant way. *'Look at me. You can't touch me or stop me. I'm not doing anything illegal.'* It's hard to say what goes on in his demented mind."

"So, we kill the fucker, you ken?" Malcolm spoke up. When everyone stared at him, he said, "And why not? He's right there in plain sight." He turned to Will. "You're a more than fare sniper, as I recall."

Will winced. Yes, that was another of his skills. He preferred flying machines, thank you very much. Being a sniper had ripped out a big emotional piece of him, leaving him feeling sick and cold. He hated killing. Except if this was what the hive required of him, if this was necessary to keep Annika safe...

Alex saved him from saying anything. "An outright execution isn't an option. We have no way to get close enough to rig an accidental death, and an assassination of the head of a presidential candidate's security would be too high-profile, especially when the body disintegrates immediately. We can't risk that kind of scrutiny."

Will was practically dizzy with relief. And he felt cowardly for it.

Val put up a bunch of pictures of young men. "It wasn't a bad idea, MacLerie, and one that I proffered already. What we need is someone on the inside. This camp is actually only for boys. The girls, I guess, only have to meet the right guy to turn them straight," he added with a shake of his head. "If we can get someone in there posing as a convert, he might learn something useful, something we can use to bring Bran down with more subtlety than double pops to the head."

"Or," Alex interjected, "we may be able to end the asshat's presidential hopes, leading to Bran suddenly finding himself without a job. He leaves for greener pastures and we nab him quietly. Either way, we neutralize the threat with the least amount of attention drawn to ourselves.

"Oh, Alex, no," Harry exclaimed. "Who would you use? Demi is known to Bran and Mackie is out of the question, for obvious reasons. It would be harmful to expect Brenin, Dafydd or even Jase to put themselves into a situation that is one step above prison. Are you sending Quinn?"

At the head of the table, the pucker factor went up substantially, but Alex was a leader, first and foremost. "I worry that Bran saw him in Wales and would recognize him. Still, getting someone inside that hell-hole is the only solution I've come up with. It's either that or we sit and wait until Bran possibly achieves his goal. Once he's ensconced in D.C., there will be no way to get to him without revealing ourselves to the world."

"There is another possibility," Emil mused.

Will stiffened. *Don't say it!*

"We could ask Damien."

Fucking hell!

"The thought had crossed Alex's and my mind, as well," Val admitted.

Will opened his mouth to say — he wasn't sure what — but Harry beat him to it.

"How could we ask him? He knows nothing about us, though. Does he?" he asked Emil.

"I haven't taken him into my confidence. I wouldn't do that without authorization," he added, clearly affronted.

"Then how the hell do we get him to agree to do this without telling him the truth?" Will demanded.

Emil shrugged. "We tell him some of it — that Bran is a wayward family member intent on mischief and we want to see what we can learn about his plans without alerting him to the fact that we're doing so. It could work."

Will leaned forward and took them all in with a sweeping glance. "Damien is *not* stupid. He'll figure out something weird's going on. Plus, it's dangerous. Why not have one of the other hybrids help, from our shipmates who are coming to Boston? I know of two born in the last hundred years, even if their fathers have bowed out of fighting."

"We considered that, as well," Alex said. "But a hybrid is still different enough from a full human that Bran is likely to detect him. Other than Annika, does anyone know a shipmate who has fathered a child that doesn't share our physical appearance? She's an anomaly, isn't she? And not only because she's female?"

Harry spoke again. "I believe Claude's boy inherited his human father's darker pigmentation. Here he could identify as African American. Except," he added with a shake of his head, "from what I know of him, he's too young to pass as a human adult."

"Then that leaves us back to using a fully human ally," Alex said.

No one was able to gainsay Alex, not even him, because fuck it all, his captain was right. Still, Will believed a hybrid was a better choice than a mere human. "Damien can't protect himself the way a hybrid could. If Bran figures out he's working for us, he's as good as *dead*." He didn't really care that his voice had risen or that he'd pounded the table on that last word.

There was silence for a few seconds as everyone stared at him. Then Alex broke it. "You've been very discreet, Willem. How long have you and Damien been involved—and have you told him more than you should?"

Will jerked back. "What? No, sir." He shook his head. "I am *not* involved with Damien, and I've told him nothing."

"Oh, Will." Emil tsked. "You should let him know how you feel. He's interested in you, too, you know?"

Will's shock rocketed up even more. "No! See? You're wrong. He isn't interested in me at all. I'm some guy he barely knows who's saddled with a child, no less. And that's my focus, totally, raising Annika. Serving our Queen."

Emil folded his arms. "He wants you. Trust me. I've known the boy for years now. He rarely goes out clubbing anymore and no one asked him to cook for the family. That was his idea." He scrunched up his face. "And when did he get that idea? Oh yeah, two seconds after you and Annika moved in." He nodded once for emphasis, as if he'd produced Exhibit A in the case of the Willem versus Reality.

Will was at a loss for words. He sat there with his mouth open and shaking his head until Logan spoke up.

"He's a good kid. He'll help if you ask him, and he's street-smart, can take care of himself."

Has everyone lost their fucking minds?

He was outvoted, however, not that theirs was a democracy. Somehow the meeting was ending and Alex had given Emil and Will marching orders to seek out Damien and ask this huge favor of him. With his heart in his throat, Will stood to obey his captain. His mind, though, searched for a way out of this crazy scheme—one that put Damien in the middle of an alien war he knew nothing about. He had no choice, though, not at the moment. He'd follow Emil and help make the case to Damien, and yet as he did so, he decided on an alternate plan that would have him undermining his captain for the first time. He hated to do it, but fear and conviction steeled his resolve. Alex's decisions were no longer the final ones. He was the captain, but Annika was the Queen.

* * * *

Damien tried to play it cool when Will trailed Emil into the kitchen. Dropping the tray of cookies he'd been taking out of the oven gave him away, however.

"Shit!" He scrambled to catch it, then swore again as he burned his arms on the hot metal and fumbled to keep the whole thing from crashing onto the floor. For a few seconds, he was like that chef on Sesame Street who was always dropping treats after he finished counting. All that was missing was the comical music — *One hopelessly crushing twiiink*.

"Let me help you."

Somehow Will had reached his side, like *Whoa, the guy was ninja fast*. The heat didn't seem to bother him, either, because he grabbed the side of the tray and helped Damien get it onto the counter. Only two cookies had bitten the dust, and Will scooped up those, as well, popping one into his mouth.

"Three second rule," the man said around his mouthful.

Damien smiled. "Thanks, dude. Losing them all would have sucked."

"Do you have a second?" Emil asked. "We'd like to talk to you."

Despite Emil's expression staying its usual relaxed state, Damien sensed something serious was going on.

"Sure thing, Chef. Is everything okay?"

"Yeah, we have a favor to ask. That's all."

Okay, curiouser and curiouser, because Will sure looked unhappy about something. He was chewing the second cookie as if it were his mortal enemy.

"I should finish this first," he said with a wave at his next batch of baking.

"That's what the new kitchen staff is for," Emil replied. "Hey, Penny? Can you take over here for Damien, please?"

"Yes, Chef." Penny was one of the four new hires. They were all pretty green, but well-trained and eager.

Damien had no trouble relinquishing his task. He didn't like how whatever was going on bothered Will, that was all. Shooting a grin of thanks at Penny, he put his oven mitts on the counter and followed Emil to the man's office. Will pulled up the rear, a solid presence at his back.

When they arrived, Damien took one of the visitor chairs and was disappointed when Will elected to stand next to Emil after closing the door. He'd had a fleeting hope that the man would sit and, given the smallness of the office, their knees would be practically touching. Yeah, leg sex... That was where his mind was at. It was practically Victorian in its prissiness, yet nothing more seemed to be in the offing.

You could make the first move, moron, his inner voice reminded him. *When did I become so shy?* Maybe it was because Will wasn't some rando in a club. If they hooked up, they'd see each other every day. And what if one night was all Will was interested in? That would suck. Damien was afraid his heart was at risk of being cut to ribbons. That was new...and scary.

He dove right into the reason they were there. It was easier than pondering his attraction and worries. "What's up, guys? How can I help you?"

The two men shared a glance before Emil spoke. "First, I want to be absolutely clear that you are free to say no. Hell no, in fact—and that refusal will in no way jeopardize your job or how we, the family, appreciate you."

"Okay, duly noted, Chef."

Emil huffed. "Good. It's, ah...weird. See... We recently found out that a member of our family, a cousin, has joined a political campaign."

Damien furrowed his brows. "Yeah, I know. Bran, right? And the cocksucker, Warren. I was there, remember, when you all collectively shat boiled lobsters in Alex's office the other day?"

Emil rubbed his forehead. "Yes, of course. I'd forgotten. Sorry. We hustled you out so fast that I'm sure it was bizarre and confusing."

It had been all of that and more, but Damien merely shrugged. "Not my business. Or I guess it is now?"

"Yes, if you're willing," Will interjected. "Which you absolutely don't have to be."

Damien smiled at the man's earnest face. "Voluntary… Got it. No worries. What do you want me to do, seduce the congressman or something? 'Cause from what I know, that's not hard. A big enough dick and he's all yours. I, ah, don't have any trouble meeting that requirement. Although," he added with wink at Will, "I bet you'd be a significant rival in that department."

Will's eyes went wide at the comment, leaving Damien both satisfied and embarrassed. He mentally facepalmed, wondering where that cheekiness had come from.

Emil cleared his throat. "Anyway, the congressman has a gay conversion camp, and—"

Damien sat forward. "No fucking way! Wow, I hate the guy even more. I had a boat-load of that shit with my own family before they realized it was never going to work and booted my gay ass out of the house. It's torture, in the literal sense of the word."

He stared at the floor, shaking his head as memories suddenly swamped him. The old feelings of hopelessness and urges for self-harm threatened to overwhelm him for a few seconds before he reminded himself he was not that scared boy anymore.

"Are you all right?"

The question and Will's closeness startled him. The man had crouched beside Damien, concern marring his lovely face, his violet eyes darker now and staring intently at him.

For a few awesome moments, he got lost in them, imagining they looked at him with something more like passion. He had to work to break the connection and shake off the effect of that focus.

He switched his gaze to Emil. "What do you want me to do, go undercover there or something?" He'd meant it as a kind of joke, real *Charlie's Angels* kind of shit. He could see by the man's expressions that he'd hit on the truth. A quick glance at Will confirmed that he also was on that page.

Damien sat back again. "Okay, wow. Fuck, but okay. I can totally do that."

"It would only be for a few days," Emil assured him. "Long enough to maybe learn something useful. Bran is up to no good. That's all we know, because that's what he does—causes trouble."

"And you want me to find dirt on him so you can make him slink back to… Where do you all come from again? Romania?"

"Originally yes," Will answered. Sadly, he'd stood and moved back. "Although Bran was raised in Wales."

"Like Brenin and Dafydd. You don't want them to go because he knows them." He was proud of being able to connect the dots, instead of getting emotionally mired in wanting Will and tracking his movements.

"Yes," Emil confirmed. "He knows all of us, but not you. And we need to be clear on this. You aren't going to do any snooping. All we ask is that you keep your eyes and ears open for a few days. If nothing pops out that is of use, then you leave. It's purely a voluntary place. They can't keep you there."

"We won't let them do so," Will clarified, and there was a fierce look in his eyes, as if he were willing to *shit, die for him* or something.

That had to be a trick of the light. Will barely knew him. Besides, it wasn't going to be dangerous. Not really. Was it?

"It could be dangerous," Will said in the next instant, as if reading his mind.

That answers that question.

"In what way?" The first sense of unease was killing his enthusiasm.

"Bran is vicious and wouldn't hesitate to make you disappear if he thought you were spying on him. I won't let him do that," Will said without a pause. "I swear I won't."

The 'I-will-take-a-bullet-for-you' vibe was back. This time, Damien believed it, wholly, and it sent a warmth through him that settled in his dick. It started to harden and an image of them sharing a night of unbridled passion before Damien went off to his suicide mission invaded his head. *Oh boy, am I being ridiculous.*

"How would you know if I needed you?" he challenged in an almost-breathless voice.

"I'll penetrate the compound every night. We'll set up a rendezvous point in there, and if they lock you in at night, I'll find a way to get to you."

Damien had stopped paying attention after the word 'penetrate' had been uttered. His hole clenched in juvenile fashion. He could hear Beavis and Butt-Head... *"He said penetrate, heh, heh."* He shook his head to get it back in the game.

"I'm sorry. Did you say you're going to break into the compound every night? You can do that?"

"Yes." The simple conviction was comforting.

"Why don't you do that instead?"

"We don't necessarily want Bran to know we're after him," Emil answered. "The idea would be for you to meet Will outside, somewhere relatively secluded to reduce the chance of being caught."

"Yeah, makes sense." He eyed Will again. The man looked and carried himself like a soldier. He trusted Will had the skills he claimed. "What about Annika?"

"She understands that there are some things I have to do that take me from her. If she objects strongly, then we may have to rethink the whole thing, of course."

There was nothing obviously duplicitous about the way Will answered, except Damien thought he detected an undertone. Was it possible Will was hoping she would kick up a fuss? And if she did, wouldn't that only mean that someone else, like Malcolm, would take over the role of Damien's protector? The man might wear a skirt most of the time, but he was like a warrior of old. He was no one to fuck with, that was for sure.

He also wasn't Will. Damien wanted Will. He said nothing about that, however. It wouldn't be fair of him to put pressure on Will. His kid came first. Damien understood that about the man and it was one of the things he admired about him. And there was nothing he wouldn't do for Emil, the man who had been more of a father to him than the asshole who'd raised him, the guy who'd looked at him with such disgust as he'd literally tossed him out of his home. The pain of that rejection still cut deep. And while there was nothing Damien could do about his past, this spying scheme was a way to pay Emil back that was more than baking cookies.

"Okay. I'm in, guys. Tell me what to do."

Emil smiled. "Thank you, Damien. I can't tell you how much this means to the family. We'll go see Val after dinner is finished and he'll go over everything you need to know. We hope you can infiltrate as early as tomorrow."

Damien nodded then glanced up at Will. He wasn't smiling. In fact, he looked like every commanding officer in every movie Damien had ever seen as he gave the order for the suicide mission. Maybe there'd be a goodbye fuck for him after all.

A boy could dream.

* * * *

Annika peered around the doorjamb, shushing Babette, who wiggled in her arms. Dafydd was on the floor playing with Idris. They were stacking wooden blocks. Well, Dafydd was stacking them. Idris seemed more intent on knocking them down. They appeared to be content, and Annika sensed no tension in the changed human. She was confident in disturbing them. The two of them were part of her hive, and although there was no one to tell her so, she knew instinctively that it was her duty to ensure that they were well. She simply wasn't sure of her welcome. It was hard to get a read on the Welshman. Although, again, no one had told her as much, she knew that he'd suffered greatly from Dracul. It was up to her to try to mend that damage.

Squaring her shoulders, she knocked on the jamb and stepped inside the room before Dafydd responded. It was harder to deny her entrance that way. She smiled brightly. "May I join you, Mr. Dafydd?" Politeness was ingrained in her as well. She never assumed familiarity, not yet. She might be Queen, but she was also young, and those more mature than she were owed certain courtesies.

Dafydd's gaze shifted from his son to Annika with obvious startlement. He started to stand, and not wanting to inconvenience him, she bent to set Babette free. Her dog raced over to Idris, who squealed with delight. The baby loved Babette, and the feeling was mutual. She attacked him by covering his face with licks. As usual, he grabbed for her fur with both hands.

His father intervened, keeping those chubby fingers from taking too great a hold on the dog. "Gentle, Idris," he said in English, then repeated the warning in Welsh. He flicked his gaze to her long enough to say, "Come in and join us."

Pleased with the reception, Annika skipped over and plopped down on the floor, careful to sweep the long skirt of her dress under her bottom. "Thank you. How is Idris coming in learning his letters?" She'd had similar blocks to learn Dutch. English had come later, as had other languages. She now knew seven, although she used computer programs to master new ones. She rather missed the blocks, though.

She picked one up and turned it around to its various sides. There was a capital C and a lowercase one, along with pictures of a cat and carrot, as well as the whole words themselves. It was all in English. "Are you teaching him Welsh?"

With his hands still hovering around Idris to keep him from playing too roughly with Babette, he answered. "Yes, but only the spoken word, as you just heard. Ric is adding in Spanish. Idris seems to be absorbing it all."

"Oh yes, I expect that as a hybrid, he will be able to easily master quite a few languages like I have and continue to."

Dafydd frowned. "He's not a Queen."

She giggled. "He doesn't have to be." She cocked her head as she considered the import of his words. "Do you think being male makes him less intelligent than I am?"

Before he could answer, Idris piped up with a series of, "Ba, ba, ba."

Annika clapped her hands. "Yes, that's it, Baby Idris. Her name is Babette. She's a dog."

"Dog!" Idris repeated and clapped his own hands.

"Very good," she praised and beamed at Dafydd. "You see, Mr. Dafydd? He's very smart. Soon he'll be speaking in full sentences, I shouldn't wonder."

Dafydd looked skeptical. "If you say so. It hasn't been my experience that hybrid sons are particularly clever."

Annika turned serious. This was why she'd come, after all. "You are thinking of your other sons."

"Yes." Dafydd's voice was very quiet. His sadness radiated off him. She felt it keenly.

"I am sorry about the older one. Father Willem has told me about him. He has been catching me up on everything that has happened since the ship crashed. I need to know these things, you understand, if I'm to lead my hive."

Dafydd gave up hovering over his son as Babette had lain down across Idris' legs and he'd mastered petting her. He looked at her straight in the eye. "If you say so. I know little about your culture. Dracul told me nothing and I didn't want to know, in any event. I don't ask about any of it. If you want to know the truth, I don't care."

"I understand. You want to live a human life again."

"Yes." The man was back to not looking at her.

"Dr. Ric will make that possible. He spends most every night here with you—and days when he isn't working. You have welcomed him into your life, so he is also welcome in the hive."

"We are…feeling our way on all things. He wants to marry me," he added, although his tone implied skepticism and Annika sensed his conflicting emotions.

"It is hard for you to adjust to a new life after so many years with Dracul."

Dafydd's gaze flicked at her, surprise clear in his expression. "Yes, it is. Ric is very patient, however."

Pleased with the open exchange, she let silence fall for a little while. They sat watching Idris alternating between his toys—the living one and the others. Babette was amazingly patient with the boy.

Annika didn't quite share that trait with her dog. "Does my presence make you uncomfortable?" She knew the answer already. It radiated off the man in such an obvious way, she figured that even a human would detect it.

"Yes."

Such an honest reply. "I understand—and I think you are very brave for saying so." When he shrugged in response, she added, "It is not my intention to bother you…or anyone. It's simply a matter of my following my destiny. I am Queen, and that means I can't do as I'd like and stay in the nursery, playing with dolls and blocks."

She turned the one in her hand over and over, still enjoying the bright colors and the cute expression on the cat's face. "I came here to see how you were doing." She paused and licked her lips. This wasn't easy, and she rather expected that much of what she'd have to do for the rest of her life would be hard. "You have heard about your son Bran?"

Dafydd closed his eyes briefly and a terrible pain showed on his face. "Yes. I know he's here, up to something that isn't good."

Putting down the block, she scooted closer to him and put her hand on his knee. She wasn't sure how to accomplish it exactly, but she was trying to give him comfort. "I promise to do whatever I can to bring him into the hive."

She thought some tension left his body, although she couldn't be sure. Reading the emotions of those around her was something she hadn't yet mastered.

"You are kind," he said. "I think perhaps that will prove impossible. To a large degree, Dracul ensured their doom the moment those boys came into the world."

"It's important not to lose hope." She removed her hand and said, "Would you like me to leave? Babette can remain and play with Idris, of course."

Dafydd shook his head. "No, stay. Please. Idris likes your being here. Can you tell?" The baby was staring at her with a sloppy grin. "He recognizes you for who and what you are, I think. And, I want to become accustomed to you too, because I'm not going anywhere. I'm part of the hive, like, by default. Unlike Bran, I was never coopted by Dracul's world view. And Ric has made it clear that he will do whatever's necessary to stay in my life, including living this alien one."

"I would that you'd be with us by choice."

Dafydd didn't respond directly, his emotions a jumble and impossible to get a read on. Instead he asked, "Do you like Legos?"

"Oh, yes indeed!" It was all right if he wanted to change the subject. She'd come to reassure him about his son, but she understood now that nothing she said was going to help. He wasn't ready to trust again and perhaps he never would be. She had to prove herself with actions, not promises.

"Idris loves his Duplo blocks. Let's get them out and see what we can build, heh?"

"A most excellent suggestion." Annika beamed back at him and happily waited for him to fetch the basket of blocks. Being Queen wasn't all serious business, after all.

She spent close to an hour of carefree fun building silly things out of the plastic blocks. Idris proved to be very adept at construction. In her mind, Annika was already assigning him a civil engineering job for the hive. It was impossible for her not to think in those terms. The planning and maneuvering were instinctive in her, and the urge to do so had grown greatly in the last few months. Resistant at first, as she'd been with most of her obligations, she'd stopped fighting it and there was peace of mind in doing so.

A knock on the door caught all of their attentions. Looking over her shoulder, she saw her father coming in. "Oh, Father Willem." She smiled brightly, happy to see him, as always. Sometimes she wished she could be less formal with him. She longed to simply call him at least 'Willem', as she'd used to. He'd said humans would find that strange and that adding 'father' to it would be more acceptable. Back on the home-world, she would have had lots of males that were mated to her mother, all of whom would be her father legally, if not biologically. Distinguishing them by name was the norm.

It was interesting, in an academic way, how her mind insisted on following rules that didn't apply on Earth. Except she really wanted to call him 'papa', but it never sat right on her tongue. Papa had always been Luuk, the human who'd made her conception and birth possible. She missed him with an ache that merely lessened occasionally in intensity, yet never truly went away. Although he didn't burden her with his problems, she knew Willem also missed Luuk, to a degree that she worried he was shutting off the potential to find happiness again.

With his hands jammed into his front pockets, her father walked over to them and peered at their efforts. "That looks like a formidable structure." Babette rose from where she'd been sleeping and pranced around his feet.

"It is mostly due to Baby Idris' imagination. I only follow his commands." Which was entirely made up of his finger-pointing and babbling.

"He can be quite demanding," Dafydd agreed. "You're very patient with him."

"It's easy to do so." She smiled at him before focusing on her father. "Is it time for dinner?"

"Not quite yet. I was hoping to speak with you."

Alone. He didn't say as much, but she could tell that was what he meant.

"Certainly." She stood and straightened her dress. "I'll see you later." She waved bye-bye to Idris and scooped Babette against her chest.

Seeing his playmate leaving sent Idris into a fretful state, his face screwing up and his arms waving. His mouth opened to wail. Dafydd grabbed him much the way Annika had her dog. "None of that now. You be nice, like." Idris' lips quivered, but he complied.

Good. It was lovely to see Mr. Dafydd being a true father to his son.

Shooting another wave, Annika left the room. Her own father followed in her wake, saying nothing until they'd reached their suite of rooms. The sitting area had been decorated to her tastes, as much as her bedroom had. She had tried not to make it too feminine, understanding that her father used this room, too. In the end, she couldn't resist turning her private environment into a place of pretty colors, tufted furniture and lacy curtains. This was quintessentially female among humans and she'd found that part of her ran strong in her instincts. It was the same reason she couldn't quite bring herself to dress in jeans and T-shirts. She was most comfortable clad in flowing dresses with fancy trim and wearing shiny shoes on her feet.

She sat on the edge of the settee with Babette on her lap. "Is something the matter?"

Her father didn't answer right away. His tension was easy to detect. He was disturbed about something and obviously reluctant, yet determined, to discuss it with her. He sat heavily on a chair and leaned forward, resting his arms on his thighs.

"I am coming to you because you are the Queen," he began. "I have a favor to ask that I shouldn't, but I can't quite help myself, regardless." He looked at her with troubled eyes. "I am being disloyal in this. I freely admit it. My concern is outweighing my sense of duty, though." Running his fingers through his hair and staring at the floor, he added, "My brain is reeling from the conflict."

"Speak plainly, Father Willem. *Papa*," she made herself say.

His gaze snapped to her face. "I don't ask this as your father but as your subject. I want your advice and intervention as a hive matter."

"Understood." She sat straighter and schooled her expression to a neutral one, letting none of her affection for the man show in her face.

"Alex called a meeting this morning to discuss the Bran situation. This human politician that he works for has a camp to try to convince young men who are gay that they are really straight. It also serves as the homestead for the guy and his wife, as well as headquarters for his campaign. We think it may be where we can learn something useful to stop Bran without, you know, killing him outright. We try to keep a low profile on this world."

"Yes, a very sensible idea." *For now.*

She didn't say that last part out loud. While she understood and applauded how her father and the others had tried to keep their existence on Earth a secret, in order to survive more easily, as Queen, her mandate was quite different. Eventually, humans would learn of them, once the hive was big enough to not only survive but potentially dominate. She was concerned that none of the men understood that in his twisted way Dracul had been right. As a more evolved species, their kind was destined to rule over humans. Her way of going about it quite simply had a better chance of succeeding. And, of course, it wasn't to hurt the humans. There would be no subjugation. All would become clear, eventually. But not now. It was too early for that revelation.

"Anyway," her father continued, "we decided to insert a human boy into the camp to see what he can learn. I think we should try using one of our hybrids, who are arriving shortly. One of them may be grown enough to pass for a human adult and be someone that can take care of himself. Bran wouldn't recognize him, either, unlike anyone who was involved with the assault on Dracul's castle. But I was overruled. The others don't believe that even a hybrid could avoid detection by Bran, that only a human will do."

Understanding came quickly. "They want to use Mr. Damien."

Her father didn't show any surprise. "Yes, I guess that's obvious, isn't it? He's the only human of the right age that we'd be sure Bran didn't know, because he wasn't with us in Wales."

"It's also obvious because he's the one you like, so naturally this plan bothers you." She couldn't help the giggle that escaped. The idea of her father being smitten by the human was too marvelous. *So romantic.* It was the perfect solution to her worry that he might mourn Luuk for the rest of his life.

He reared back at her observation. "No, it's not... I don't... He and I aren't—"

"You should be." Putting Babette on the sofa, she slid off and over to her father. She plopped onto his lap, much the way Babette had on hers. He didn't hesitate to wrap his arms around her and hold her close as he'd done for her entire life. There had been no lack of affection in her childhood, and her rapid approach to maturity didn't change how much she loved being cuddled.

They sat there for long seconds, hugging, her father kissing the top of her head. "I love you so much that it's almost a physical hurt. You are the center of my life, and that would be true even if you weren't Queen." He sighed. "It's been hard since losing your papa. I wish you'd had more time with him, so that you could have known him better."

Annika had very clear and wonderful memories of her human parent. He'd died when she'd been young, yet they'd spent a great deal of time together as he'd prepared for his end. *'Take care of Willem. He's going to need you when I'm gone, and eventually, he'll rely on you to make hard decisions.'* "I have many memories of him and others that are yours that you've been kind enough to share with me." She laid her head against his chest, so solid and secure. "And I believe he wouldn't want you to be alone for the rest of your life."

"You are my focus," he said with a little squeeze for emphasis.

She leaned back to look him in the eyes. "I'm hardly Baby Idris. I don't need constant care, and look at how Mr. Dafydd is with Dr. Ric. They love each other and find time to be together."

But her father was shaking his head. "It's different. They're building a life together, and Ric knows about us and what Dafydd went through. There are no secrets between them. It's still going to be long and difficult road for them, with no guarantees for success."

She realized she had to be firmer with him. "And yet with all that to face, they are still trying. You are looking for excuses, reasons to deny yourself. You've always done that." She grimaced. "I don't like it. It doesn't help me if you are unhappy."

"I'm not!"

"All right," she conceded. "It doesn't help me if you are less happy than you could be." She pressed forward. "I see the way you look at him, and I also see how he looks at you. You want each other."

Her father ran his hand gently down the back of her head. "It's not like in the movies you watch, sweetheart. Damien and I aren't in love."

"Oh, but it's exactly like in the movies!" she exclaimed. Really, males could be ridiculous sometimes. "Remember in *Frozen* how Anna falls in love with the evil prince that she just met at the ball and everyone is telling her that it's crazy? You need to get to know someone before you decide if it's love and if you want to get married. You and Mr. Damien need to spend time together. That's all."

Now her father had a pained expression on his face. "My darling girl, it's not the same…at all. Damien and I are, um, attracted to one another, yes. We both have certain physical needs that might be satisfied by engaging in…" He closed his eyes briefly. "How did our conversation end up here?"

"Oh, Father Willem, you are talking about sex."

He winced. "God…"

"Why are you distressed? You're the one who said I should come to you for explanations when I was ready."

"Yeah, as an academic exercise. I am not going to discuss that with you in the context of my life."

"Why ever not?"

"Because it's embarrassing?"

"Huh." Annika folded her arms, irritated at the way the discussion was going. "Does that mean that when I have questions about my eventual desire for males that I can't talk to you?"

"No! I doesn't mean that at all. I want you to always feel free to come to me with any questions or problems. Although, in this case, you might be better talking to a woman…like Kitty. She would understand better than I and she knows our secret—which is a really important point. Damien knows nothing of our true nature. I shouldn't become personally involved with him because it risks exposing us."

"The others have taken the humans into their confidences, like Ms. Kitty—and like you did with Papa."

"It's hard to do. You never know if they will be accepting or out you to the world."

"And yet you did it once and it was worth the risk, wasn't it?"

Her father's eyes clouded with emotion. "Yes. Yes, it was."

Clasping his face with her hands, she said. "Isn't it time to take that risk again? We wouldn't be here talking about your fears for Alex's plan if you didn't care for this boy."

"You're right, of course." He took her hands in his and kissed both palms. "Going behind Alex's back feels wrong, but I couldn't resist the urge. That says something right there about how much in denial I am about Damien."

"This isn't a betrayal. I'm Queen. Talking to me is always the right thing to do. In this case, however, I defer to Alex. He knows far better than I what the proper course of action is in matters of conflict and aggression. I will learn, eventually. Not yet, though. I want to side with you because you are my father, but Alex has done a remarkable job of containing Dracul and his followers. He knows what he is doing."

She got off his lap and stood before him. "You should go to him, tonight. Mr. Damien, I mean, not Alex." She inwardly shook her head at the image of Alex's hearing about Will's concerns and his hopes that she would intervene. As honorable a drone as he was, he was going to have trouble accepting her supremacy. It was inevitable that they would clash, although she had no doubt that she would prevail. A thousand years on Earth wasn't going to have altered far more millennia of evolution.

This wasn't the time to focus on that problem, however. "Once I'm tucked into my pretty bed with Babette curled up beside me and I don't need you anymore, go tell Mr. Damien how you feel, including your worries for him. I bet he will be extra careful to please you, because I am certain you matter to him."

Father Willem took in a deep breath and let it out slowly. "You are a wise Queen." He stood and held out his hand. "Shall we go down to dinner?"

She took it. "Yes, indeed. Come, Babette."

There was more that she wanted to say but she decided to hold her tongue instead. She didn't think her father was ready to hear the whole of the truth. He didn't merely want the human. He was falling in love with him—and that was fine with her.

Chapter Five

Will couldn't quite believe he was doing this. His daughter had actually talked him into pursuing Damien. He shouldn't have been surprised, really, about her matchmaking. Queens were very instrumental in the various pairings within the hive. It was usually older ones eyeing who would do well with whom. Adolescent queens, not so much. But Annika was an anomaly in many ways. Her observations about his attraction to Damien were predictable, given how rapidly she was taking on her mantle of power. He just couldn't shake the weird feeling that his daughter was in any way involved in his sex life.

Jesus, she practically ordered me to go get laid.

It was his own fault. What had he been thinking, bringing the problem to her anyway? Abject fear for the boy had been the driving force. And while he didn't think seducing him would help with that at all, it might be useful in making sure Damien welcomed Will's protection while he did his infiltration. No way was Will going to allow anyone else to be the boy's guardian angel during the whole thing. Damien would probably be more receptive to his lover keeping tabs on him that someone else.

Or, this could all be a rationalization for acting on the desire to fuck Damien that had been plaguing him since he'd moved to Boston.

It's wasn't very late, barely eleven. Annika was tucked under the covers of her canopy bed with the furball by her side, as she herself had described. She was absolutely angelic in her sleep, with her pale blonde hair fanned out on her pink silk pillow and her white eyelet coverlet pulled up to her chin, with only the lacy collar of her nightgown showing. Her beauty took his breath away, and he loved her with an intensity that, as he'd said, almost hurt.

He hated the fact that Luuk had had so little time with her — that his enhanced life could be struck down by a human ailment that Will's blood was supposed to have immunized him from. He should have been here to see their daughter grow into a woman, to become the Queen. He missed the man so much, his bed cold and empty, no matter where he lay his head. Sometimes he still reached for his lover in the middle of the night, only to come up with a fistful of bedding. More than the sex, it was the intimacy he truly missed. Perhaps he could find a measure of that with Damien.

He found the boy in the kitchen — not the family one but the big commercial area that served the club. He was alone, which was a relief. Will was out of practice asking a man for company and didn't want an audience. *God, what if he turns me down?* That would suck, especially given the hours he'd spent working himself into a lather over the asking part. But there was no need to get ahead of himself. There was a mutual attraction, so it was likely Damien would welcome the advance. Will didn't need anyone else to point that out to him.

The club music was piped into the kitchen. The Doors' *Break on Through* was playing. Damien was cleaning up and moving to the beat. It was such a delightful surprise that Will stood and watched. The boy had moves, as good as the go-go boys for sure. His slender hips, draped in the white chef's jacket, were swinging back and forth as he moved around the kitchen. The synthetic keyboard chords echoed throughout the space, and Damien added little steps back and forth in time to the rhythm. *God, he's adorable.* And Will had loved the sixties, especially living in Amsterdam. Those had been the happiest, most carefree days of his life.

He'd met Luuk back then and had fallen instantly in love.

Except Luuk was dead, and Annika was right about his not wanting Will to stay alone forever. He'd have felt the same if the situation had been reversed. In fact, they had discussed it, knowing that Will might have to leave at any time to join Alex in a fight. Will had made Luuk promise to find some else, to continue to live his life. And that had been before Annika's unexpected birth. He knew that being with Damien wasn't any kind of betrayal. It was still hard to make his feet move.

He did it, though, approaching the unaware boy as the song reached its crescendo. Damien executed a whirl at the last note and ended up facing Will. He came to an abrupt stop and stood wide-eyed, staring at him.

Then he grinned sheepishly. "I didn't realize anyone was here."

Will tried for a casual smile back. "I didn't want to interrupt you. You were obviously enjoying yourself."

Damien shrugged. "Well, you know, I love the classics—The Doors, Jimmy, Janis, Cream, Guess Who. I can't stand still when they're playing. Tonight's retro night, so... I mean, don't get me wrong, I love a lot of heavy metal and grunge, the alternative rock stuff. It's all good. But, man, give me that synth keyboard and I'm in heaven." The boy stopped and shook his head. "I'm babbling because you're being here with me alone is freaking me out."

Alarmed at the statement, Will took a step back. "I'm sorry. I didn't intend to bother you."

Damien rolled his eyes. "No, dude, it's because I want you to be here so much. I, like, fantasize about your being with me just like this—no one around, the two of us staring into each other's eyes. Then you come up to me and wham, I'm in your arms and you're kissing the shit out of me." Damien stopped and barked out a laugh. "And now I'm freaking you out because you're here for like a sandwich or something."

Will didn't let the conversation go any further. He did exactly what Damien had said, went to him and took him in his arms. He wasn't gentle because he didn't think Damien wanted that. Instead, he locked him into a bear-hug and attacked the boy's lips. It was full-on tongue down the throat time. There was no way he had the patience to finesse it. He'd generally known that the human had a pierced tongue, but it still surprised him to find it massaging the tip of his own, the steel ball providing a unique stimulation. He liked it, though, and kept coming back to it, tickling it and enjoying the sensation.

Damien hesitated only a second before responding in kind, with his arms wrapped tightly around Will's torso and his leg entwined with one of Will's. The position allowed Damien to rise up to align his shorter body with Will's taller one better, grinding their hips together. Their hard cocks pressed and rubbed, even with their clothing still on. *Fucking hell*. Will thought he would come from that little contact alone.

He had to slow things down before he did, before he bent Damien over one of Emil's prepping stations and fucked him right there. God, it was a tempting thought, but there were any number of people who could walk in and Will had to show some common sense. It was hard, though. After so many years of celibacy, his sex drive was like a bursting dam. There was little to hold it back.

Breaking the kiss, he huffed, "We have to find a private place."

"Storeroom," Damien panted out.

Before Will could respond to that suggestion, Damien was already taking the lead, uncoupling them in order to grab Will's hand. He tugged him across the kitchen and into one of the rooms where Emil stored his dry supplies. Damien opened the door then kicked it shut again. They were plunged into darkness, which was rather arousing, actually. Then there was little time to ponder that before Damien was in his arms again.

This kiss was no less intense than the last one, except now Damien was working Will's T-shirt, shoving it up to expose his chest. Damien found Will's nipples and made him moan as the human rubbed and plucked at them. Will wanted to do the same, but settled for working his hands under the chef's jacket in order to slide them past the waist of Damien's jeans. They were loose enough that he could reach the boy's perfect high, tight ass. He cupped it and used it to press him even closer.

"Hm-m," Damien moaned. He broke the kiss and whispered, "Fuck me. Right here against the door. I want your dick inside me. *Now!*"

Will latched onto Damien's lip and tugged before saying, "The condom's in my front pocket." Humans needed such things to feel safe, even though there was nothing Will could transmit to him. The club had plenty on hand and he'd grabbed a few on his way to the kitchen, along with a small tube of lubricant.

He'd barely said the words before Damien had pushed him away and was undoing his jeans, lowering the zipper and freeing his hard dick. At the same time, Will was pulling out a condom and the lube, covering and slicking himself. It was fast, efficient and being done in the kind of dark that humans couldn't see in.

Then Damien was back to kissing him before saying, "You're ready for take-off, Captain. Just don't trip on your partially lowered pants," he added with a chuckle.

Will almost said something about Alex being the captain before mentally kicking himself. This beautiful, sexy boy was offering his ass on a platter. Well, against the door, but the point was, all Will had to do was point and pierce. Because yes, Damien had turned and put himself in the perfect position, jutting his ass out in invitation. His naked ass, because in the last half-second, he'd dropped his own jeans. The paleness of his flesh was visible to Will's alien eyes. And by taking the boy from behind, Will's natural inclination to sink his fangs into the jugular was somewhat hampered.

What the fuck am I doing thinking? Analyzing? He slipped one finger down the crease of Damien's ass to locate and press against his hole. With a groan, Damien pushed back to take the finger in more deeply. The puckered ring was soft and pliable. The tight channel was also loose and welcoming.

"What are you waiting for?" Damien demanded. "I'm not into the whole BDSM thing. I don't like being *tortured*."

Will smiled at the admonition right before he sunk himself balls-deep into Damien's beckoning hole.

Oh God. It was amazing. To experience that tight heat clasping his cock made him light-headed from the pure pleasure. He stayed right where he was for a few seconds to simply revel in the complete rightness of it all. Then Damien whined and clamped his hole like a vise in obvious demand. It got Will moving, because it wasn't all about what made him happy. He treated the human to a few hard, long thrusts and had intended to keep those up, but he came. Like an uncontrolled explosion, he filled Damien's ass with pent-up cum. Well, filled the condom, really, except Will liked to picture it otherwise.

He did it once, twice, always thrusting, and was on his third orgasm when Damien jerked and cried out. Will had enough sense left to bury himself completely before reaching around to clasp Damien's dick and milk it through the boy's climax.

They stood there, panting and shuddering with the aftershocks. Will allowed himself to lower his head to place his mouth along the side of Damien's neck. He kissed, even though he wanted to bite. He soothed his necessary disappointment by sucking the skin with his lips, knowing he'd leave a mark, just not the one he would prefer.

Damien spoke. "I knew it would be great. I've wanted you from the moment I first saw you." He paused. "I hope that doesn't freak you out."

Will licked his way up the side of Damien's neck and around the shell of his ear. He would have loved to nip at the lobe, but the boy's small gages were in the way. "Not in the least. Will it, as you say, freak you out, if I ask you to come to my room and spend the night with me?"

Damien chuckled. "Hell no. Fulfill all of my fantasies, why don't you? Except, um, Annika?"

"Sleeps soundly through the night. She won't come out of her room until morning. Not even her dog rouses her before then. And," he added in order for his daughter to not became an issue, "our walls are very thick. She won't hear us, so long as you don't do any screaming."

"Ha! That part might be hard. You're amazing. You do know that?" Will didn't know how to respond to that assertion. "I mean, do you ever get soft? It felt as if you came a few times and it still feels like I've got a club up my ass."

"Am I hurting you?" Alarmed, Will tried to pull out. Damien made that hard by following and slamming back into his chest. Will had to hug the boy from behind to keep him steady.

"Hell no! Dude, you're like a sex god. I can't get enough of you. Maybe we should stay here for the night."

Will chuckled and gently decoupled them, despite Damien's mew of disappointment. "I think we've probably already violated some number of sanitation codes for kitchens. Let's go where we'll be more comfortable and have better privacy. I find," he confessed with only a little embarrassment, "that I crave you again, too."

"Then, what are we waiting for?"

* * * *

Will woke from his dreamless sleep to the feeling of silky wet warmth sliding up the length of his cock. He smiled before opening his eyes, knowing whose mouth was tending to him in such a delightful way. Having stumbled into Will's room, they'd fucked again, more slowly and face-to-face, which Will had appreciated. They'd collapsed and fallen asleep with Will's dick still embedded in Damien's ass. At some point, Will had roused sufficiently to disengage and toss the condom into the wastebasket by his bedside. Thank God, he had it there because he lacked the strength to get up and go to the bathroom.

He'd felt satiated and amazingly content.

Except now the fog was lifting from his brain and his body was waking up oh, so delightfully. The touch on his cock was lazy, a slow arousal, although Will's dick didn't do slow. It was already hard as steel, ready for more play. God, it had been so long since he'd enjoyed another man's touch—except he wasn't going to go there. Luuk wouldn't have wanted to be an uninvited guest while Will entertained Damien.

He slid his hand to where he expected to find his lover's head and touched the strands of slightly stiff hair. Damien gelled it into a funky array that also showcased the blue streaks. He didn't understand the humans' universal desire to change their appearance. Will wondered if he could convince him to leave it natural. It was baby fine, and he bet it would be soft to the touch. The ink on his skin and the piercings were another story. They were not easily changed, and he would never ask it of the boy anyway. He got the fact that they were an expression of Damien's rejection of the life that he'd been kicked out of. It was his way of telling the world that he existed and he was proud of himself.

Will's eyes popped open when Damien took the head of his cock into his mouth. The sight of the boy blowing him was erotic enough to make him come right then and there. He held it back with effort. He wanted to make it last.

Damn, but the boy knew his way around a dick, that was for certain. And oh holy fuck, talk about body modification. The tongue piercing served a very useful purpose, the metal ball teasing Will's cock in a most unusual way, an indescribable boost to the already-intense sensations of being licked and laved, sucked and nibbled. He arched as the pleasure threatened to peak. Not wanting to come alone, he used the strands wound around his fingers to gently tugged Damien off his cock and up his body.

When they came face-to-face, Will captured those lips, tasting his own cum. He rolled them over, grabbing both their cocks in a single grip. As he kissed Damien deeply, fucking his mouth with his tongue, he jerked the hard shafts as one. The pre-cum leaking from both of them eased the way, although, for his own part, Will was willing to scourge the skin off his dick to achieve another mind-blowing orgasm with the human. He wanted to make it good for Damien, and when the boy erupted into Will's hand, crying down his throat and thrashing beneath him, he figured he'd succeeded.

As they both panted their way back to normal breathing, Will amused himself once more by playing with Damien's hair. The human's heartbeat was still fast, and it was nice to listen to, even though he couldn't do more than that. Nothing was likely to end their night together faster and more horribly than for him to show his true nature. He'd forgotten how hard that was, to hide himself, to act like any human man getting laid — no blood, only freakishly amazing orgasms, not that there was anything wrong with that. Quite the contrary… Will hadn't felt this happy since losing Luuk. It was only that Damien's scent was driving him wild, and he was desperate for a taste of him. His blood would be sweet, Will knew for a certainty.

But there was no point in torturing himself with thoughts of what he couldn't have. So he focused on what was right in front of him—the warmth of Damien's body, the smoothness of his skin, the way his fingers skittered lightly over Will's abdomen, teasing his dick indirectly into another erection.

"Are these stretch marks?" Damien asked in a voice thick from being well-fucked. He tilted his head to look at Will. "Sorry. I don't mean to make you self-conscious. They're sexy as hell." He grinned.

Caught by surprise at the question, Will hesitated, choosing to focus on that last bit. "Sexy? Seriously?"

Damien's grin widened. "Yup. Everything about you is." So saying, he dropped his head against Will's torso and licked a trail up one of those stretch marks. "Did you used to be overweight?"

Oh, thank God. That was the perfect cover. "Um, yeah, I was," he admitted. "It was a long time ago, when I was a kid." He inwardly cringed at how awkward his response sounded to his own ears.

Damien rubbed his cheek against Will's stomach before resting it there. "I get it. I was a chubby kid myself. When I hit puberty, that all went magically away somehow. Of course, other problems replaced it, like how I really had the hots for the captain of the baseball team. I was crap at hiding that too, so you know that I got beat up a lot."

The image his casual words created inside Will's head made him furious. "Little shits. Say the word and I'll track them down and show them how much it hurts to be picked on."

Damien chuckled, his warm breath tickling Will's stomach. "You'd have to put my entire family on that list, too."

Hearing that enraged him. He slammed his lids shut so Damien couldn't see his pupils turning red. Holding back a howl was like choking on rising bile. "They hurt you?" he bit out, dreading hearing the answer, yet wanting to give his new lover an outlet for his grief.

Damien blew out a long breath. "My daddy was quick with his belt. Every time I came home bloodied by the other boys, he made sure my backside matched. *'You bring this on yourself, boy. I need to get that devil out of you.'* I sometimes wonder if old dad was a pedophile or something. He seemed to really enjoy pulling down my pants."

Will mauled his sheet with one hand in order to keep from digging his fingers into Damien, as his anger against the boy's family increased. "And with all that, they also kicked you out of your home, didn't they?" He knew something of the tale, and it was the same with most of the boys who worked with Alex, including the ones who were now members of the family.

"Yeah, well, I got pretty secure in my sexuality. No one was going to convince me I was sinful or sick."

"You are far from being either." Without thinking, Will flipped them both so that now Damien lay on his back and Will covered him. Using his inhuman speed, he covered his dick, as well. He wouldn't allow his actions to ever frighten this boy. Thankfully, Damien didn't seem to notice anything except how his body was being claimed, because Will slid his cock inside Damien's welcoming heat with one powerful thrust. He forced his anger to give way to passion, knowing his darkening pupils would look more violet. He wanted to be able to look his lover in the eye.

Damien's eyes went wide and his mouth opened in an O, before morphing into a smile. "I do love the way your dick fills me."

Will rolled his hips once. "No one is ever going to hurt you again. I won't let them." The vehemence in his voice surprised him, as did the almost sacred vow he was making. Strike the 'almost'. One night, just a few hours really, and he was feeling fiercely protective and territorial.

Damien chuckled warmly. "I'm not that vulnerable little boy anymore. I learned to bulk up with muscle instead of fat and I only had to fight back a few times to get my message across. That was true for my father as much as with the boys at school. They were all cowards in the end. They only cared about my being gay if they were sure to be able to beat their homophobia into me."

Damien squeezed his hole, making Will groan. "I like how you make me feel kind of delicate," he added, running his hand up Will's biceps. "So much raw power. I've never been with a man as big as you."

Will returned the compliment. "I like how I don't have to be careful with you. I'm not afraid I'll crush you." As much of a distraction as being inside Damien was, Will still had enough brain cells left to devote to his concerns. "I don't want you to go to this camp," he confessed, "especially after hearing what you've already endured. A place like that could really do damage, send you back to those awful days."

Damien cupped Will's cheek. "It's sweet that you're worried, but I know what I'm doing. There is no way these people can touch any part of me. I'm going to let their bullshit roll off me. It's the guys who are there because they think it's going to help that I worry about. That kind of thing, as you say, can do horrible harm. Anything I can do to shut it down is worth the risk."

Then there was no more talking for a while, as Will plowed Damien with long, slow thrusts. He wanted to draw out the pleasure. Things had been too fast and furious so far. This time needed to last. "I won't let anything happen to you," he vowed in a voice thick with passion and something more that he wasn't ready to consider closely yet.

"I believe you. It's one of the reasons why I'm willing to do this. Yes, I'd do damn near anything for Emil, but I trust you, Will. I know you, more than you know—more than maybe I should. It's how I feel, regardless." Damien's eyes narrowed to slits and his grin turned sly. "Now, shut up and drill me into the mattress, dude."

Will was happy to comply.

* * * *

"You've come to the right decision. This is a safe place and we can help you." The guy doing Damien's intake was short and skinny, with red hair and freckles sprinkling his nose. He was cute, in a nerdy kind of way, and oh so earnest, so desperately wanting to keep Damien from bolting, so that Hades Hill, as he thought of it, could save him, body and soul.

"I'm Elliott, by the way, and I'd like to be your friend if you'll allow me."

Earnest Elliot. That nickname wrote itself. Damien tried for an expression somewhere between apprehensive and hopeful. "I'd like that. I want to change my life. The other guys I know are leading me down a bad path — clubs, sex, drinking, drugs."

That last part was a lie, at least it had been ever since Damien had been taken under Emil's wing. He'd done no more molly or anything other than the occasional pot brownie. But people like this guy thought that gay always meant being dominated by other vices, so he might as well lay it on thick.

"We can help you with all that. You only need to show me your ID. The Commonwealth is on the wrong side of this and doesn't allow us to help underaged boys."

"Hey, no problem. I'm twenty-one, actually." He took out his license and handed it over.

Earnest Elliot smiled. "That's great. You're making a very mature choice."

"Thanks."

Then there was paperwork he had to fill out. He sat on an ass-numbing visitor chair — the camp already trying to make him hate that part of himself — and dutifully filled in the necessary blanks. It was too bad for the clever bastard who'd bought the furniture that Damien's posterior sweetly ached from the total reaming Will had given him. The hard plastic merely served to press all the right spots, proving that there was a whole lot of ignorance as well as self-loathing going into this shitty place.

And how had his time with Will happened? After so many days spent in unrequited lust, somehow Damien's fantasies had come true without any warning. *All. Night. Long.* He wondered what Earnest Elliot would think if Damien 'confessed' what he'd been up to merely hours before. Maybe that would make him even more convincing, like an alcoholic hitting rock bottom before seeking help. Of course, his inner twelve-year-old snickered at the word 'bottom'.

"Here you go. Is there a tuition or anything? Because I don't have a lot of money." He tried to make himself look pitiful. He knew the answer anyway and was only trying to act like someone who was unfamiliar with the whole thing.

"There's no cost. Good people—God-fearing ones—have been very generous and will fully fund your therapy."

"Oh, that's good." He sighed with relief. "I think I heard that a member of congress or something runs this place? He must be very generous, too."

"Congressman Warren," Earnest Elliott confirmed with a nod. "He and his wife are wonderful. They've devoted their lives to helping people like you get back with God and find your true path in life. And he wants to spread his efforts to the entire country in so many diverse ways. He's running for President."

"Really?" he said, wide-eyed, because Earnest Elliot seemed to be looking for some kind of response. "That's impressive. I guess I should register to vote so I can help him get into office."

The boy nodded. "That would be best. Now, I have to ask for your mobile phone. There can be no contact with outside influences that can interfere with your getting better."

"Um, okay," he said, reaching into his back pocket. He'd known about this already and had a new mobile to sacrifice, while his own was carefully hidden inside the lining of his bag. "It will be weird being without it."

Elliott gave him a wise look, even as he took the thing and put it into a drawer. "When you've recovered from your disease, you'll find that most of what you have on your phone is pure poison, and you'll be ready to get rid of it. I also have to check your bag. We also don't allow certain other things here. We do it with everyone, so don't take offense. Then I'll show you around. It's nearly time for supper. We can dine in the hall with everyone else, and I'll take you to your room afterward."

"Swell, thanks." He'd known about the search, or rather Will and the others had suspected as much. There was nothing to find. But he was impatient throughout it anyway. He wanted to look around. He wanted to help Will, despite the limitations the man and the rest of his family had put on this little adventure.

'I won't come to see you tonight,' Will had told him, a walk-back of their earlier assurances. *'Val has a lot of experience in security and he figures you'll need at least twenty-four hours to know how they handle things. You might be locked into your room — or you might have a roommate. We don't want you taking any risks by sneaking out, unless you're sure you can do it without detection. That doesn't mean I won't be out there, because I will be. Text me if you need me to get in there and get you out. I'll be by your*

side in a heartbeat, and if they get to your phone, just scream. I won't be any farther away than your cry for help. I promise.'

Damien had stared into those very worried violet eyes and had reassured his lover that he would be very careful. That he believed him, totally, even though he knew the guy wasn't Superman or anything. He would have said anything to ease Will's worries. While he couldn't be sure, he believed that the night they'd shared together had meant something to the man as much as it had to him. Being bold in the kitchen when he'd been embarrassingly caught shimmying around had paid off. He'd seen something in Will's expression that had shaken off his inexplicable shyness, no more timid glancing and longing hopes of being seduced. He'd taken as much as given, and the experience had been unlike any other.

God, he didn't think he could stand it if Will brushed him off as a convenient diversion. But he was getting ahead of himself. There was no reason to believe that, especially after Will had let him stay the night, only gently showing him the door right before Annika woke for the day. Damien would have insisted upon that, anyway. And during the final meeting with the other family members and Logan that morning, while they'd discussed what they hoped Damien would accomplish here, Will hadn't been aloof. He'd kissed Damien, briefly, yet very publicly before the meeting had started and he'd sat him right by his side. That wasn't the behavior of someone ashamed or indifferent about what they'd shared. It gave him hope.

And although he'd promised not to take chances, he was determined to learn everything he could, because it was important to Will. That made it important to him.

* * * *

Mackie curled his feet under his butt and beckoned to Annika. "Come here and let me braid your hair."

They were well into a *Frozen* loop and he knew the girl loved having her hair done in similar styles to the characters. She might be the Queen but, first and foremost, Annika was the girliest girl Mackie had ever met. He'd asked Val if that was the norm on their planet and his husband had said no, that their species didn't have such rigid gender norms when it came to things like hairstyles and clothing. Annika seemed to have adopted a hyper-femininity that might be some weird byproduct of her hybrid nature. Whatever the reason, Annika was all about the frills and the pretties, and turning her beautiful blonde locks into various braids was fun. She liked the look and he enjoyed the process. It had become their thing to do, particularly when watching TV.

That didn't change, either, with the surly Merlin curled in the far corner of the couch. With Damien gone, there was no risk of the hybrid letting the family secret out by saying or doing anything weird. He spent most of his time in his suite with his beleaguered father while Lucien and Harry valiantly trying to undo all the damage living with Dracul had caused to the kid's world view. Mackie found him intolerable, and that was saying something coming from a former brat. Merlin pushed his every button, getting on Mackie's last fucking nerve.

Except any time Annika was around… She kept him not merely in line, but she also caused him to change his demeanor in meaningful ways—like now. There was no way the kid liked this movie, and yet when

Annika asked him to join them, he'd complied without protest. Mackie had figured he would endlessly snark about the plot and the songs. He'd been wrong. Merlin sat quietly, watching, saying nothing and—bigger surprise—petting Babette. The dog didn't seem to mind him in the least.

Without taking her eyes off the screen, Annika maneuvered into the space in front of him, giving him access to her hair. Mackie considered what his next move would be for a few seconds before he started gathering up the strands and weaving them. It was soothing work and his stomach seemed to be accepting his meal of plain mashed potatoes. He'd found an eating rhythm not unlike plaiting hair. If he fed from Val then topped it off with bland food, his stomach would keep it down.

Out of the corner of his eye, he saw Val approach. He was dressed for going out—not to the club, not in a suit, but in leathers. "Where are you going?" Mackie asked his husband.

Val paused by the side of the couch, a look on his face that almost appeared angry. For a brief moment, Mackie thought he wouldn't answer him. Then, "Out. I have some errands to run."

God, that's practically a non-answer. "Will you be gone long?"

Val shrugged. "Don't wait up for me, if that's what you mean. Call if you need feeding—and don't overdo it." He nodded at Annika, although she was paying no attention, before continuing on his way.

Mackie felt a rush of sudden tears. His husband might as well have said, 'none of your fucking business' for all the information he was giving these days. Despite being completely attentive to Mackie's needs, he was also distant, cold almost. *He's shutting me out.*

"He is afraid," Annika said while still watching the movie, "about you and the son you carry."

"Is it a boy for sure?" he couldn't help asking, his worries about Val temporarily replaced by parental curiosity.

Annika nodded. "A drone, yes. Not another queen."

He felt relief at that news. He didn't want the responsibility of raising a girl hybrid, nor did he question whether Annika knew what she was talking about. She seemed to see the world with more clarity than a mere human or even her male relatives could perceive. Her effectively supernatural abilities were both unsettling and comforting. It meant that she probably had insight into Val's feelings that even Mackie, as his husband, couldn't determine.

"I don't know how to ease his fears," he admitted. "I try not to be too much of a burden, but my body isn't cooperating."

"It is not your duty to help him. You are the one carrying his seed. He must cater to you."

"He does. I mean, he feeds me regularly and that helps a lot. I just don't want him to worry about me. That's all."

"Maybe he's going to see his piece on the side," Merlin popped into the conversation, with a remark that instantly infuriated Mackie.

Before Mackie could response, Annika placed a delicate hand on his arm. "Merlin, that is not only inaccurate, but it is also mean speculation. Apologize."

Merlin grimaced, shot Mackie a frown then said, "Sorry. I was being bitchy."

"You certainly were," Mackie ground out.

"Mr. Valeriu will find his own way," Annika continued, taking his attention away from the brat. "Once it is clear that you and the babe are doing well, he will worry less. That was how it was with Papa."

"At some point, Will stopped being concerned about your other father's pregnancy, you mean?"

There was a slight hesitation before she said, "Yes, eventually."

"When you were safely out, I bet."

Another hesitation. "No, before that."

Mackie finished the braiding and sat still, as a thought occurred to him. "Say, how exactly were you delivered? I know Harry has to cut my baby out of me. No birth canal and all that. But, Harry wasn't there when you were born or he would have said something to Alex. So, who helped out your fathers?"

This time, Annika was silent for so long that he thought maybe she wasn't going to answer, had gone back to focusing on the movie. "I don't know," she finally said. "I think perhaps they did it all on their own."

"Will has medical training?"

"Maybe…or Papa did." She flashed him a smile over her shoulder. "Shall I go and get a mirror so I can see what you've done?"

"Sure." Reaching for the remote, he paused the movie. It didn't matter how many times she saw it, she never wanted to miss anything.

He relaxed against the pillow behind him as he waited and couldn't shake the feeling that neither Val nor Annika were being entirely truthful with him.

Chapter Six

From where he hid in the woods behind the camp, Will kept track of the comings and goings. Kitted out as he was with the latest human and Val-created tech, he could practically see inside the walls of the buildings. He kept his focus there, although he couldn't tell where Damien was. The heat sensors only highlighted humans, not specific ones, no matter how much Will longed to form a connection with his lover through the distance separating them. The only positive part of this first night's surveillance was that he could tell Bran was both there and isolated. His body registered as different from the others and no human was in the room where he'd settled in the last hour.

Thank God he doesn't have his foul hands on Damien.

Of course, that was cold comfort. There was no telling what the humans might be up to. He'd lobbied unsuccessfully to put a tracker on the boy. Val had the ability to do so. And while it was likely that it wouldn't be detected any more than the phone tucked between the material of the duffle bag they'd given Damien, there would be no acceptable answer for having it. Hiding his mobile would be something any human might do. Being wired like an informer for the human authorities would definitely pique Bran's interest. Unlike everyone else there, he would know that it was likely an Alex move, which in turn could endanger Damien.

More than this long-shot scheme was already doing... *God...* Will couldn't settle down. Worry crawled all over him like ants. The urge to text the boy for an update was almost too hard to resist. Only the knowledge that such a thing might put Damien in the kind of danger he worried about stayed his hand. Under no circumstances was he to contact Damien, not unless it was to say *I'm getting you out of there right fucking now!* He had to be patient and wait for the boy to contact him, when and if it was safe to do so.

Waiting was hard, but what on this planet hadn't been? At least he knew that Annika was well looked after. Mackie was entertaining her in the living room, and Dafydd had surprised him by offering to see her to bed, not that she needed the kind of help that Idris did. Still, there had rarely been a night when Will hadn't overseen her bedtime routine. The separation was hard, although not as much as he'd feared. He had a family with him now to help him raise his daughter. His Queen. If he hadn't been afraid to reveal her to the others, he could have had this help from the very start. In hindsight, he'd worried for nothing. They'd all been missing having her. Annika was a balm to each of them.

Knowing that her future was secure gave him the opening to face what he hadn't been able to for many years. He was lonely and needed someone more than his daughter and his shipmates in his life. He craved having a man in his bed, in his life. Being with Damien had made that more than clear. He wasn't going to be able to remain celibate and alone. With that knowledge came the fear that he'd held at bay. Without conscious thought, he ran his fingers along the lines that Damien had traced during the night. Here was the one thing that held him back from embracing the joy that begged to be let out.

Last night, there'd been no worry. Condoms and Damien's exuberant willingness to be topped had allayed any fears. If they got fully involved, however, where Damien learned Will's true origin, would that last? Could Will bind himself to another human without risking what was now something that was a known possibility? He wouldn't be caught unaware this time. Did he want that for himself? Why was it so difficult to accept his own nature?

The issue was too hard for him to face now. It was enough that he'd taken the step to allow himself some pleasure. The focus had to be on keeping Damien safe, not on his own existential angst. Adjusting the heat-seeking goggles on his face, he concentrated on the camp below. This was how he'd spend his night, guarding his lover by watching for trouble. The future would come eventually, but not now.

* * * *

"You'll be bunking in with me," Earnest Elliot said with a sweep of his arms, like Vanna showcasing a vowel.

The room was practically a cell, with two high windows that would be impossible to climb out of, two narrow cots and two rickety wooden bureaus, on which lay two folded towels. It was like a prison version of Noah's Ark, except here there would be no sex.

Putting his duffle down, Damien forced a smile. "It's great…cozy. I can, um, really do some serious thinking here." *Yeah, such as how the fuck did I get into this situation? Oh, right, because I'm at least halfway in love with Will already, even after only one night and though he's still mourning his dead partner, and I'd do anything for him.* Not that he said any of that out loud, of course.

Earnest Elliot wasn't finished with the tour, though. "You can put your belongings into that bureau." He pointed to the one on the right, as if the one on the left having personal stuff wasn't a clue that it was Elliot's already. "We like to pair up newbies with more experienced campers."

They liked to refer to this place as if it were an overnight, fun-filled camp for adults, instead of the hellish prison it really was. They had nature-based group names with a heavy dose of masculinity such as 'the bears' and 'the bucks'. The counselors promised full days of healthy activities, like canoeing, along with trying to convince their campers that they were deranged. *Yeah, right…macramé and self-loathing. Fun, fun, fun.*

Dinner had yielded his first useful results. Warren and his wife had joined their 'boys' in the large dining hall. They'd sat on the dais at one end of the room while the campers had spread out on long picnic-style tables and benches. The food had been bland, naturally. Damien had amused himself by mentally listing the various seasonings he would use to make it all more palatable. Halfway through the meal, the man he was there to spy on had come slinking in. That was the only way to describe it. Will's cousin had appeared at the end of the dais, almost as if he'd materialized out of nowhere, and taken a seat beside Warren. He looked exactly like the other Stelalux men, except his expression was set in granite and he wore sunglasses, even inside. *Weird.*

Although nothing of note happened for the rest of the meal, Damien's heart had galloped with excitement and fear. He really wanted to come through with something useful for Will, but at the same time, he appreciated even more how much Will's admonition to not take chances mattered. He'd said this man, Bran, was dangerous, and boy, was that an understatement. The guy could play death in any avant-garde stage production with no makeup required. Stealing glances at him sent shivers down Damien's spine.

Elliot was still talking. "I've been here for nearly a year and stay on because the program really works. My impure thoughts and impulses have all but vanished." He dropped his gaze and his voice briefly. "I continue to struggle and that's okay. No one expects years of damage to be repaired in any kind of predetermined timeframe. You can stay as long as you want."

Damien figured as young as Elliot looked, he must have run straight to this horrid place on his eighteenth birthday. He nodded his head. "Great! I'm really looking forward to, um, making progress."

"Good." Earnest Elliot grinned broadly for a second before becoming serious again. "We don't give anyone their own room for a reason. You have to get used to seeing another man—me—naked without, you know, reacting. It's normal for men to be around each other without their clothes on. You know, lockers and whatever. Here we learn to give each other privacy and not allow our bodies to betray us."

Damien was nodding again while thinking *Seriously, dude, I don't get a boner every time I see another guy's dick and ass.* God help poor Elliot if he did. It was just rude. "Sure, I understand," he said, because his roomie seemed to be looking for some kind of response.

"Excellent. And we learn to sleep with another man nearby without again, reacting inappropriately. Also, I'm sure you've read all your intake papers, but remember that there is no self-polluting. God wants us to save our bodies for our wives. Otherwise, it's a slippery slope from that to fornication with men."

Self-polluting? Gee, Elliot is both earnest and old-fashioned. And if whacking off led to straight men fucking each other, then same-sex relationships would be mandatory by law. Jesus Christ, this is going to be tougher than I'd thought when I volunteered. He bit the inside of his cheek to keep from responding. He just kept nodding like an idiot, hanging on to every pearl of wisdom dropping out of his roommate's mouth.

"Anyway, I'm here to help you in any way I can. I'll guide you through your meals, workshop sessions and physical activities for the first couple of weeks until you settle in."

"Okay, thanks." He waited, because clearly Earnest Elliot had more to say. He just wasn't getting to it quite yet.

The boy sighed heavily. "Look... This is tough...at least at first, and I want you to know that it's particularly hard at night."

I will not snicker at the word 'hard'. I will...not. The inside of his cheek was almost bleeding from the force he had to use to bite it.

"So, if, in the middle of the night, you find yourself in trouble, maybe the urge to, ah, touch yourself becomes overwhelming, then come to me. Crawl right in next to me. I promise I won't be mad. I'll hold you until the crisis passes. That's what real men do for each other without going so far as to violate God's law. We're like trench buddies in a form of war. Soldiers give each other comfort all the time. There's no shame in it."

And that's when Damien's irritation at the guy turned to pity. Elliot wasn't so much earnest as absolutely miserable, and he was keeping himself in this hell in a futile effort to change feelings that would never go away.

Damien held out his arms. "Real men can hug, right? I mean, I have to admit that I'm kind of scared. I'm afraid I'll fail," he added, keeping up the pretense of wanting to be there. "Do you mind?" he added, gesturing with his arms.

Elliot's face lit up. "Of course not! Real men can hug without it being an abomination."

The boy came to Damien and practically fell into his arms. Damien gave him the same affection he'd given lots of guys who struggled with addiction, homelessness and domestic violence. It was easy to do and cost him nothing. He didn't worry about getting hard, either, because contrary to what the people running this place thought, he wasn't aroused by the touch of any and all men. Only certain ones…

Will. Yup, that was the one at the moment, and he suspected that his desire for Will would never go away, even if the guy himself did.

So no, hugging Elliot didn't make him hard. Too bad the same couldn't be said for poor Elliot. Damien simply ignored it and let the boy cling to him for as long as he wanted.

Eventually, his roomie broke the embrace and stood back a little red-faced. "Go ahead and get settled. I have to see Congressman Warren. I report to him every evening. He has been my personal counselor since I first came here and he's gracious enough to continue with that, even though he's so busy. I, ah, don't know what I'd do without his kindness. It's, um, my life-line, you know? I won't be long," he added with a visibly hard swallow.

"Okay. Thanks. I'll see you later."

"I won't be long," he repeated and scurried out of the room.

Rolling his eyes, Damien opened his duffle, pulled out the few clothes he'd packed and dumped them in one drawer. "All unpacked," he muttered to himself before lying down on his cot. *Lumpy and hard, the perfect combination.* He briefly wondered if he could get away with jerking off, then decided against it. But he was hard—and not because of Elliot. He was thinking of Will—again. He was out there, watching, ready to come to Damien's rescue. He had absolute certainty of that and knew, as well, that it would be difficult not seeing him for a whole twenty-four hours.

* * * *

Annika felt only a minor amount of guilt over her actions. With her father gone for the night, she had an unexpected opportunity to do what needed to be done. Mackie was back in his room, sleeping—thankfully, not sick. The others were working, leaving only Dafydd at the family building to watch over her and Merlin to keep her company. She'd had no trouble pretending to retire for the night before slipping out again, while coopting Merlin to her cause. That hybrid drone chafed at confinement and was happy to do the impermissible. His father was easily gotten around. Poor, sweet Dafydd and Alun didn't deserve this kind of duplicity, but the good of the hive overrode all other considerations.

She hushed Babette as they crept through the connecting tunnel between the two buildings, the family quarters and the pretty club where human men went to enjoy themselves. She would have loved it if this underground part led directly to the basement of the club. Annoyingly, she had to first go up to the street level, then back down through the secure door. It meant she had to be very careful not to let the others see her. It wasn't easy, but she had the benefit of the noise and the distraction of the business. Plus, she knew that most of her hive were occupied in some fashion with their work. They weren't expecting to find her there, so she had more chance of avoiding them. Merlin was a solid presence at her back, equally stealthy. He was a difficult boy, but she trusted him to do her bidding and he would be able to protect her if it became necessary.

She'd chosen her red velvet dress, hoping it helped her blend into the décor. It also made her look her most regal, she thought. Reminding her quarry of her position in as many ways as possible was critical to her success. She only had to get there without being seen. If someone caught her on the way back, she could always claim curiosity as the reason for her journey, and her goal would have been achieved. That was what mattered. Babette was a bit of a concern, but her presence also gave an excuse for why she'd gotten up. Dogs needed to go out sometimes after dark, and naturally Annika wouldn't want to interrupt the men at their work. She'd already instructed Merlin to back up any story she told, and having the boy with her made more sense than her venturing out on her own.

Luck was with her. Other than a startled human woman—one of Emil's cooks, rushing to deliver a tray of food—she and Merlin met no one. The kitchen worker shot Annika a quick smile without pausing. It was easy from there for Annika to reach the basement door, enter the code she'd seen Alex use on her one trip to this place, then slip through it.

Neither she nor the boy needed light to see the way, which was good, because that could possibly attract attention. There was some risk that Harry was in his lab. Opening her hearing, she listened for his heartbeat or footsteps. Nothing. There was only the one she was going to see occupying this level. Babette whined and wiggled in her arms. She shushed the creature and rubbed her head in comfort while they descended.

Another door with another keypad lock and she was in the room filled with weapons. Here she dared to turn on the light.

"Whoa!" This from Merlin, who stopped dead in his tracks and looked around with obvious awe.

"Pay attention," she admonished. "You are here for a purpose and that doesn't include gawking at this...stuff." She didn't like things that killed, although she understood the need for them.

Merlin's expression turned mulish, but as always, he obeyed.

Although the dog briefly voiced her unhappiness, Annika nevertheless tied her leash to the leg of a table by the entrance. She needed to be the Queen, not a little girl with a pet. Plus, while she was willing to risk being hurt herself, she wasn't going to put her precious Babette in harm's way.

She strode across the room to the last barrier to her goal, Merlin still sticking to her heels, then paused and took a deep, cleansing breath. If she was supposed to be free of fear of her subjects, she was failing. There wasn't enough of the emotion to stop her, but it did give her a moment's pause before she opened the last door.

Her subject was on his feet before she became fully visible, his gaze flicking only briefly past her — to take in Merlin, no doubt. The bright light in his cell emphasized its starkness, as well as the nakedness of the man. He held a book in front of him, shielding her view of his most private parts, not that she cared. She wasn't a human child, after all, although it was a touch of almost gallantry that would be appreciated on this planet. So she chose to ignore it and focus on what mattered.

Except, Mr. Petru, as she knew he was called, lunged as near to her as he could get and dropped to his knees in the next second. "My Queen," he said and bowed his head. His fingers remained clenched around the book and its position didn't waver. The metal collar around his neck dug in with the way he pulled to the farthest limit of the chain that kept him from getting any closer.

Annika opened her mouth to tell him to get up then thought better of it. His devotion to her station, if not her personally, was a critical test of what she could accomplish.

"Look at me," she commanded instead, and she did so in the tongue of his world.

When his gaze met hers, she relaxed a hair. She could see his feelings laid bare. If his submission to her was an act, she couldn't detect it. It seemed unlikely, given how good she was getting at knowing the hearts of her subjects. The man waited for her to speak again. Now that she was here, her carefully thought-out script flew from her head. This man needed bluntness, not graciousness.

"I am here to inform you of your role in my hive." She channeled Elsa in her tone, although it was hard, given the chasm of differences in Earth languages and that of her alien father. She was delighted when Petru bowed his head.

"I serve you, my Queen, however you decree."

"Very prettily said, but words don't mean much on this world. You've been here a long time indeed. How do I know you can be trusted to follow the dictates of our people?" She'd almost said 'your people' and caught herself just in time. It could be hard having this duality in her identity.

Petru rattled his chain. "Words are all I have to give you, my Queen. Set me free and I will prove my loyalty."

Annika trilled out a laugh. "I don't think so." She deliberately took a step closer to show she wasn't afraid. Of course, with Merlin practically plastered against her back, it was easier. That was the reason she'd brought him. His presence helped, although she doubted he could best Petru, so fear did skitter up her spine. But demonstrations of fearlessness and confidence were helpful. "The time for your release will come, of course. Not by my hand. You are under the domain of the captain, for so long as I permit it. When you are let off your leash, he and his men will ensure that you don't betray them. However, I require that you do just that when the time comes."

Petru shook his head, a human gesture, she believed, and one that she used herself without much thought. How long, she wondered, had it taken her men to adapt to Earth's ways? How long would it take humans to adapt to theirs, once she demanded it?

"I do not understand, my Queen."

"You don't have to. However, I will explain this much to you, although it should be obvious to you all. I am Queen. I have only one biological imperative, despite the human DNA within me—to form and grow a hive. Living in secret from the humans was the right decision at the time that the captain made it. The situation has changed."

In the pause that followed, Petru's face lit up and his eyes turned shiny. "You are going to subjugate the humans, succeed where Dracul failed over and over again." He laughed. "Oh, my Queen, that is too delicious."

Annika turned her expression flinty. "Do not get ahead of yourself," she snapped, satisfied when he instantly sobered.

"Of course not. My apologies," he said with a bow of his head.

"Dracul made that mistake. This isn't his planet to dominate, and you have no real notion of what it means to rule a hive. The humans will live far better lives under my beneficence than they have ever known. There will be no subjugation, only gentle herding in the right direction."

"I understand, my Queen. I have been under the influence of that madman for too long. I have promised Alex that I will go quietly away after we defeat Dracul once and for all. Naturally, I will break that, if you wish."

"I insist that all of my men fall into their ordained roles. That includes you and Alex. There will be no hiding away among the humans. I don't know how matters will play out, so I am warning you now that, at the right moment, I will call upon you to do as I say."

She did take another step closer, almost putting herself within his reach. "From this moment forward, you are my creature and no one else's. Do you understand?"

He stared at her again and his fervor was back in his eyes. "Yes, my Queen. I am yours, only yours. I merely ask for you to grant me the boon of having my boy back."

"A human, yes?" She nodded. "If he wishes it. There will be no more forcing humans to do anything, except those that I dictate," she added, although whether that was to reiterate that to Petru or herself was hard to say. This power didn't sit as easily with her as she would have liked.

Stepping away, she shepherded Merlin farther into the larger room, and taking the door in hand, she added, "You will say nothing of this visit to anyone."

Petru placed a finger to his lips and nodded as she shut him into his bright prison.

Merlin moved in concert with her as she headed back to Babette. "I will keep quiet about this, as well," he said.

"Naturally." She dismissed him with a flip of her hair, a move she'd gotten from Elsa. "Don't touch anything!" she said when he ran his hand over a shiny gun.

"I know how to use it," he replied with his usual petulance. "When it comes time for you to take over this planet, you'll need warriors who can fight for you."

As she reached to untie Babette, she narrowed her eyes at him. "It won't be like that."

"No?"

"Certainly not. Besides, I have warriors already."

Merlin raised his chin. "Then why did you have me come here with you instead of one of them?"

Annika hugged Babette close to her and peppered her with kisses before answering. "I don't have to explain myself to you. However, as you undoubtedly know, I must ease my warriors into the new way of doing things. Plus, you were bored."

"I don't like being a prisoner any more than Petru does."

"Stop being difficult and you won't be. And be nicer to your poor father." She led the way out of the room.

Merlin snorted as he closed the door behind them. "He's…"

"Your father," she repeated. "He deserves respect and appreciation for all he's done for you."

They quickly climbed the stairs. "If you say so."

She shot him a glare before opening the door back into the club. "I most certainly do."

Her luck didn't hold out on the way back to her room. She and Merlin met Dr. Ric in the living room as they both entered the building. They stared at each other in surprise for a few seconds. Before she could explain her late-night wanderings, the human asked, "Annika, what are you doing up? Dafydd texted me that he had put you to bed almost an hour ago."

She held up Babette's leash. "My doggie needed to pee," she replied, deliberately using childish language to reinforce in the man's mind that she was young. Humans underestimated the minds of their offspring, and she was far more advanced than her physical form indicated. "I didn't want to disturb Mr. Dafydd, and Merlin was awake and happy to accompany me."

The doctor furrowed his brow, glanced suspiciously at the boy. "Oh, I don't think anyone expected that." He looked in the direction she'd approached from and his frown deepened. "Going outside at this time of night isn't a good idea, even with Merlin. He's not entirely safe, either, at his age."

Except, of course, he hadn't found her in the alley or out on the sidewalk. She'd come from the tunnel that led to the club. That wasn't a place to walk a dog. She changed tactics in an instant.

"I'm very sorry, Dr. Ric. I just lied to you."

"No kidding. Did you two sneak into the club to watch the dancing? I know you've wanted to."

"Yes." She latched onto his explanation, which was essentially what she'd intended to claim. The fact that he'd thought of it on his own proved it was a good excuse.

"I wanted to see it, too," Merlin interjected, then shrugged when Dr. Ric looked at him. "I'm bored being trapped here."

The truth woven into the lie was an excellent touch. She would have to reinforce her approval later with the boy. She lowered her gaze. "I know it was naughty of us. My father leaves for one night to do important work and I take advantage of his absence."

"You know that Dafydd took his responsibility to watch you very seriously?" The human's tone was stern. Of course it was. He was worried about his man's state of mind more than Annika getting into mischief. "And Alun doesn't need the extra worry, either," he added to Merlin.

Given the importance of her activities for the hive, she could not feel guilty over what she had done. But she didn't want to hurt these nice humans more than necessary. "I know," she replied contritely. "He was very kind to me, too, reading a bedtime story to both Idris and me. *Paddington Bear*. I do love the classics, and Baby Idris seemed to like looking at the pictures."

That mention of father and child served to distract the doctor. He smiled. "Dafydd's relationship with his son has improved greatly. I think the baby simply loves the sound of his father's voice. He could probably read sports results and it would be fine.

"None of which explains away your sneaking out," he continued, the sternness returning. "I understand that among your kind, you are special. You're still a child, as far as I know, and my concern is for Dafydd, first and foremost. This thing with Bran is hard on him. He doesn't say much…"

"You're worried about him." Annika was happy to keep steering the discussion back to Mr. Dafydd. "I am, too. I promise I won't do this again. It was a whim, and now I know that I don't like what goes on in that club."

"I did," Merlin said with a smirk.

"Not helpful, Merlin," Annika chastised.

"Neither of you should, at your ages," Dr. Ric scolded.

"Very true," Annika agreed. "I guess I'm a little unsettled. My father has rarely been away all night before and never since we arrived in Boston."

The human's expression morphed into compassion and understanding. His sincerity radiated off him. "Oh, of course. I understand. Let me take you back to your room and we'll say nothing more about it. I'll see you to yours, as well, Merlin."

"I don't need babysitting."

"Nevertheless." Dr. Ric held out his hand to Annika as he smiled.

She took it and returned the look. Now the guilt was setting in. Being duplicitous, playing on the human's emotions, didn't make her happy. She needed to get used to it, however. Being the Queen was going to be a lonely place for the rest of her life, one in which she did things that she didn't like and with no one to confess to.

* * * *

Will was in his element—slipping from shadow to shadow, silently and invisibly making his way to the compound. The waiting was over. This night, he could see for himself that Damien was okay. There had been a brief sighting of the boy earlier in the day when all of the campers had headed down to the small lake situated on the property. They'd stripped to their skin for a quick dip in the cool water. Yup, having a whole gaggle of gay young men skinny-dipping was somehow supposed to be therapeutic. Frankly, Will was inclined to believe that whoever set the curriculum was merely trying to satisfy his own prurient interests under the guise of 'help'.

And who was that again? Oh yeah, the closeted politician whose own peccadillos had him sucking off randos in Boston clubs. Was the guy trying to sink his career? Probably. With self-loathing came self-destructive behavior. In any event, Will had been grateful for the peek at his lover, to know for sure that he was not locked up being bombarded with a water cannon or some other sadistic shit. He'd still sweated his way through the hours that followed until their time to meet. The text that Damien had sent giving him a thumbs-up thirty minutes before had helped a lot. The relief had left him almost dizzy.

At the moment, however, he was concentrating on the mission. Val's surveillance told him exactly where the security cameras were and what was their range. He had no trouble avoiding their line of sight and was able to get right up to the fence where they thought a blind spot was. Crouching behind a large bush, he opened his hearing to detect anyone nearby, nevertheless. It didn't appear that the camp actually posted guards, but one couldn't be too careful. It was already crazy that they enclosed what was supposed to be a voluntary experience as if it were a prison. The idea of a patrol in addition to the high wire fence wasn't completely far-fetched.

These people had the fervor of absolute certainty that they were right. He'd seen that in humans before, and they could do anything to justify their goals. That included keeping others confined against their will, if necessary. Fear for Damien swamped him for a moment. What if they'd found out that he was a mole? What might they do to him if they had?

Except he was getting himself into a lather based on nothing. Damien was smart and he hadn't been in the camp for more than a couple of days. He knew his job — to keep his ears open without going anywhere or doing anything he wasn't supposed to and try to figure out where the asshat's campaign kept their records. There was no reason to worry about his getting into trouble, not unless Damien had taken unnecessary risks, despite his clear order to the contrary. And now he'd just ratcheted up his worry again.

Just fucking move, moron.

Standing, he ran toward the fence, leaped over it and landed on the other side in another crouch—the right side, the one with Damien on it. How quickly his life had changed, where he wanted to be wherever his lover was. For years, it had been all about Annika, but he'd spent an entire night and most of the day away from her. Nothing bad had happened. He'd found her at dawn, tucked into her bed with Babette. Neither of them had stirred when he'd peeked in. She'd been her usual perky self at breakfast and hadn't batted an eye when he'd told her he was returning to the camp and wouldn't see her for the rest of the day.

'Please do not worry about me, Father Damien. I will spend the day with Mackie once Mr. Val decides he's fit to come down. And Mr. Dafydd and Dr. Ric will take excellent care of me.'

The two men in question had been there, feeding Idris, although without Damien to pamper them, breakfast had been bagels and cereal. Something, a look, had passed between Annika and the doctor in particular. Will hadn't been able to figure it out, but nothing seemed out of place, so he chose to accept the truth that his daughter was fine with his being gone so much. At the moment, it was Damien who needed him more.

With that thought in mind, he sprinted toward the rendezvous point. Nothing stirred, nothing shone. The security for this place really was for shit. Then again, as far as the assholes who ran this place were concerned, there was nothing but a bunch of confused queer men here and everyone knew they wouldn't have the guts to do a runner. Yeah, right. In their insular world, gay men were never cops or soldiers or just plain ballsy like

Damien was. He was ten times the man that Congressman Asshat was, if for no other reason than he'd had the courage to come out to his family and find a way to survive when they'd kicked him to the curb. How many other kids in this place had been treated the same and had come to this place out of desperation to be welcomed back?

The idea that humans could treat their young in such a cruel manner infuriated him. It made him want to track down Damien's family and rip their throats out. There was nothing that could justify turning your back on your child. Even if they did something you couldn't forgive, you had to at least love them and do your best for them. The love he'd felt the moment when Luuk had placed Annika in his arms had been alarming in its ferocity and continued to be so. He would do anything for her, to keep her safe or help her with her troubles. Even if she came to him and said '*Screw this whole Queen thing. I just want to be like a human girl*', he would fight Alex and all of the others if necessary to give her what she wanted.

These thoughts and emotions weren't going to get the job done, however. Amateurs they might be, but he couldn't afford to get complacent. Instead, he raced to his destination and slid behind the old potting shed where Damien knew to meet him. This spot had no security cameras and there were enough bushes in the back to give them more cover if anyone came wandering around. Although he'd surveilled the place himself the previous night and had spotted no guards patrolling, one never knew what might have changed since then.

With the wind blowing toward him, he smelled his boy before hearing his familiar tread. Damien darted around the side of the shed and right into Will's waiting arms. He couldn't help himself. He pulled the boy in for a deep kiss, inhaling his sweet smell and tasting his equally delectable mouth. He went instantly hard and had to really fight the urge to take him down to the ground and push into his tight ass. He was actually shaking with the effort to keep himself in check. By the time he broke the kiss, he was panting, as well.

Damien was in much the same condition. "Wow," was all he said as they stood with foreheads pressed together, catching their breath. "I guess that answers my question."

"Which one?" Will huffed.

"The one where I wondered if you could possibly miss me as much as I was missing you." He grinned, his white teeth gleaming in the moonlight.

Will chuckled softly then took one of Damien's hands and placed it against the spot where his hard dick strained against his worn fly. "Every fucking minute."

Now it was Damien's turn to chuckle and kiss him, which led to more long seconds in which they fought to consume each other. It was up to Will to find the strength to shut off the reunion. He tugged Damien down so that they were both sitting on the ground behind the shed, out of view. And if, hey, that meant creating a smaller footprint by having Damien sit on his lap? That was the price they had to pay for their covertness.

It was a stupid temptation, but Will couldn't help it. Holding the boy, touching him, even in a non-sexual way, eased his worry. "What have you found out?" he made himself ask, because that was the purpose of his visit.

Damien relaxed against Will's shoulder, the trusting gesture of affection pleasing Will enormously. "Well, the food here sucks. I mean it's like the kitchen staff isn't even trying to put something decent on the plate. I know they'll say it's hard to fix good meals for a large crowd but come on. I do it all the time at the club and… Jesus, have some pride in your work, people."

Will smiled as he kissed the top of Damien's head. "I mean, outside of the food service part."

Damien sighed. "I know. It's just… Everything here is so depressing. It's easier to fixate on the crappy quality of the food than how sadly unhappy everyone is. The 'campers', I mean. The staff are mostly relentlessly cheerful and so goddamn smug that you just want to smack them. Except most of them are female, as it happens, so I'd never give in to that temptation. And they're really good-looking too. Pretty and ultra-feminine in appearance. And stacked, you know? I guess the idea is to expose us poor, deluded homos to the real deal, hot women that are there for the taking if we can only shed our pesky perverse natures."

Will was surprised by that statement. "You don't mean these church-goers actually employ women to 'service' you?"

"Not in any overt way. We're mostly learning all about how our bodies are temples that we must save for our future wives. No self-polluting, as they call it, and no premarital sex of any kind. But I get the feeling if I approached one of those women and asked her to help me 'get over' my gayness by giving me a hand job, she'd have me in the broom closet in record time."

"Good lord, what a fucked-up place this is."

"You got that right."

"How are you holding up?" Will's worry for his lover increased. He'd expected possible physical restraint or cold showers or the like to be employed in this awful place. Psychological torture could be far worse. Risking Damien had never been his first choice—or, any choice he'd make, for that matter. He'd been overruled, however, including by Damien himself.

"I'm fine, really. I know who and what I am, and I love myself as I am way too much to buy into any of their bullshit. Please don't worry about me. We've had this conversation before," he added with a pointed look.

Will barked out a soft laugh. "I know, and it's impossible for me to stop fretting over your welfare, especially after everything you've told me about your past." Revealing that was the verbal equivalent of his initial assault. He wore his feelings for Damien on his sleeve, no doubt about it. He found he couldn't care much about that. It wasn't as if he wanted to hide them from the boy. It was more that he couldn't quite forgive himself for falling for another human, despite his internal vows not to do so.

Damien twisted his head enough to place a quick kiss on Will's lips. "You're very sweet. I promise you that I'm not at risk of buying into their nonsense. Now, do you want to hear what I've discovered? It's not much."

"Please."

"Okay, so this place is just as advertised. Their focus is on converting those who want it, although I'm not convinced everyone here really wants to be 'saved'. Sure, legally they're adults and signed themselves in, but I get the sense that a lot of these boys were dragged here by their families and basically given an ultimatum—get 'cured' or get out. You know?"

Yes, Will did know.

"Anyway, as far as Congressman Asshat, excuse me, Congressman *Warren* is concerned, he and his wife — *please call me Cathy* — do keep an extensive suite of rooms on campus and have been here both days since I arrived. This is definitely their home base and a few office rooms in the main building are designated for their campaign, too.

"Both Mr. and Mrs. also do personal counselling for some of the boys. I'm not sure if either of them have any kind of degree, not that there is one that would be sanctioned for this conversion crap. Anyway, my roommate and personal guard, for lack of a better word, still sees Warren for his personal therapy."

He wiggled his butt, trying to look at Will more closely, and didn't that movement drive Will's dick crazy? "The thing is, when he comes back from his nightly sessions, he's kind of subdued and obviously unhappy. I know it's only been twice since I've arrived, but I swear that kid is so beaten down afterward. And yet he keeps pretending that this is a great place…" He sniffed. "I'm worried about him. This isn't good for him…or anyone."

Will petted the boy's head, much as he did with Annika when she needed soothing. "I promise you, baby, if there's any way we can shut this whole shitty thing down, we will. All it takes is finding the right leverage."

"Yeah, I know." Damien swiped at his face to clear the moisture that had been gathering in his beautiful green eyes. "So, your, um, cousin? He's also here, tags along with Warren like the way Babette sticks to Annika's side. And no offense, but he creeps me the fuck out. Inside, he occasionally takes off his sunglasses, I think to scare the crap out of all the boys. Anyway, his eyes are nothing like yours. I mean, you have gorgeous Liz Taylor eyes and I could stare at them forever. On him, they just look dead."

Damien shuddered with that pronouncement and Will hugged him closer. He was ridiculously pleased at the human's praise of his eyes. "No offense taken," he said in the silence, understanding that some response was necessary. "His nature is perverted, as we warned before sending you in. He has the temperament to do a great deal of harm. We must stop him before he does. Family honor and all that." That was the official line for their checking up on Bran's movements, and Damien did seem to buy it. Tremendous guilt ate at Will, nevertheless.

Damien shook his head. "I don't understand how such a nice family could produce that evil-looking spawn. I guess that's how it works sometimes. And he's different than the rest of you in another way."

"How so?" Will had a feeling he knew the answer already.

"Let's just say he's the perfect guy to be working security here, in that he has zero interest in the boys. There's no gay gene there. The way he leers at the girls, staring at their racks and asses... Yikes!" He shuddered again. "If I had a daughter, I wouldn't want that letch anywhere near her."

Yes, as Petru had warned, Bran was different. Not pursuing human females had been the one point Dracul and Alex had agreed on. They were too hard-wired to view them in a certain way. Preying on them hadn't been a real option. Of course, Dracul hadn't cared about millions of females being hurt and killed through his machinations over the years. That kind of remote violence toward females was okay, apparently. It was the upfront and personal type that none of their crewmates could stomach, at least up until now. However Dracul had raised his son, Bran had decided to take a different path. The likelihood of their being able to contain the guy using Annika's influence was diminishing, the more they learned.

"Okay," he finally said, "this is good intel, useful. We should probably think in terms of getting you out of there tomorrow. I'll come in the front door this time, pretending to be your boyfriend, and…"

Damien looked at him, a flash of hurt crossed his face. "Pretending?" He turned away in the next instant and tried to wiggle out of Will's embrace. "Sorry, that was bitchy of me. I can be a needy little fuck sometimes. I've been working on it."

Will silenced whatever else Damien might have said by pulling him hard against his chest, taking his chin in a firm, grip and putting the kid's mouth right where he wanted it. This time when he kissed the human, he waited until they both convulsed, desperate for air, before releasing him.

Damien rested his forehead against Will's chest and gasped like a landed fish. "Jesus, I guess I'm forgiven."

Will squeezed him hard enough to make him squeak a little. "There is nothing to forgive. I expressed myself badly. What I meant to say is that I'll pretend to be your *outraged* boyfriend, coming to collect you before they put stupid ideas in your head. Although frankly, I prefer the words 'lover' or 'partner,' as they typically say in Europe. I'm a bit old to be called a boyfriend."

"Um, okay." Damien smiled broadly. "Whatever works for you, I'm onboard with." He dropped his gaze. "I've never been in a relationship before, not really. I don't know the rules. I thought maybe I'd jumped the gun."

Will shook his head slowly. "Not in the least. I haven't been with anyone since Luuk, Annika's father, died. I didn't think I wanted another relationship. Being with you has changed my outlook." He kissed the boy again, this time keeping it light and reverent. "You make me feel again, and that scares me."

This was hardly the time and setting for such a heartfelt conversation, and he was acutely aware that he had no right to draw Damien any further into a relationship without revealing his true nature. But, like Damien, apparently Will was also *'a needy little fuck'* because God, he couldn't help himself.

Damien cupped Will's cheek. "We'll take it slow. I can appreciate how hard this is for you, and your being Annika's father adds an extra layer of difficulty. I adore her, by the way. It's hard not to. And you're not so old."

Now they were really treading on dangerous territory. *You have no idea,* he started to say, although he had no plan on how to end it.

"It doesn't matter." Damien gave him another quick kiss. "And I'm not going anywhere tomorrow. It's only been two days. I need more time to learn anything that might be useful."

Will knew that was what Alex wanted. He couldn't shake the feeling that leaving Damien in this hideous place for much longer was dangerous. In fact, it was all he could do not to pick up the boy and race out of there.

"Okay," he forced himself to say instead. "As long as you're sure and take no chances. Don't try to rifle through their offices or anything. We're only looking for weaknesses and obvious information to use against Bran." Clasping Will's face with both hands, he stared hard at him. "When we said that Bran was dangerous, we meant it. Deadly so. Everything you think you see in his eyes is real. It is *not* your imagination. He has no moral compass. You are like a bug to him, and you can't assume you're safe simply because there are so many people around."

"I understand." A spark of fear showed in Damien's eyes. *Good, let him be afraid.* Hopefully it would make him more careful.

Will nodded and expressed the sentiment. "Good." Then he kissed him again and, damn, this time he didn't stop. They ended up sprawled flat on the ground, Will grinding his pelvis against the human's.

Until Damien pushed on Will's chest hard enough to make him stop. "I-I can't afford to climax in my pants," the boy gasped. "If my roommate smells cum on me, I'm in trouble."

Will grinned. "Then I'll makes sure not to spill a single drop."

He didn't wait for Damien to react. He merely slid down and undid his lover's fly. The hard cock sprang free the moment he had the zipper lowered. He wasted no time sucking it into his mouth and swallowing it all the way down.

He kept his eyes open as he lavished attention on the shaft, using his tongue to stimulate the underside. He cupped the balls with one hand while sliding his forefinger underneath to tickle the puckered flesh that his cock so hopelessly wanted to breach. To his delight, Damien slapped his hand over his mouth to muffle the moans he wasn't successful in stifling. Will pressed the tip of his finger inside, crooked it and rubbed the bundle of hard flesh he found. Damien bucked up, giving Will the perfect leverage to swallow over and over again, his throat working that dick. When Damien let go, Will made good on his promise.

Chapter Seven

Val had started his nightly walkabout early that evening. Mackie was happily hanging with Annika — and Merlin, surprisingly — in the living area as part of their new nightly routine since Will spent nearly every hour surveilling the camp and meeting with Damien. They were watching that movie that made Val's ears bleed, so he felt free to make his escape. He tried not to dwell on the hurt look on Mackie's face each time he shut down his boy's questions. He couldn't tell his husband about what he was up to. This was his private time.

The calm that came from his DC Comics-like excursions was working wonders for all concerned. At least it had the potential for doing so. It made Val more relaxed, which Mackie should pick up on eventually, making him happier. He didn't want to be a burden on Val and no amount of reassuring words was helping. Actually being in a good frame of mind should do the trick. But letting Mackie in on what he did at night definitely could make matters worse. Mackie would worry, even though there was no reason to. Val knew what he was doing. There was no risk to him, only to those he preyed upon.

He had to be careful for a while yet this night. There were still revelers milling about the streets, closing time for a lot of the bars having just occurred. It wouldn't be that hard for someone to glance up and see him doing his Nightwing imitation. He'd been both careful and lucky so far. Those who had seen him up close had been drunk and-or homeless, so there were no cell phone recordings and no reliable witnesses. He knew he was taking a risk that would have Alex shitting screeching monkeys if he found out, but his activities had taken on an addictive quality, as well as being therapeutic to his husband's condition.

There was a rhythm to it all now, even after just a few nights. He knew to rein in his journey, to stop and listen for sounds of someone in distress. It was actually a horrible indictment of the human race in general—and the city of Boston in particular—how many people needed help. There weren't enough cops, obviously. Part of him wanted to seek out Duncan and apprise him of the situation but that was just his little bloody do-gooder lurking surprisingly within. The saner, logical part of him knew that not only did Duncan already know the state of his city but he was also unable to do anything about it.

Enter Val.

He found his fight quickly. As he crouched on a roof top somewhere in Chinatown, he caught the sound of a female whimpering pitifully. Another voice, a masculine one, followed. "Shut up. Don't move, do as you're told and maybe I won't slit your throat when I'm done."

Val didn't wait to hear any more. He leaped over the edge and down in his now-familiar method of entrance. This time, he didn't bother to scope out exactly what was happening and making sure, as he'd always done after the first time, that there was no one to see him do this inhuman feat. The woman who was in distress couldn't wait for even a second more for him to come to her rescue. That it was a female in particular being attacked in an obvious way had his fury rising unchecked.

He found them seconds after he'd landed. The man had his victim pressed into the back corner of the alley. She was dressed for clubbing and so was he, except his attire came accessorized with a switchblade that he held up to her throat as he fumbled with his fly with his other hand. This was how the fucker had intended to end his evening the moment he'd left his home, do doubt. A consensual hook-up wasn't his thing, apparently.

It didn't really matter how he'd maneuvered her into this hellish, stinky alley. All Val cared about was that the fucker wasn't going to get his way — and he wasn't going to be able to ever do this again. Val had already decided the outcome without fully realizing it, probably because he'd simply had enough of human shit. Plus, given that the man wasn't even trying to hide his face, Val was willing to bet the woman was supposed to leave this alley feet first and straight into the morgue.

He was on the guy in an instant, using his natural speed to reach him then grab him by both the back of the neck and the arm that held the knife. He brought it up and back to an unnatural angle, so that it snapped the bone. His quarry howled with shock and pain, and that was music to Val's ears. As he pulled the man away, he told the woman, "Run!" She looked at him with wide eyes that were streaming with tears. She appeared to also be momentarily shocked and frozen in place.

He repeated his command a second time as he continued to drag the rapist to the other back corner of the alley. The woman finally reacted, sprinting as fast as her high heels allowed. Val waited until she'd cleared the mouth of the alley before slamming his opponent against the wall. He held him up off the ground, enjoying the way the guy's legs flailed. Val's gaze focused on the wild pulse at the base of the man's throat. Thirst overtook him and he let his fangs descend, then grinned.

As he looked in the man's terrified face, he couldn't help but laugh. "Not so much fun being on the receiving end, is it?"

The man's lips flapped in silent protest. Val allowed him to play the landed fish for a few seconds longer before striking. His fangs sank into the font of the neck, piercing the jugular on one side. He allowed some blood to slide down his parched throat, but he didn't want to feed on this polluted blood, so he ripped the flesh off and spat it out before dropping the dying body on the filthy ground. He watched the man bleed out and felt nothing but satisfaction. He was certain that murder had been on the menu. All he'd done was change the ingredients.

It took no time for the human to die, a merciful death considering Val hadn't violated the man's body first. But with the blood-lust subsiding, the enormity of how the night had turned out hit him. He'd done something too extreme to go unnoticed. The wail of sirens coming closer didn't help any, either. On impulse, he picked up the knife the man had dropped and slashed what was left of the guy's throat on the sides. It wasn't much. It might help disguise the teeth marks. Probably not. *Shit.* He wasn't one to dwell on what had been, however.

He took one quick look around before leaping back up to the roof.

When he got home, he found Mackie curled up in their bed, sleeping peacefully. Val silently went to the bathroom. He'd already ditched his bloody shirt. Stripping the rest of his clothing off, he showered, setting the spray as hot as he could stand it. He wanted to purge the stench of his victim from his hair and skin. Never mind that there was really nothing like that on him. It just felt wrong, sliding into his marital bed without cleansing himself.

Long minutes later, when he did join Mackie, the boy rolled toward him and murmured incoherently. Val wrapped his husband in his arms and held him close. He needed the comfort as much as Mackie, because this time, coming home from his nightly escapades, he didn't feel that peace he'd come to crave.

* * * *

Will knew something bad was up when he saw Demi's man, the cop, coming storming into the club. The doctor, Ric, was hot on his heels, looking very grim indeed. From across the room, Val stiffened around the same time, having also seen the men's arrival. Duncan paused long enough to point a finger at Val, then gesture toward the back. Apparently a meeting with a capital M was required ASAP in Alex's office. Val didn't hesitate. He followed Ric.

Will didn't hesitate, either, to join the parade. This was one of the rare hours when he wasn't out watching the conversion camp. Whatever was going on, it must have to do with Bran. Being a warrior of the hive, Will had to answer the call of duty, even though he really wanted to go back to that damnable place and see if he could talk Damien into leaving and coming right back into his arms. Or, barring that, keep an eye on him. He lived now for their brief meetings behind the shed, trading blow jobs. And damn was that tongue piercing a delightful addition to the party. He longed, though, for more, enough for Will to get inside Damien's precious ass. Damn, but he'd gone from *who needs sex* to *how can I possibly last a whole twelve hours without it?*

The shit hit the fan before Will had even crossed the threshold to Alex's office. Malcolm was there already, sitting on the couch, his mouth agape as Duncan stopped in front of Alex's desk with his finger pointed once again at Val.

"Who the fuck let him off his leash?" Duncan was incandescent with rage.

Will quickly shut the door. Whatever this was about, none of the humans wandering about needed to hear it.

Alex straightened from his normally relaxed pose. "Would you care to rephrase that, Sergeant, in a more coherent and less insolent way?"

Duncan dropped his arm but not his attitude. "Oh, no. You don't get to play lord of the manner, Stelalux. I've put a shitload of my life and career on the line by joining your merry band. But this is insupportable, and I would have thought you'd care about making such a big, fucking, *unnecessary* mess in your own backyard."

"I really have no idea what you're talking about." Alex's icy tone sent a shiver down Will's spine. He rather admired how the human cop didn't cower in the face of it.

"I do." Val's quiet admission got everyone's attention. He stood to one side, his back pressed against the wall, looking very un-Val-like. Will had always thought this particular drone was born to fight. Nothing fazed him. At the moment, however, he had an almost-defeated air about him.

"Well, color me fucking surprised," Duncan bit out.

"Trey, please." Ric put his hand on the cop's arm. "We need to hear him out." He switched his attention to Val. "You really have put us both in a difficult position."

Duncan snorted. "Don't sugarcoat it, Paz. If we both don't end up losing our jobs over this, we'll be the luckiest fuckers in town."

Alex's eyes took on a reddish hue. Not a good sign. "Val, explain."

Val only hesitated a second before saying, "I killed a man last night."

"What man?"

He shrugged. "A human. A rapist. And he was trying for murderer, too." He looked at Duncan. "He wasn't going to leave that woman alive after he'd…done what he was in the process of trying to do. God, I hate rapists."

Malcolm spoke up before anyone else could respond. "Well, I cannae say that anyone in this room would argue that point with you, but I dinnae understand. Where did this happen, and why did you kill the fucker instead of incapacitating him?"

"Because I wanted to kill him." The answer, stated in such cold terms, sent another shiver through Will.

"You didn't simply kill him, though, did you?" Ric said. His quiet voice held censure. "You ripped his throat out, then did a half-assed job of making it look like you'd slit it and maybe rats had chewed on it."

Duncan barked out a laugh. "Yeah, rats. Somehow in the few minutes it took that poor woman to call the cops and them arriving on scene, rats got at the body. That's the best we could come up with. I suppose we should thank you for at least trying to muddy the evidence." Duncan put his hand on Ric's shoulder. "Do you have any sense of the risks this man has taken, making sure he got the autopsy and falsifying records? If anyone takes a closer look at his pictures and report..."

"They probably won't," Ric volunteered. "But if they review Trey's interview of the woman, they might notice how he steers her away from a more accurate description of what her savior looked like and how he might have entered that alley. I believe she initially said that you seemed to appear out of nowhere."

"But, of course, that's impossible. I have her believing you ran in from the street." Duncan shook his head. "Because the alternative is you jumped three stories down from the roof."

The silence that followed was interrupted by Alex letting out a string of compounded and creative swearing. It wasn't Alex's usual style, but apparently this wasn't a usual situation. *Seriously, what was Val thinking?*

"Wait," Will said suddenly. "You knew it was Val the moment you entered the club. How?"

Duncan raised an eyebrow. "I knew it had to be one of you, and the victim at first described someone with a Mohawk. I was like 'are you sure in the dark it wasn't a hat or maybe the guy was completely bald and the moonlight was playing tricks?' Fuck! I had to make a traumatized woman think that her memory was faulty. I hate myself for that, and I hate you too!"

Duncan paced as far away from Val as the room would allow. "I would have known it was Val anyway. Who else? No way it was Alex or Emil or Harry. Could have been MacLerie, but he's been trying to get away from fighting." He glanced at Will. "I barely know you, except you are all about your kid, so… Besides, Val has always been like a quivering mastiff, waiting for the order to kill."

"I can't disagree with your assessment of me," Val said quietly.

"You do need to explain this, however," Alex said, his eyes had gone back to violet. "Why ever would you do such a thing, especially now, when we are the middle of dealing with Bran?"

Val didn't answer right away. He stared at the floor and said, "I'm not sure how to explain it. I, ah, needed to take the air one night. Mackie… He's struggling, you know. The pregnancy is hard on him. It's too soon. He wasn't supposed to change for a few more years. I thought I had time."

Everyone remained quiet, letting him get it out at his own speed. He was obviously in distress and Will couldn't help but feel sorry for him.

"I went up to the roof one night, like I used to. I decided to take my version of a stroll around the city. It was…fun. Then I happened upon a few assholes trying to roll an old homeless man. A vet, actually. Logan, I think, knows him. Anyway, it was no big deal. I broke one's wrist and battered the rest. They fled and I felt…amazing." He snorted. "Fucking amazing.

Suddenly, all the shit with Mackie, which made me feel impotent, was more bearable. I started going out every evening once he was settled, looking for trouble." He glanced up at Duncan. "It wasn't hard to find. This city has a lot of unaddressed crime at night."

"No shit," the cop replied. "Why don't you try petitioning the city council for the funds necessary to hire more police. And while you're at it, try convincing the good citizens to pay extra in taxes, because money doesn't grow on fucking trees. It has to come from somewhere."

Alex put up his hand. "Understood, Sergeant. So, Val, you turned into a vigilante? Cracking heads and breaking bones made you feel less impotent, as you say?"

"Yes, sir."

Alex sighed and shook his head. "You could have come to me, or any of us, to let us know what you were feeling."

Val barked out a laugh. "Not my style, sir. I would have thought you'd know that by now. I used to take my frustration out in battle, because I hate being marooned on this planet. Then I used the playroom to keep the edge off."

Val cleared his throat. "Mackie has been my balm this last year. Except now he's hurting and I'm just so goddamn fucking terrified of losing him." His voice broke and the effort it took to bring himself back under control was painful to watch.

God, Val has always been a rock wall of emotion. Will felt terrible that he hadn't noticed how much his friend was hurting. In hindsight, it hadn't been so hard to pick up on. Val had been hovering around a sick Mackie much the way he did with Annika. And he got it, the way Val felt as if he couldn't do anything useful. Will often felt as if he were watching a frightening thing unfold as his daughter entered into full Queen mode. He was powerless to stop it, didn't know for certain what the outcome would be and could only stumble through it to the best of his ability. And Luuk's slow death had been more of the same. So, yeah, he got how Val felt.

On impulse, he walked up to Val and put his arms around him. "I'm sorry I didn't notice you needed help. What can I do now?" He pulled back, although he left his hand on Val's shoulder.

Val looked at him with surprise. "You have enough on your plate. The Queen…"

"She's starting to shut me out. I turn around and she's off somewhere. I look in her eyes and I can't tell what she's thinking anymore. I understand your feelings of impotence. I really do."

Ric spoke up. "What this family could use is some therapy. Really?" he added when they all looked at him as if he'd sprouted horns. "What? Is that not a thing on your world?"

"The Queen is our therapy," Alex answered. "She is what keeps us all emotionally anchored." Leaning back in his chair, he added, "I'm beginning to think we've all been slowly going mad on this world without one. Perhaps Dracul's only failing is that he got to that point earlier than the rest of us."

"I didn't mean to imply that you were clinically insane or anything," Ric sputtered.

Alex smiled briefly. "No, of course not." He eyed Val. "Although ripping out a human's throat and leaving the body in plain sight *is* crazy."

"I'm sorry, sir. What can I do to remedy this situation?" he asked Duncan. "I don't want you or the doctor to suffer for my indiscretion."

Duncan shook his head. "It's done. Nobody on the force likes a vigilante but we're not going to cry over this asshole's death, either. So long as no more bodies show up or anything else that implies someone is doing our work for us on a regular basis, the whole thing will be relegated to the unsolved files." He gave a pointed look at Val.

"Understood. There will be no repeat."

An idea occurred to Will. "Why don't we go to that well-planned home gym of yours with the padded walls and do some sparring."

"What with watching over Damien and everything else, you've got enough on your plate. Thanks, though."

"I could use an outlet myself," Will confessed. "I'm not happy about Damien being in the belly of the beast." That was more information than he would have liked getting out at the moment. It was the right thing to say, however.

Val nodded. "I can appreciate the need. I'm happy to distract you with pain and humiliation at my hands." He grinned, letting his fangs show.

Will gave him the same right back. "And I was thinking that maybe my beating your ass in hand-to-hand will cool your jets some."

Val, bless him, dug deep for some more humor. "In your dreams, Dyke Boy. I can still take you."

Alex clapped his hands once. "Excellent suggestion. Work off your mad, Val, then go spend time with Mackie. We may have lived a long time without the influence of a queen, but I have found a large measure of peace with my Quinn. Just the scent of him eases me in the most delightful way. I expect if we asked Harry, he could confirm that having Lucien and Demi in his life filled the unnamed void, as well."

"Indeed, Captain." Harry had opened the door without Will noticing and slipped inside the room. "My husband and son are both the center of my universe and my touchstone." He glanced at Will. "Annika's presence is the icing on the cake, as the humans would say."

Harry focused on Val. "Mackie needs feeding and I said I'd find you." His gaze swept the room. "I feel I've missed something."

"I'll fill you in later," Alex said. "Go," he ordered Val.

Nodding, Val moved to the door. Will followed. He wanted to see Annika—needed to see her. More, though, his desire to go to Damien had increased with all this talk of what the males of their species required. There was no fooling himself any longer. He was in love with the boy.

* * * *

"Where have you been?"

Crap, Earnest Elliot was awake.

Damien finished quietly closing their door before answering. "I couldn't sleep, so I went for a walk."

Elliot sat up, his hair sticking out in all different directions, folded his arms and frowned like an old woman. "Leaving your room at night is against the rules. You know that."

Damien tried to look contrite as opposed to well-blown. "Yeah, I know." He'd already considered this possibility. Once he went under, Elliot slept like the dead, but even heavy sleepers could wake unexpectedly. Damien had a cover story.

"See, um, I was feeling weak," he said in a confessional tone. He went over to sit on his bed, slipping his sneakers off right away. "You get me?" He pulled his T-shirt over his head before waiting for a reply.

Elliot's gaze tracked his movements, and once Damien was bare-chested, he just sat there and let the guy get an eyeful. "I thought a walk might help. It seemed like a better idea than what I used to do to help get to sleep—you know what I mean—or waking you for support. You work so hard all day."

Then he unsnapped the jeans that Will had minutes ago done up and stripped down to his boxer-briefs. Because they were talking, Elliot didn't avert his gaze the way he had previously on other nights. He just sat in the same pose, staring…and staring… God, Damien felt like a total shit, using his body to distract his keeper. It did the trick, though.

Finally, with a huff, Elliot responded. "That was considerate of you, but really, that's what I'm here for. I wouldn't have minded." Damien suspected that was true. "Did it help?"

"Oh yeah, I'm like totally under control now." He made a sweeping motion toward his crotch, where his limp and satiated dick lay tucked in for the night. "Fresh air and some quiet exercise did the trick for sure."

Elliot finally relaxed his arms and looked away. "Well, that's good. Don't do it again. I like you, Damien, and I get how sincere you are about changing. Rules are rules, though. Jeremiah—Congressman

Warren — is very strict. He holds everyone to the same high standard he sets for himself."

It took a herculean effort to hold back a snort over that statement. Damien had seen with his own eyes the asshat's hypocrisy. "I understand," he said, as solemnly as he could.

"And his head of security misses nothing."

At the mention of Bran, Damien saw an opening and possibility to gain additional information. Elliot had been in this place and part of the campaign for a year. "Say, what's his story? He's scary looking and sounds kind of foreign." Which was a lie, because he'd yet to hear the guy say anything. He was only going on what he knew about the Stelalux family.

Elliot scrunched up his face. "I'm not sure where he's from. Wales, maybe. He joined Jeremiah's campaign only a few months ago. Back then, the congressman was only planning on running for re-election. The presidency was something whispered about, but I thought it was for further in the future. Mr. Nyx showed up around the time the plans became accelerated. It was a good thing, too, given the hateful accusations being made online — and the threats. It's hard for some people to hear the truth," he added primly.

"He's not married, is he?"

"No. Cathy said something about how he'd once been engaged with this girl who died tragically. I guess he's still not over her. Besides, the campaign schedule is going to be grueling. There won't much time for dating. I'm sure he'll find someone nice to settle down with once Jeremiah is President."

"You think that's really going to happen?"

Elliot's eyes lit up. "Oh yes. He's God's chosen one. I'm sure of it."

Holy fuck. Damien hoped Elliot was wrong about that.

* * * *

Val looked over from where he was scarfing eggs scrambled by Emil and called out to Will. "Hey, you just getting in?"

Will stopped with one foot on the first step leading to the second floor. "Yeah, I'm going to escort Annika to breakfast then go back out there."

Val shook his head as he speared more eggs. "I'd thought my nightly travels were crazy. You can't keep this up, brother."

"Amen to that," Emil muttered, flipping a pancake in its pan.

Will looked annoyed. "If Alex will agree to let Damien leave that place, I won't have to."

Val shrugged. He was as frustrated as everyone that nothing useful had been discovered so far. "Not my call, but I feel you. This sitting around and waiting isn't in my nature." He held up his hand before Emil could say anything. "And yet, I'm being a good boy. My lesson has been learned."

Emil nodded once. "You're a fucking lucky one, too, that the whole thing seems to have blown over."

Yeah, early days and all that, but nothing had popped on the cover-up by Duncan and Paz in the last couple of days. He really needed to do something to show his appreciation. He'd ask Mackie for his advice, because he was now fully in the loop on the matter. Val had confessed all to his husband and hadn't that been a fun conversation? His bratty sub knew how to excoriate him with looks alone, and he hadn't confined himself to those. Words had been spoken. Lots of words. The very thought of it had Val wincing and his balls shrinking.

At least he left me with my sperm-makers intact. Between the unexpected pregnancy and his brief foray into the land of insanity, that had been a close call.

He lifted his mug and drained it. "How about after breakfast we spar like you offered? I need about an hour then I'll be free. I'm eating here because the smell of eggs doesn't sit well with Mackie's stomach. I'm going to feed him soon then give him some plain pancakes. He and Annika can do their usual thing while we pound each other into the ground."

Will started climbing. "Fine. I can spare about an hour before going back. That fucking place is wearing on the boy. I'm not sure how much more he can take."

Emil waited until Will was out of sight before saying, "Do you think he realizes that he's fallen in love with my sous chef?"

"Probably not." Val put his empty plate and mug in the sink. "The bigger question is, how will Damien react to Will's true nature? That's always the tricky part—or at least it's where I got stuck in my own life. It's hard to say how a particular human will take it. You know Damien best. What do you think?"

Emil handed him a plate with two pancakes on it. "Damien is a survivor with bigger balls than most of the men swaggering around the club, professing to be Doms. He'll handle it."

"Assuming he feels the same way about Will. Otherwise, the entire subject is moot."

Emil grabbed his own coffee and sucked some down. "Oh, he does. Count on that. He was really wild at first, always looking for a party, burning his candles at both ends. Since Will arrived, Damien has seemed more...settled, I guess. I wonder if he will eventually give us another queen."

Val pondered that possibility. It had occurred to him, as well. "A better question is what's going to happen to this planet if more queens are born? I'm not sure how this all shakes out with only Annika in the mix, but we both know that one Queen can birth a lot of young. Add more, and how long would it take for our kind to overrun humans?"

"Is that a rhetorical question or are you asking me to do the math, because I never once imagined that it might happen before learning about Annika. Frankly I don't think I have the guts to consider even now how our kind might populate this planet, do you?"

"Val shrugged. "Stream of consciousness for now. I'm not sure I want to run the numbers, either. Not yet. Oddly, I'm not really worried about it. Maybe I'm too focused on dealing with Bran, then Dracul, whose resurrection feels more likely with each passing day, for some reason."

"And all of it's easier than worrying about Mackie," Emil said in his quiet, yet reassuring way.

Val closed his eyes briefly. "Yeah, that."

Without saying more, he headed upstairs and was relieved to find his husband still in bed. Most mornings, he couldn't get back fast enough and found Mackie in the bathroom. Right now, the boy was beginning to stir, his eyelids fluttering. Val was already scoring his wrist as he raced to the bed. He slammed the plate onto the nightstand and knelt as he offered his blood. As usual, Mackie latched on with single-minded purpose.

The sensation of his blood being pulled through his veins calmed him as much as it settled Mackie's touchy stomach. It also aroused Val, his cock turning to steel within seconds. He was careful to keep it pressed against the side of the bed. The last thing his poor husband needed was a stiff dick in his face. Sex was off the table for the foreseeable future and, given how it was responsible for this entire shitty mess, he couldn't be upset about it.

No, it wasn't the sex's fault. It was an activity, not a living thing that had reached out to invade Mackie's body with Val's child. It was Val's greedy need for it that had caused all this trouble. After swearing off human men as long-term partners for centuries, he'd allowed his insatiable desire for Mackie to override his better judgment, and this was the result. It didn't matter that Earth had entered its twenty-first century, that Mackie wasn't Robbie and that Harry had what amounted to a hospital-level medical suite on the upper floor.

Val couldn't shake the almost paralyzing fear that everything was going to shit. He would lose Mackie the way he had Robbie, and he'd be cremating another lover and child. With an un-warrior-like sob, he bowed his head over his boy.

"I can't lose you. How would I ever survive?" He didn't even care how pathetic he sounded. His fear was that great. It overwhelmed other thoughts and emotions, such as pride and his urge to protect his husband from all bad things, including his insecurity.

Mackie landed his small hand on Val's head. At the same time, he broke the seal of his lips against Val's wrist. Val licked his skin closed without looking at him. The touch was light, soothing. It made Val feel like a small drone again in his mother's care. It was completely unmanning and yet, he made no move to stop it.

"I won't die, Val. I'd never do that to you."

Val could only shake his head. This was beyond both their controls.

"I *won't*," his feisty sub insisted. "And I can't tell you how much it means to me that you are confiding your fears. This shutting me out while you went looking for trouble was making me crazy. I thought…" There was a hitch to his voice that broke Val's heart.

He forced himself to move then. His boy needed him, too. *Time to man-up.* In a blink of an eye, he was on the bed with Mackie cradled in his arms. "I'm sorry, baby. So very sorry. You have enough to deal with. You don't need to worry about the shit jamming my head."

"It's part of being married, you big dope." Mackie sniffled. "Not knowing what you're thinking or feeling or doing hurts me. It's worse than this puking marathon. You'll have to trust me on that score."

It was hard to accept, but he had to—as his husband had said—trust him to know his own mind and the limits of what he could handle. "I will. Promise," he added when he got the side-eye.

"Good. Hand me a pancake."

Val complied and watched with relief and satisfaction as the boy consumed the bland food. He couldn't resist placing small kisses in the top of his pretty red head. "Don't you dare die on me." It was a stupid thing to say, yet he couldn't keep the words from coming out.

Mackie, bless him, simply giggled. "I promise." He finished his pancake and wisely lay against Val's chest to see if it would stay down. "This doesn't mean I'm not still mad at you over the stupid stunt you pulled, going vigilante to clean up the streets of Boston."

"I know, but I am done with it. And if it makes you feel any better, I have a date with Will in a short while in the gym. He's going to try to pound some sense into me."

"Good, tell him to give you a good kick from me."

Val laughed, enjoying the moment of carefreeness. "I will." He sobered. "I love you." He didn't say that nearly often enough.

"I know." Mackie snuggled closer, his complete trust in him all the reassurance Val needed.

* * * *

Will stood naked in the middle of the sparring room, stretching his muscles and waiting for Val. He'd kept his breakfast light, not into mimicking Mackie's wonderful world of technicolor. Annika had noticed and had merely shrugged when he'd told her his plans with Val. She was already a wise Queen, not interfering in her men's lives any more than was necessary. She appeared happy, too, even with his long absences. He shouldn't have been surprised, but it was an abrupt change from their lives to date. He supposed it was merely another sign that she was maturing rapidly.

Val didn't keep him waiting for long. He entered, stripping off his own clothing with the kind of speed they could only employ when pesky and uninformed humans weren't around. Although they hadn't discussed it, they'd had the same idea — to fight in the traditional way. The human need to battle while dressed had amused them at first. It made sense, of course, when weapons were employed. Hand-to-hand demanded something more personal. Will's palms itched with the desire to get hold of Val's flesh.

"I promised Mackie I'd give you the chance to take a good shot on his behalf." Val cracked his neck as he advanced on Will.

"My pleasure, I'm sure. I trust he's doing well this morning."

"Yes." The relief in Val's eyes was obvious. "He's currently playing with Idris, along with Annika and Merlin in the living room. Her control over that particular hybrid is a relief," he added. "Mackie may have turned a corner on this morning sickness thing. At least I hope so. Harry said it can happen that quickly but not to be surprised if it changes again."

"Any break is welcome, I'm sure."

Will didn't give any warning. Small talk and reassuring male bonding time was over. He struck with what he knew was a 'gimme' by Val, his foot hitting Val square in the chest. The man went flying right into the padded wall. The room shook ominously. Will had only a split second to consider that before Val used his momentum to launch back and plow into Will's mid-section. They both went down with dual grunts, then popped up again.

They locked onto each other's shoulders, digging their feet into the equally padded flooring, each trying to push the other. Neither gained much purchase, being more evenly matched than Will would have thought. Truthfully, he'd assumed Val would outmuscle him. Perhaps he was only toying with him. That thought had barely formed before he found himself flipping over Val's head to land hard on his back. The mat may as well been missing, given the jarring his body took.

He rolled onto his side and pushed to his feet, even as he struggled to regain his breath. "Fuck, that hurt."

Val bared his teeth. "It wouldn't be much fun if it didn't. I'm getting serious now, dude."

Will wheezed. "That's what I was afraid of." Except he wasn't as bad off as he was acting. It allowed him to get another shot in. He went low this time, flipping Val, tit for tat.

Val bounced, skidded, then came roaring back for more…and more. They both did. There wasn't a spot of flooring or wall that one or both of them didn't hit with some part of their body. Will's muscles ached and his ears rang. He never once thought of throwing in the towel. It had been ages since he'd been able to truly let loose. Their limbs became blurs of movement, even to their superior vision. Will's focus narrowed to taking his next breath and beating Val's out of him. Their cocks were hard and dripping, clashing like clubs, giving a spike of pleasure along with the pain.

In the end, though, the outcome had never truly been in doubt. Val outweighed him and had more experience with combat. He brought Will to the mat one final time. No amount of wishing allowed Will to throw the guy off. He tapped out the only way their kind knew—by exposing his neck, offering Val a clear path to his jugular.

The strike came fast and hard, causing Will to climax. They both did. That was normal, too. This kind of fighting always ended thusly. Val, though, took only a few pulls before retracting his fangs and licking the punctures closed. Then they lay side-by-side, panting in sync, regaining strength.

Will almost fell asleep. No surprise… He'd barely slept in the last several days. Between watching over

Damien and keeping an eye on Annika, he was being pulled in two different directions, day and night.

"Jesus, I needed that," he finally said.

"I as well," Val agreed. "You are a more formidable opponent that I expected."

"Thanks. I think."

"No offense. As a pilot, you are unequaled. This is different."

"Agreed. I guess I'm channeling my abject terror at how Damien is in Bran's lair. Well, the asshat's. I'm not sure what worries me more, the damage Bran can do or the type Warren can. It's not a good place for the boy, regardless."

"I hear you on that, but let me give you the benefit of my recent experience. These human boys bring out our protective instincts, yet they are both courageous and mini-warriors. They can handle themselves in surprising ways."

"I know that. I've seen it myself. Except it was fine when it was your boys, not mine. It's different now."

Val chuckled. "Of course it is. I also get how hard it must be for you to open yourself up again after losing someone."

Will closed his eyes at the stab of pain. "I didn't think I could ever love again. I was determined not to get involved with another human. They are so very fragile." He winced. "Sorry... You don't need that reminder."

"No, it's okay. I, um, had a good talk with Mackie. I, ah, need to learn to lean on him more. He was reassuring. Does Damien know how you feel?"

Will snorted. "I'm not sure *I* know what I feel."

"Yes, you do."

"Yeah," he sighed. "I love him. How the hell did that happen?"

"It sneaks up on you. Don't be stupid like me. Tell him and trust him to take you as you are."

Will shook his head. "What if he recoils in horror? It happens. No matter how close we get to them, some humans can't handle the truth."

"I'm betting Damien isn't one of them." A second later, Val sprang to his feet and offered Will his hand.

Will accepted the help and stood with a groan. "I need a shower. Nothing has to be decided now, anyway. Keeping him safe is my priority. I'll worry about the future once Bran has been neutralized."

He raced out of the room, his respite from the fight already a distant memory.

Chapter Eight

Damien wasn't sure how much longer he could sit through the inspiring, yet completely insipid movie playing in the rec room. He really didn't want to be there. Not that it was compulsory or anything... It was purely his own idea to attend instead of reading in his room or something. Not that the selection of books in this place was much better than the approved movies. Even TV shows were forbidden, given how much they were under the influence of the 'gay agenda'.

The problem was, Damien didn't want to see Elliot in their room. He wanted to catch him right after his therapy session with Warren. Something wasn't right. The boy put on a good front, yet with each passing day, he appeared more withdrawn, troubled. Damien was worried about the kid, as annoyingly self-righteous as he could be. And Damien sensed there was something there that was important to ferret out. His stay hadn't otherwise yielded any useful information. He was beginning to think he needed to take risks, to stick his nose into private places, to do that very thing he'd promised Will he wouldn't.

With one eye on the sun-shining rays of hope as some footballer found Jesus, and the other on the hall leading to Warren's office, he waited for his roomie to reappear. The hairs on the back of his neck stood up. He swung his gaze around to find the source of his sudden unease and landed on Bran. The guy was lounging in the dark corner by the doors that led to the patio. His glasses were off for a change. It was dark in the room for the purpose of watching the movie. It was impossible to tell, nevertheless, who or what the guy was looking at. Somehow, Damien felt sure it was him.

He made himself look away and ended up eyeballing some pimple-faced kid instead who was staring at him. At his arm, really.

"Why do you have the mark of the devil on you?" the boy demanded.

Damien glanced at his newest ink, the one that Annika had labeled 'pretty'. "Dude, it's a dragon. Red, yes. Tail, check. But no cloven feet, only claws. Plus, I don't think the devil breathes fire, only throws people into it—but what do I know?"

The kid opened his mouth to argue the point. Damien was already getting out of his chair. Earnest Elliot was coming down the hall, looking like…shit, actually. He walked a little as if he were drunk, which was crazy because alcohol was one more thing that was forbidden in Hades Hills. In fact, Elliot headed straight, sort to speak, for the refreshment table, where he downed a cup of watery lemonade. Damien knew from experience that the stuff was pure mix, not a single real lemon in it and not worthy of a sip, let alone a whole cupful.

Damien moved to meet him there and arrived while Elliot was emptying his second cup. "Are you all right?"

Startled, Elliot sloshed his drink. "I'm fine."

Yeah? Once more with feeling, dude. "Are you sure? You seem upset."

Elliot gave him the side-eye and nodded. "Of course. It's just my therapy. That's all. I wish it was making better progress, but the congressman tells me that I'm too hard on myself. These things take time."

Elliot crushed the cup with his fist and threw it in the waste basket. The aggressive move was totally out of character, as was his next question and the tone he used to ask it. "What are you doing here? You usually go straight to our room."

He must have realized the harshness of his question and switched to his usual helpful self. "Are you, ah, socializing more? Because that's great if you are. Being with other boys, having wholesome fun, is a major step in your rehabilitation."

For God sake's, Elliot, give it a rest. He didn't say that out loud, of course. "I thought maybe I'd enjoy the movie, but…" He shrugged. "I don't like sports much."

"You should learn to. It's what—"

"Real men do," he said in unison with the guy. "Yeah, I know. Look," he added with a sigh, "why don't we turn in? I know I'm bushed, and you seem to have had enough for one day, too."

He didn't even wait for any kind of capitulation. He simply took his roommate by the arm and led him to their room. Elliot didn't give so much as a token struggle against it. He was completely docile as Damien escorted him to what little sanctuary that they possessed.

Sitting on his bed, he watched Elliot undress with slow, jerky movements. "Dude, are you sure you're okay, because you kind of look like Rocky after losing to Apollo Creed. Minus the bruises, of course." Except the guy's lips looked kind of puffy.

"I told you I'm fine," Elliot snapped.

Damien put his hands up. "Okay, dude, whatever you say."

Once again, Earnest Elliot returned. "I appreciate your concern, but really, you should focus on your own recovery."

Damien had to hand it to the place. They'd totally coopted the strategies and buzz-words of addiction treatment. They really hammered at the idea of sexual orientation being a disease. Damien would have made some kind of appeasement if Elliot hadn't winced once he sat on his own bed. He'd recovered immediately, trying to turn that frown upside down.

"It's good of you to worry about me. Congressman Warren has that burden. And I know what I have to work on to make myself wholly well."

"Sure, whatever you say." There was no point in pushing it. Not yet. Damien was now certain that he'd found a weakness. The only question was how to discover fully what was going on without hurting Elliot. The kid was a pawn, another kind of victim.

"Thank you. Goodnight." Elliot slid under the covers without bothering to wash his face or brush his teeth, testament to how exhausted he truly was.

"Peace out, dude."

Within minutes, Elliot was tucked in and breathing deeply. Damien resisted the lure of joining him. Glancing at his watch, he was glad to see he had only two hours to wait before he could sneak out to see Will.

The thought of it made him smile. He believed he had something finally of use, perhaps. Plus, the thought of what Will had in store for him made him hard. As therapy went, a blow job was a great way to end his day.

* * * *

Will silently had a meltdown as he stared at his phone, excoriating it for not showing any text from Damien. It was more than thirty minutes past their rendezvous time. His hands shook from the effort not to text his lover to see if he was okay. A parade of horrors marched across his brain, where in each vignette, Damien suffered more and worse agonies. The boy was never late. If anything, Will had been the one to frequently apologize for tardiness, driven by this push-me-pull-you loop he was in. Val had been right about his being unable to keep this up for much longer. But unless and until Alex agreed to pull Damien out of this torture chamber or Annika managed to finish maturing in the next twelve hours, he would have to.

And still, no text. Will was seconds away from rising and storming the building when his phone vibrated.

Coming. Sorry!

When Damien arrived a few minutes later, Will didn't give him a chance to say a word. He grabbed him and brought him down in a controlled tumble to the ground, attacking his mouth—and his everything else. Will didn't give a good damn about information or keeping cum off his boy. *His. Boy.* He wanted Damien to smell like him. Will wanted to *drench* the kid in his scent. A drumbeat of 'mine, mine, mine' replaced the scenes of torture in his head.

He tore off their clothing, enough to expose the necessary parts, that was. Buttons popped and he might have broken Damien's zipper in his haste. *Too damn bad.* He'd buy him a thousand other pairs and didn't care what Earnest Elliot, as Damien's roommate was known, might notice. He had some presence of mind to pull a condom out of his pocket, and at the last second, regained more sense with the ebbing of his fears. So he covered Damien's dick instead of his own and sat on it.

"Oh fuck!" Damien's newly liberated mouth uttered the exclamation in a hoarse whisper.

Will silenced him with his tongue, doubled over as he rode the human's cock with punishing strokes. He ripped his shirt in two to get a clear path to his own dick. He jerked himself hard and fast. As he came, he clenched his hole, tugging Damien's shaft on a long upswing. His efforts sent his lover over the edge with him. Damien arched into the stroke at the same time as Will dropped down completely. It caused him to lose touch with the boy's mouth, but he simply couldn't resist grinding the last of his climax out of him. Will stayed seated on the cock long after the spasms eased for both of them.

God, he wanted to bend over again, not to reclaim Damien's lips but to sink his fangs into the boy's neck. Not doing so was something like a death, denying him the essence of life. But he had some control left, barely. So he settled again for placing his lips over the jugular, although he was careful not to leave a mark. *Mustn't leave any love bites. Fuck, this whole thing sucks.* He had half a mind to march inside and rip Bran's throat out and be done with it. And why the hell not? He'd leave behind a pile of unidentifiable dust and whatever clothes he found the fucker in.

Problem. Solved. Except that would make him like Val, and even Dracul, to some degree. They were creatures of the hive and not wired to act independently as rogues who were only interested in what made them happy. Besides, how horrible would it be for Damien? Such an act wouldn't go unnoticed. Damien would stick to his side if he tried such a stunt. He'd learn Will's true nature and that would probably lead him to be horrified or disgusted. Will wouldn't have to worry about someone else taking Damien from him. He'd make the boy go screaming as far from him as possible.

No. Killing Bran here and now would only serve Will's interests and no one else's. So, he didn't.

"Don't scare me like that," he whispered into Damien's ear once he had his breath back.

Damien grabbed him in a bear hug. "I'm sorry. I fell asleep."

Will kissed him. "I was scared shitless for you. This is madness. I have to get you out of here. I don't care what Alex says. You don't have to do this." Yeah, it was an indirect way of achieving his goals. Damien wasn't of the hive. He had his own agency in this.

He eased off of his lover, careful to keep any and all bodily fluids away from the human.

Sitting, Damien grinned. "That was totally awesome. I feel really bad about scaring you like I did, but holy fuck, dude, that was some wild ride."

Okay, that was a bit of a dodge. Not exactly an *You're absolutely right, I'm checking myself out of this madhouse right the fuck now.*

Damien's face morphed into a frown. "Did you hurt yourself? I mean, you didn't use any lube."

More dodging. Will had felt the burn, but it had been nothing. "I'm fine. Really." He emphasized his answer with a fierce kiss.

Damien melted into his embrace. "I guess I figured you as a total top. I was wondering if I was going to get a chance at having your ass."

Will inhaled deeply. "I like variety. No set rules. I'm glad you enjoyed it. I-I couldn't help myself. No blow job was going to do it for me."

"No complaints here, dude. Plus you made sure I don't return to my room stinking of sex."

A growl escaped Will. "Such madness. As if what two consenting adults could be doing is anyone else's business."

"Preaching to the choir, my man. The suckitude of this place is off the charts. It's making poor Elliot more miserable every day."

"I can't help him. You can't, either. He has to want to leave here. In the meantime, I don't suppose I can talk you into leaving?"

"No effing way, Will. I volunteered for this because it matters, not only to your family but to kids like Elliot. It's personal now that I've seen the damage they're doing. I want to shutter this place for good."

Will knew when to retreat in a fight. "Okay, I hear you. Is there is anything you know that we can use to accomplish that?"

Damien shook his head, then changed halfway through to a nod. "Maybe. Something's going on with Elliot."

"I know you want to help him—"

"Hear me out." He turned to sit cross-legged, facing Will fully. "Warren is his personal counselor, something he only does with 'special' boys, the ones he thinks have leadership abilities. Or that's the excuse he uses, except I've seen Elliot after those sessions—which, by the way, are always in the evenings. That makes some sense, given that Elliot is part of the staff, too, and does a lot during the days."

"And?" Will prompted when Damien fell silent.

He licked his lips before continuing, which only served to distract Will. "I may be totally off base with this, but I swear that whatever is going on behind Warren's closed door is bad. It's hurting Elliot—and not only mentally. I think he's using some kind of physical punishment. Surely that's illegal."

"I don't know. I'd have to check with Alex and Val. It sounds wrong, obviously, but I've learned that humans don't have to make sense."

"Humans?"

Will kicked himself mentally. "We humans. You know that as a species we kind of suck."

"No argument here." He paused again. "It could be even worse, like maybe he's having Elliot give him what he's missing from not going to the clubs anymore. I have to assume that his extracurricular activities are off the table during his presidential campaign."

"There's some logic there."

"Yup, unfortunately there is."

"Do you think Elliot would admit to any of that?"

Damien's face fell. "Probably not. He's drunk a lot of the Kool-Aid. I'm surprised his face hasn't turned bright red by now."

"I fear we are back to not having anything of value."

"Crap." Then he said something that made Will's heart skip a beat. "I think Bran was watching me this evening. I can't be sure—" He stopped on a squeak as Will grabbed him by the arms and squeezed.

"Why the hell didn't you lead with that?" He could barely keep his voice in check.

Damien's eyes widened. "Sorry. It didn't seem that important compared to what I thought I'd learned about Elliot shortly after the guy creeped me out lurking in the corner of the common room. I could be wrong. It's easy to get paranoid in there. I swear I've done nothing worth his notice."

Will looked off in the distance, his moods and instincts whipsawed with each new piece of information. "This ends tomorrow." He'd made his decision. If Bran was suspicious of Damien, that put his life at risk. Alex would understand pulling him out. Everyone would.

"I told you I want to see this through."

Will glared at him. "And I've told you—we've all told you—that Bran is dangerous. Seriously, he will kill you if he thinks you are a threat. He doesn't operate by even the low standards that I expect Warren does."

Damien finally looked seriously scared. *Excellent.* "Okay, I hear you. I could be wrong, though, and I don't want you to upset Alex because I'm jumping at shadows. I don't exactly get how your family works, but I can tell that he's like, the boss."

"That's not entirely true. It doesn't matter, in any event. My feelings for you will override Alex's judgment on this. I'll make sure of it."

"Your feelings?"

Will winced. He really hadn't intended to show his hand quite yet. "We'll talk about that once you're out of here. There are things about me that you need to know before we take our relationship any further."

"Okay. That's fine, so long as you understand that I'm falling in love with you already."

Oh, sweet Jesus. "Wait until you hear what I say before deciding if you want to tell me that again."

"Okay," the boy said for the third time. Damien wiggled out of his hold and righted what he could of his clothing with Will's help.

When they were done, Will wanted to hold him in place and made an aborted attempt at doing so, before letting him go. Damien smiled at him. "I'll see you tomorrow?"

"First thing in the morning. I'll be coming through the front door."

"They may not let you in."

"Let them try and stop me." He made sure his expression showeed his lover his determination. It worked.

Backing away, Damien chuckled. "Okay then. Tomorrow morning." He blew a kiss and was gone.

Will sat, watching him leave, unable to move himself. He couldn't shake a sense of dread. He wasn't sure he could make himself return to the club, to even ask Alex's permission before he pulled Damien out—or Annika's, for that matter. Every fiber of his body was telling him that his lover was in imminent danger. His feelings, including his growing love for Damien, felt like a far more important thing than hierarchy and power. Maybe he'd been on this planet too long, or perhaps he'd never been a good member of the hive, despite his high birth. Regardless, his path was clear if he could keep his shit together for a few more hours. Come dawn, he would be on the move.

* * * *

Damien's heart sank when he realized that the light was on in his room. Elliot had woken, again, and it would be harder to explain his late-night wanderings this time. Damn, he'd been lucky since that one time, with Elliot sleeping soundly through his comings and goings. Of course, what difference did it make, given that Will was determined to pull him out of the camp within less than twelve hours anyway? Damien was willing to bet his man wouldn't wait for breakfast before storming the battlements for him. The depth of the man's devotion pushed all kinds of sappy buttons that he'd had since pre-puberty.

"Sorry, dude," he was saying as he opened the door. His words died on his lips when he saw his roommate lying on top of his bed—not under the covers, not anymore. He was paler than usual and, considering the blood dripping down both his arms, that wasn't surprising.

"Elliot!" Even now, his instinct was to stay quiet, not wake the others. He didn't trust anyone in this place to provide the right help.

He rushed to the bedside, saw that the boy was already unconscious. "Oh, Elliot, what did that fucker do to you?"

This was Warren's fault. There was no doubt about it. But blame could wait. Damien dithered for a few seconds before choosing to grab his phone from its hiding place. *Help room quick quiet*, he texted to Will before tossing the phone on his bed and returning to Elliot's side.

Pulling off his T-shirt, he tried to rip it in half. It was fucking hard to do. How had Will manage to make it look so easy? He gave up and wrapped it around the nearest of Elliot's wrists. He was just turning to get another one from his drawer, when miraculously there was Will. His keen eyes took in the situation in a fraction of a second. Then there was a moment of obvious hesitation before Will dropped to Elliot's side. He took the unbound arm first and raised it to his face.

Damien frowned. "He's slashed his wrists," he said, because it seemed as if his lover didn't understand what had happened.

Will turned troubled eyes on him. "I know. I'm sorry. I wanted you to learn this a better way."

Damien opened his mouth to ask what the hell Will was talking about. He shut it with a click of his teeth as he watched Will stick out his tongue and begin lapping at the slits Elliot had made in his skin. Vertical cuts, because this kid was serious about killing himself.

"What the fuck...?" His words died as he realized the blood was slowing and the wounds were closing.

Will drenched the boy's flesh with his saliva, and when he was done with the first arm, he pulled off Damien's hasty bandage and repeated the effort. Stunned, Damien backed away until his legs hit his cot. He fell rather than sat, his gaze fixed on what was happening mere feet away.

"I don't understand." He swallowed hard and tried again to ask a question that didn't quite form in his mind. "What are you?" he finally croaked out.

Will didn't answer. Not with words. Instead, he turned his head, licking the spots of blood from his lips, his white fangs gleaming. *White. Fangs.*

"Holy fuck! You're a vampire?" He giggled because that was crazy.

But Will didn't join him in his mirth. He merely nodded.

* * * *

Will had never hated being Earth-bound more since the crash, in the very literal sense of the world. Speeding eastbound on the Mass Pike toward the help Damien's friend needed, he couldn't stop wishing that they were in the air. A chopper wouldn't necessarily be faster in populated areas, but he could go in a straight line and without having to keep one eye out for a state trooper pulling him over. He was speeding *just* a bit, because time was not their friend.

Calling an ambulance had been discussed and discarded as an option. The camp had a small medical center to handle minor problems. Both Damien and Will had been concerned that the Warrens would try to contain Elliot's suicide attempt in-house, given that their concerns were obviously all about *their* needs and not those of the boys they coopted. Plus, with Bran on the prowl, there was an unknown variable about how he would react to finding one of his enemies right at his doorstep.

The good news was that Harry was on his way, heading west as Will went east. They were minutes away from the Natick exit, where they'd agreed to meet. The doctor had plasma and every type of blood to aide Elliot in his immediate needs. After that? Well, it didn't bear thinking about. Will had no idea what they were going to do. Fortunately, that decision was above his pay grade, although he had his own problem to solve.

He glanced in the rearview mirror and looked his quandary right in the eyes. Damien sat in the back of the SUV, holding a blanket-wrapped Elliot in his arms. His lover had said little after the big reveal, only enough to agree to the plan about taking Elliot quickly and silently out of the compound. He hadn't blinked when Will had leaped over the fence while carrying Elliot, as if the whole blood-licking event had set his bar for 'whoa' to a very high level. But when Will had started to set Elliot down to go back for Damien, the human had thwarted his efforts by climbing over the fence. His nimbleness and raw strength was impressive for a human his size. Will took pride in his lover's abilities, although there was no guaranteeing that he still had the right to think of Damien in those terms.

As a form of silent rejection, that simple act of escaping unaided by Will had cut deep. So also had Damien's jerking his scraped palm away from Will's grasp. The boy had wiped his hand against his jeans rather than let Will lick the abrasion closed. Damien's reaction to learning Will's true nature wasn't a surprise. It had been Will's fear all along. Perhaps there would have been no way to make that big reveal and have it go all right.

In the heat of the moment of trying to save Elliot's life, the information dump had been too great a shock to Damien. That had been especially true, given that Will hadn't been able to keep his fangs from descending. Much like his dick, the damn things had minds of their own. Despite the medical emergency, all his instincts had reacted to blood on his lips and tongue. His fangs had naturally thought there was a party to be had. There had been no hiding his nature. Of course, Damien thought he was a vampire, which was bad enough. How much worse would this get once he learned the full truth?

The one bright spot was that Damien didn't look away. He stared back at Will with a steady gaze. His thoughts and feelings were impossible to read in those brief moments when their eyes locked. Will counted that as a small win. At least there was no obvious fear or disgust. That might be down to shock. Will hoped not. There was nothing to be done about it at the moment in any event. He returned his attention to the road, because driving was all he could do of any use.

Elliot whimpered, incoherent words passing his lips. That was hopefully a good sign. The kid wasn't in a coma, it seemed. He hadn't lost a lot of blood by Will's estimation. Damien had come back in time and had done the right thing by texting him. He'd been in the process of leaping over the fence to leave. The sound of the text coming in had been enough to have him twirl mid-jump and race to the building where he knew his lover would be. He'd read the text on the fly, although its brevity had made him more worried, not less. He was a little ashamed that when he'd seen that it was Elliot, not Damien in distress, he'd been relieved. Grateful. A living Damien who hated him was infinitely preferable to the alternative.

Damien murmured reassurances to his friend. "We're nearly there. Help is on its way. You're going to be fine."

"No, no, no," Elliot whined.

Yeah, for someone who'd attempted suicide, Damien's words were probably not that reassuring. Jesus, what had led the boy to take such drastic steps? Will answered his own question—that fucked-up place. Even if Damien's theories about what Warren was up to with Elliot were wrong, therapy of the kind they promised in their brochures was sufficient to send a sensitive person over the edge.

Conversion didn't work because sexual orientation in humans was not a choice. This outcome wasn't surprising. The inevitable failure of the program would lead the boy to blame himself. He was the defective because he couldn't change instead of the process being a giant lie from the beginning.

"How much longer?" Damien's strained question had been directed at Will.

Looking at him again in the rearview mirror, Will said, "Five minutes."

That wasn't a reassuring underestimate, either. The exit loomed in the near distance. Will crossed lanes over to the right and picked up speed. There was very little traffic and these machines were built with humans' slower reflexes in mind. Driving them was child's play. He took the exit, tires squealing as he rounded the curve and merged onto the local road. The medical van that Harry had tricked out with brilliant foresight sat in the dark far back of the deserted parking lot of a big-box store. Will pulled up beside it and stood on the brakes.

Emil was the first to come out of the van. *Good call.* Damien knew him best and hopefully trusted him, despite the obvious point that Emil was the same creature as Will. Harry was hot on his heels while Val stayed in the driver's seat, undoubtedly keeping watch. As much as he wanted to keep tabs on Damien, Will did the same. The spot wasn't that remote and there were always police patrolling the area. Too bad Duncan wasn't with them. The cop could talk their way out of any awkward situation.

"We're going to take good care of your friend," Emil was reassuring Damien.

"Is Harry really a doctor?" Damien barked out the question in a skeptical and accusatory tone that made Will wince. He'd given fair warning to his crewmates about what Damien did and did not know, species-wise. Harry's medical credentials hadn't been raised, but it had been a fair question.

"I am," Harry confirmed. "I know how to take care of a human. I promise you that."

Damien didn't say anything more. Will caught their movements out of the corner of his eye. They transferred Elliot's still-limp form from the SUV to the van. Damien scrambled out after them. He paused outside and leaned over the front seat. Will whipped his head around to look straight at him. It was hard. He was so sure he'd see hate there emphasized with an *I don't want to ever see you again, monster!* That was not what greeted him. Damien's expression was hard to read, but there seemed to be a lot of conflict in there.

"I have to go with Elliot. When he wakes up, he'll need to see a familiar face." Damien swallowed audibly. "I don't want him to be afraid."

It took a moment for Will's brain to accept that the words he'd been expecting weren't the ones he got. Was the human explaining his choice because he thought that the alternative was to stay in the SUV with Will? Did Damien even consider that a choice? Will expected he would welcome any chance to get away from him. Then again, no matter what, the boy had to ride with monsters. What difference did it make which one? Yet, he was explaining his decision as if he wanted Will to understand.

So, Will nodded and said, "I get it. I'll, ah, see you soon."

Damien also nodded before shutting the door and climbing into the back of the van. Val took off with a spray of gravel. When the van cleared its spot, Emil was left standing there. He came over and got into the passenger's side.

"I figured you could use the company."

Putting the SUV into Drive, Will said, "Don't you want to be with Damien? He's closest to you and could use the emotional support."

"I'm not the one he's closest to and I'm not sure how much comfort any of our kind would be for him at the moment. He's in shock, I expect, but his worry for his friend is probably holding his meltdown at bay. For now, Harry is the only one who can give him any reassurances. I can't even give him answers, frankly. There was no time to discuss any of this with Alex beyond the immediate need to get this kid medical care. I'm sure he'd agree, though, that whatever explanation has to be given, it's your right and responsibility."

Will pulled out onto the road, heading toward the Pike again. It was the fastest way to get to Boston. The van was already a dot in the distance. "When did you get to be so smart?"

Emil flashed a grin. "I've been through this particular shitshow before."

"Right, with Jase."

"Yup. Humans are surprisingly resilient. Damien loves you. He'll adapt to this new reality."

Will did a double-take. "You can't know that—the 'his loving me' thing. I only heard from him tonight that he was falling in love with me. That's 'falling' not 'fallen', and that was when he thought I was human.

Whatever he felt then is surely gone, now that he knows what I really am, except he thinks I'm some mythical creature. He doesn't even know my true nature." He barked out a laugh. "Once Elliot's safe, Damien is going to make like the Roadrunner."

Emil was quiet for a few seconds, then said, "My mistake. I thought you loved him too."

Will sputtered. "I do! That's what makes this whole thing suck at a tsunami level. He's not merely one more human that might try to out us. He's become central to my life. After losing Luuk, I thought that was it—no more love, no more sex. It was all about raising my daughter, the Queen. Then Damien got under my skin, spreading through my body like bacteria that I was helpless to fight off."

"Wow. Here's a little advice, Willem. Never express your love for the boy in those terms to him. It's not exactly Hallmark-worthy."

Will barked out a laugh. "Yeah, no kidding. I make it sound like I resent him, and maybe part of me does. Along with the love is a terror that has me by the balls. I don't think I could survive losing another human lover like I did Luuk. I know now that my blood is insufficient to keep him healthy."

"That was an anomaly, though, surely. Have you spoken with Harry about it? A changed human shouldn't have been susceptible to cancer. It was a fluke, had to be."

Will was already shaking his head, clenching his fingers around the steering wheel in a death grip, all his fear and guilt vomited out of him. "But it wasn't. It's my blood, my genetics that did it—and can do it again. I never changed him—not completely, perhaps not at all. There was no autopsy or anything."

"Annika."

"*I* gave birth to her!" He pounded the wheel with one palm and his breath wheezed out of him. He struggled to rein in his emotions. Losing his shit wasn't going to help anything or anyone, Damien included. He took in deep breaths and let them out slowly. Emil, bless him, said nothing, merely sat there until he was ready to speak again.

"It took nearly a thousand years, but our species' survival mechanisms finally kicked in. I have no idea if feeding Luuk my blood was a factor at all, and I didn't realize what was happening to my own body, if you can believe that."

He grimaced. "No, that's not true. I did feel the changes and ignored them. So long as my masculine traits remained visible, it was easy to pretend that my insides didn't feel like they were being churned. As it was, it took me a couple of months before I faced reality." He barked out another laugh. "I actually thought I was putting on weight and started running to get rid of my *belly*.

"It was Annika all along, growing inside me, not that I knew I carried the Queen. I assumed it was a boy and was terrified when Luuk handed me a baby girl. I was frightened that Alex would react badly to my change and her existence." He swallowed past the lump in his throat. "That he might kill me and my child to stop the spread of our kind."

Emil tsked. "How could you think such a thing about him?"

"How could I not?" he countered. "He'd been battling Dracul with a single-minded determination for centuries to keep humans safe from our domination. My changing was reason enough to worry. When I birthed Annika, I went into survival mode. A Queen poses more risk to the humans than Dracul ever could. Despite her being a hybrid, we have to assume that she could birth hundreds more offspring from the crewmembers left alive."

All this had been the unspoken truth for months. When he realized he couldn't keep Annika a secret anymore, that she herself wouldn't permit it, he'd all but pleaded with Alex in MacLerie's castle to trust him to prevent Annika from getting out of hand. *'She's a hybrid, Alex, not a full queen. And she listens to me, has never given me any worries. She's not a danger to this world, Alex. I swear she isn't.'* It had been the truth followed by a series of lies. He had no idea what she would do now that her maturity was nearly upon them. And he knew with certainty that his influence was on the wane.

"Alex is a good man," he said quietly. "I looked in his eyes and saw that he didn't have the heart to destroy her. Not then. She's growing, though, faster than I expected. Time has nearly run out." He glanced at his friend. "I don't know how this is all going to end, and loving Damien is just one more complication. Unless I'm very careful, I know that he will impregnate me the same way Luuk did. Between us, Annika and I may have the capability of populating this world with queens. That makes us more dangerous than the H-bomb."

They drove in more silence until Will exited off the highway in Boston.

"I expect," Emil said finally, "that Alex has worked this out already. He's the smartest drone I've ever met, and now that you say it, it all seems obvious that you birthed Annika. I'm frankly embarrassed that I didn't think of it myself." He turned to look at Will directly.

"Every one of us loves Annika. She is our Queen, but we would love her, no matter what. We will not hurt her. I promise."

Will made himself shoot his friend a reassuring smile. It was hard, because while he wanted to believe him and he didn't question his sincerity, he also knew that under the right circumstances, anyone could justify doing anything. And he very much suspected that his adorable little girl was going to push them all to their limits.

Chapter Nine

"He's sleeping normally now."

Damien made himself look at Harry. It was hard, given what he knew about him, about all of them. "Thank you."

Elliot still looked way too pale against the oddly black pillowcase. They'd been brought to a medical suite on the top floor of the family's building. Damien had never seen any part of it other than the open living area — and Will's bedroom, of course — and was surprised to learn how much of a fortress the place really was.

They could survive a nuclear war here.

He'd been allowed to stick by Elliot's side during his care, which had involved a blood transfusion to replace what had been lost. It wasn't surprising to see that they had a supply of it in all types handy. Vampires needed it to survive, after all. And didn't modern takes on the tale show 'good' ones using blood banks instead of sucking humans dry?

Harry interrupted his thoughts. "He's safe here. You both are. I'll be in my office. If you need me, please press that red button." He pointed to the same kind of device for calling nurses that one could find in any hospital bed.

Not trusting his voice to say more, Damien simply nodded. The chair he sat in was wide and comfortable. He leaned forward, however, in order to take Elliot's hand in his own. He wanted the boy to know, even in sleep, that he wasn't alone. It wasn't a sufficient distraction to keep Damien from thinking of Will, of how vulnerable he'd been each time they'd made love. And he thought of those times in that way. It wasn't only fucking. He knew the difference, despite never having fallen for another man. Sex with Will had felt different than any other experience in his life, because there had been feelings involved right from the beginning.

He instinctively put his free hand on his neck. Had Will ever sucked his blood? He didn't think so, unless vampires really did have the ability to erase memories. There was no scar there or any kind of mark. From what he'd seen of Elliot's wrist, Will's saliva had taken care of the worst of it, but Harry had still used butterfly bandages to bind the cuts more tightly. Surely there would be some remnants if Will had pierced Damien's jugular.

"I never fed off you."

Damien jerked in surprised and turned to see Will standing a few feet away on the opposite side of the bed. *God, they're fast and quiet.*

"It requires consent. At least, that's how Alex and the rest of us have chosen to conduct ourselves."

Damien knew he should be afraid, and yet somehow he couldn't quite work up that emotion. He was mad, yes, because he'd deserved to know such fundamental information about his lover. He felt not so much betrayed as disrespected.

"You should have trusted me with the truth," he found himself saying, quietly because he didn't want to disturb Elliot.

Will nodded. "Yes, although it wasn't my secret to tell without permission." He pulled up another chair and sat so that they were speaking across Elliot's limp body. "I really should have resisted getting involved with you at all."

Those words stung. "I don't think you get to resent this situation. I'm the injured party here."

Will looked surprised. "I agree. I merely meant that I shouldn't have put you in this position. I'm sure it's frightening and confusing…"

"I'm more pissed than anything else. Not as much as I could be, though, given that you saved Elliot's life. Thank you for that," he added more primly that he'd intended. He sounded like a prat.

"Helping humans has been our mission for a very long time." He seemed tired, in more than a physical way.

"How many years is in a 'long time'?"

Will hesitated before answering, making Damien believe that he would lie. If he did, it was a whopper and the complete opposite of what he expected. "A thousand years."

Damien sat with his mouth open for a few seconds before closing it and swallowing past his heart, which had become lodged in his throat. "Seriously?" he croaked out. "Vampires live that long?"

"We're not vampires. There's no such thing," Will replied matter-of-factly.

"But, the"—Damien gestured to his mouth—"fangs."

"I do have fangs that descend, sometimes of their own volition, in order to drink blood, which is an important part of our diet. I'm long-lived, with keen senses and tremendous strength, compared to a human. All those things gave birth to the vampire legend. But we aren't the mythical monsters you're thinking of."

Damien almost said 'of course not' because he didn't think of Will or Emil or any of them like that. Again, perhaps he should, but he knew them too well to see them in such a negative light. They were different, though, and not apparently human, by their own viewpoint.

"What are you, then?"

"Aliens."

Damien snorted and would have laughed out loud, except Will was totally serious. He could see that. Plus, the answer made a lot more sense. He'd always been one of those people that believed there were alien species out there that could make contact—and maybe had already visited Earth. It wasn't completely bonkers to think so.

With his hand still holding Elliot's and his gaze fixed on Will's, he said simply, "Tell me."

* * * *

"Where am I?"

Damien pulled out of his slump against the bed and blinked sleep away from his eyes. "Hey, you're awake." Which was a mega dumb thing to say, but he was operating on fumes, for the most part. "How do you feel?"

Elliot's gaze flicked to his bandaged wrists. "Disappointed."

Damien squeezed the hand he was still holding. "No, it's okay. You were under tremendous stress, and it's just a good thing I came back into the room and found you in time. I'm sorry I left you alone," he added, because he felt guilty he hadn't been there for his roommate—and sort of friend—when he'd needed help the most.

Elliot stared hard at him. "No, I'm disappointed that it didn't work. I was supposed to be free now, free of sin and weakness, and—" His eyes filled with tears.

"No! No, Elliot. *No*," Damien practically shouted with dismay. "Your being alive is a good thing, the best thing ever. You are *not* a sinner, not damaged. You have worth, and fuck that hypocrite Warren for making you feel differently."

Tears rolled down Elliot's cheeks. "He was trying to help me."

"Bullshit!" Damien fought to get himself under control. He was totally out of his depth, but also desperate for Elliot to appreciate that killing himself was not the answer.

He took a few calming breaths before continuing. "Elliot, please believe me when I tell you this. Warren is gay, actively so. He's not someone who 'cured' himself, either. While he counsels you and others that you can change your sexuality, he's going regularly to gay bars and getting his freak on with any random guy willing to get his dick sucked with enthusiasm."

Elliot's eyes went wide before he shook his head. "That's not true!"

"It is. I've seen him myself. That's why when my friends—the people who saved your life, actually—

asked me for help, I agreed. Warren is the worst, self-loathing and destructive. He made you feel like killing yourself was the only option, when the better one is to be who God made you."

"He was helping me," Elliot insisted quietly. "I was the one who couldn't make it work."

"Helping how? By telling you over and over that all you had to do was pray your gay away? Or was he beating it out of you?" He'd seen something of Elliot's mostly naked body and there hadn't been any visible bruises. That didn't necessarily mean anything. He knew Elliot had been in pain after his 'session' with Warren.

"No, by showing me how disgusting and painful it all is."

Huh? "I don't understand." Although he was getting a sick feeling in the pit of his stomach that his 'out there' theory earlier was true.

Elliot licked his lips. "Could I have some water, please?"

"Sure." Damien grabbed a covered cup on the nightstand that contained water. He helped Elliot lift his head to suck through the straw.

Elliot dropped his head back onto the pillow. "Thanks. That helped, except I swear I can still taste it and I know it's vile but I can't quite hate it the way I should."

"Easy there." Damien took hold of Elliot's hand again. "I don't understand what you mean."

Elliot let out a sob. "The cum. It lingers in my mouth, no matter what I drink or how much I brush my teeth. I can taste it still."

Sensing that a whole boatload of important shit was about to be said, Damien worked to stay calm. He really wanted someone else there. Harry made the most sense, although it was Will who came to mind. After telling him that fantastic story of how an alien ship had been marooned on Earth and the crew splitting into warring factions, he'd left to give Damien some peace and quiet, as well as time to let the truth sink in.

Man, it's crazy and yet totally believable.

"Tell me what Warren made you do," he demanded in the gentlest way he could.

At first, Elliot took so long to respond that Damien thought he wouldn't at all. Then the dam broke and there was no stopping it until all the poison spewed forth. When he was done, Elliot closed his eyes and cried silently. Sitting there helplessly watching this boy's suffering, hearing what had been happening right under Damien's own nose, he was suddenly glad that he counted super-aliens as his friends.

* * * *

Duncan and Anderson walked into the middle of Chaos Central. The entire living room was filled with irate boys and their equally pissed-off partners. Only Harry and Damien were missing. Val had to keep a tight hold on Mackie to keep him sitting on his lap. With the morning sickness almost under control, he didn't want his husband making himself literally sick with this problem. Pacing and ranting were not going to help the kid upstairs any. For once, this was a purely human issue, and their cop friends were going to take the lead.

Frankly, Val had been outvoted on this. He'd sided with Will, who wanted to storm the conversion camp, rip it apart and toss its leader into the nearby lake. Oh, and turn Bran to dust, for good measure. It was an awesome plan, but Alex's logic had put a damper on it. There was a way to handle the situation that accomplished what they wanted—bring down the asshat, which would flush Bran out so that he could be dealt with under the radar.

Demi had latched onto his man and was haranguing him about taking care of this problem *yesterday*. Like all of the boys, he could relate to the pathetic soul who thought his life was worthless, even though Demi hadn't suffered the depravation and abuse that the others had. It made Val hold Mackie closer, thinking of how much he'd suffered before finding Club Lux and him. It wasn't only the boys, however. Kitty had pulled Anderson aside, and while that particular pairing still caused Val to scratch his head in disbelief, the detective was hanging on to her intense discourse. She was giving him his marching orders, no doubt.

It was Annika who brought everyone to order. "Quiet, please." Her little girl voice cut through the others like a meat cleaver. Even the humans obeyed her command. Val had thought Will should shield her from current events, but he'd been at once overruled on the issue. The guy had been right to allow her to participate, clearly.

Duncan walked to the center of the room. "Thank you. First of all, I understand how mad you all are, but I have to establish if the law was broken. It's not clear that I have jurisdiction over what happened, other than getting a protective order to place Elliot in a facility. He's the only one who has obviously done something illegal so far by trying to kill himself."

"Trey!" Demi screeched, his arms folded.

Duncan winced. "Demi, baby, please. I didn't say I was going to do so. I'm merely pointing out that running a shitty conversion camp for adults isn't a crime in the Commonwealth. Being a crappy counselor isn't, either. Before I try to arrest a sitting member of Congress, I have to believe he's guilty of something illegal."

"Oh, he for fucking sure is."

Every head turned as Damien trotted down the stairs. He looked around the room, his gaze landing on Annika. "I don't think what I have say is appropriate for you to hear, honey." He got major props for worrying about the girl.

Will came over to his daughter and putting his arm around her shoulder, he said, "Would you please go to your room? Your being here is going to make matters more difficult for Damien."

Oh, so it's like that, huh? Damien apparently got a gazillion more votes than Val.

The Queen surprised him. With a regal nod, she scooped Babette into her arms and headed for the stairs. She paused only to place a quick kiss on Damien's cheek before leaving. No one said anything until she was no longer visible. Val would have bet anything that the girl wasn't out of earshot, not that he raised the possibility. He was as interested as anyone to hear what Damien had to say.

Before speaking, however, the boy went to the kitchen island and picked up one of the sandwiches that Emil and Jase had made, and which no one was eating. Except Damien, who took a big bite, chewed, then washed down his mouthful with water.

"Sorry. I'm starving."

"Take your time, dear boy," Alex soothed. "We understand you've had a difficult night."

Damien nodded as he chewed. "Difficult, right." He swallowed and asked, "Just so I'm clear on this, who's the boss, you or Annika?"

Will took a step toward him. "Damien."

"No, it's quite all right," Alex interjected. "Your boy has questions. He deserves answers."

Will shook his head, his face a picture of misery. "He's not—"

Alex spoke over him. "Annika. She is our Queen. I am her loyal subject."

Damien stuffed the rest of the sandwich into his mouth. "Got it. Makes sense. I mean, Will gave me the thumbnail sketch, but I'm still trying to wrap my head around it all. You know?"

"Certainly. Perfectly understandable."

Quinn pressed his head against Alex's shoulder. "We'll help you, Damien. We humans have all been there. We get it."

Damien cleared his throat. "Yeah, thanks." He focused his gaze on Will. "Will and I need to do more talking first, but thanks for the offer."

With a sigh, he hopped onto one of the kitchen-island chairs. "My issues aside, Elliot is the more pressing problem." He nodded at Duncan. "You asked if Warren broke any laws and again, yes he did. The reason Elliot tried to kill himself is because Warren's counseling involved making Elliot suck his cock so that he could experience for himself how disgusting having a man shoot in your mouth is. Too bad that Elliot didn't react the way he should. He loved sucking dick, which only made him loathe himself more." He paused and took a long drink from his water bottle. "Apparently I misjudged the asshat."

Val couldn't help grinning over the use of his nickname. Mackie burrowed closer to him, shifting his attention to his husband. Perhaps he would bring him to Annika's room. All this trouble couldn't be good for him. He dismissed the notion in the next instant, knowing that while Mackie was young, he wasn't a child. He'd handled far worse in his life than this sad tale of abuse.

Damien continued, "Because I'd always seen him in a more submissive role, I hadn't considered that he might prey on these boys in the way he did. If you'd have asked me, I would have said that he sucked them off, maybe beat them or something, because Elliot was showing signs of pain. I just didn't imagine he'd use his body as punishment against them. And it's worse. He also, um, fucked Elliot—without lube, so that it would hurt as much as possible. That was also supposed to be a form of aversion therapy." His face screwed up in an obvious effort not to cry. "Too bad poor Elliot is so screwed up that he liked it anyway. He hates himself for it."

Understanding the complex relationship between pleasure and pain, Val could imagine how confusing the coerced experience would have been for the boy. He hoped the kid would find the freedom and confidence to figure out what he really liked and to accept that there was nothing wrong with him if he did enjoy some pain.

"Oh, Damien." Jase made a move to offer him comfort.

Will beat him to it. With the speed of their kind, he was by Damien's side before Jase had taken a single step. Jase stopped and leaned against Emil while Will made the bold move of pulling Damien into a tight embrace. There was a collective holding of breaths before Damien melted into him rather than recoiling.

No one said anything more for a long time. Duncan was the one to throw fuel onto the fire.

"Look, Damien. I'm sorry about your friend, but I'm not sure any laws were broken here. Sure, Warren is a total shit for what he did, and maybe he committed fraud. I'm not sure it's a police matter."

Damien turned his face away from Will's chest and stared at the cop. "But it is. You see, Elliot told me that he came to the camp from Pennsylvania when he was still seventeen. His parents brought him with his blessing—or so he says. Anyway, it's illegal here, isn't it, to take someone under eighteen into a conversion camp then to use sex coercively as a form of therapy? On a *child*?"

Duncan's expression turned flinty. "Yeah, that's a horse of a different color. If Elliot is willing to state this for the record, we've got the congressman by the short-hairs."

Damien straightened, although he kept his arm around Will. "He said he would, although I should be with him. He trusts me, even though he shouldn't. I lied to him."

"Not in a way that mattered," Will finally interjected. "When he needed you, you were there for him."

"You did more than I did. it's a good thing you're a blood-sucking alien vampire." The words were spoken without heat, almost affectionately.

"They're going to be okay," Mackie whispered to him.

"Yup." He kissed his boy's head and held him that much closer.

Will seemed at a loss for words. He did the same to Damien as Val had done to Mackie. Val couldn't help echoing the idea in his head. *They're going to be okay.* It made him stupidly happy to think it.

"He told me something else," Damien added. "He's not the only one. The camp has been taking underage boys from the beginning. They falsify the records with the blessing of the families to get them 'treatment' earlier than the law allows. If you dig into them, you'll find the truth easily enough, I expect."

Anderson joined his partner. "Sounds like the perfect thing to take to Jefferson. Sexual exploitation of minors is his thing, after all."

"Yeah." Duncan didn't look happy. "Let's get Elliot's statement first. Then I'll bring Jefferson in. He's a vice cop," he said to the room at large. "The best."

"He helped with the whole Cadoc thing," Demi reminded everyone.

Oh, yeah. That was where he'd heard the name before. An old flame of Duncan's, if memory served. *Awkward.*

Damien slipped off the stool. "I need to come with you. I promised Elliot I'd stay with him while he was questioned. He needs me." Glancing over his shoulder, he said, "And I need you, Will, if that's okay."

Will pressed a quick kiss on his boy's lips. "I won't leave your side."

"I should certainly hope not, Father Willem," Annika called down.

Val winced. "This is going to be one fucking bumpy ride."

"We'll handle it," Mackie reassured him, moving Val's hand to his stomach.

There was barely a noticeable thickening of his husband's body, but right at the moment, Val could swear he felt their son.

* * * *

Shocking news out of the Worcester County area today, as police descended on the controversial so-called gay conversion camp run by Congressman and Presidential candidate Jeremiah Warren. Warren was seen being taken into custody on charges of enrolling underage boys, in violation of Massachusetts law. Although the police have given out very little information, we have been told that further charges may be pending involving the sexual exploitation of some of those boys, as well as adult men who were coerced into sexual situations under the guise of therapy.

Alex turned the TV off, mercifully. The last few days had been very hard on Damien. Will wanted him to have some respite. They'd needed closure on the asshat piece, and this news report, complete with awesome images of said asshat being taken out by Jefferson in handcuffs, had been a welcoming sight. The solution to the human problem was in motion, whereas Bran remained an open issue. Until they'd neutralized him as a threat, Will couldn't relax and plan for a future—one that involved Damien, assuming the human was interested.

He and the boy had been virtually inseparable since that night they'd whisked Elliot to safety. But it had been a platonic relationship, neither making any move to reestablish their sexual connection. They'd slept together in Elliot's room, Damien in an extra roll-away hospital bed and Will on the floor. He didn't give a good damn where he laid his head, as long as Damien was in reach. The boy had wanted Will there for help and security, which made him feel astoundingly grateful. The truth was that being near Damien gave Will needed relief. It hadn't been hard to keep himself in check, either. Having Damien willingly by his side and often in his arms, seeking comfort however he wanted, was sufficient for the time being. It meant that his alien nature wasn't so repugnant that Damien couldn't overlook it. It gave him hope for a future together.

"So, now what?" Damien asked, his shoulder pressed against Will's, given that they sat next to one another. The casual contact was like a balm to Will's nerves.

"We go after Bran," Val answered. They were all there in the conference room, including Logan and the cops. After handing the case over to their colleague, they'd managed to return to help with the family's problem.

"Indeed." Alex sat at the head, as per usual, still in command, despite his declaration that he served Annika. He'd made a point of stopping Will briefly to impress upon him how they needed to have a little chat, as he put it, after the Bran problem had been contained. Will wasn't looking forward to it, but after his confessional with Emil, he didn't feel quite so worried.

Alex continued. "We are sure Bran will leave tonight. Given the amount of attention on the organization and the congressman no longer being a path to power, he'll move on."

"Once the media has left, of course," Val added. "He'll want privacy and darkness, scurrying away like the cockroach he is. He has to make choices when he leaves, as to direction."

"Won't he simply go to the Pike?" Duncan asked. "He might not want to come to Boston, given you're here, but westbound sends him to New York. There are lots of path he can pick from there."

Val shook his head. "If he goes in the opposite direction, he can take back roads north. We can't predict what he's thinking. We have to assume he has a Plan B already, although why we give him that much credit, I'll never know."

"He got this far," Anderson said. "He found someone who had a decent chance of getting him within a few feet from the nuclear codes. Seems to me you all have been underestimating Dracul's kids."

"He is quite correct."

They all turned toward the doorway in unison. It would have been comical, if not for the tragic look on Dafydd's face. He entered the room clutching Ric's hand. He looked paler than usual, and Will could only imagine how hard all of this was for the poor man. Having been forced to kill one son... The idea that he was likely going to have to watch the other be destroyed must be agony. No matter how miserable his existence had been with Dracul, Dafydd had carried those sons inside him. Will understood how that felt, the bond that formed even when the pregnancy had been forced. Dafydd was too sensitive a person to feel nothing.

Alex stood. "Dafydd," he said, with the kindest tone Will have ever heard his captain use, "you are welcome here, of course, but nothing we are discussing will please you."

"I know." Dafydd went to an empty seat and perched on the edge. Ric stood behind him, their hands remaining clasped. "I want to help. You saved my life, after all"—he glanced at Ric and flashed a smile—"even if I didn't appreciate it at the time. I want to help," he repeated.

Alex inclined his head and sat again. "What can you tell us?"

Dafydd licked his lips. "Bran is clever, far more than Dracul could appreciate. Unlike Cadoc, who was impulsive and pleasure-driven, Bran is patient. He plans far in advance. I imagine that he set this whole thing in motion years ago. When he leaves tonight, he won't be running away from anything but toward something. He'll have a place to hold-up and regroup. Stop him now or you'll be right back to this situation in a few months."

Will leaned forward. "We're hoping Annika can persuade him to—"

"No," Dafydd interrupted. "It won't work. I'm sorry. I know you're probably counting on her bringing everyone back into the hive. That assumes a certain sanity, I suppose, for lack of a better word. I used to think Dracul was merely evil and that his sons inherited that from him. Now, having spent time with Idris, I believe the twins' behavior was learned."

"I agree," Harry responded. He smiled. "Idris will be a fine young man because he's being raised by good parents."

"You are kind to say so," Dafydd said with another smile at Ric. "I wouldn't have agreed with you not so long ago, as you know. But I have given it a lot of thought. There was nothing I could do to stop the twins from being what they became.

"And observing all of you and having found out a lot from Harry, I can see how much you are driven by your biology. I can well believe that your Queen's presence is sufficient to bring Petru to heel. And it may work with Dracul, as well. His biology may demand it of him. I can't see it happening with Bran, though. Although Annika clearly holds sway with Merlin, he is still young and malleable. Bran is neither of those things."

He fell silent for a moment then looked directly at Will, for some reason, as he continued. "He's part me, after all, and Annika has no effect on me. She is a sweet child, who frankly makes me nervous, because she is so obviously different from a human girl. How could she possibly compel Bran to change his learned behavior?"

"We hope," Will started to stay, then stopped when Dafydd shook his head.

"I'm sorry. I don't mean to upset anyone, but I want you to know two things. One is that you must cover all possibilities when you go after him." He stood and headed for the door, Ric keeping a tight grip on him. The Welshman appeared fragile, yet determined.

"And the other thing?" Alex asked.

Dafydd paused. "You'll have to kill him. I know that for a certainty, and as of this moment, he's dead, as far as I'm concerned. Whatever happens, please don't tell me the how and the why or the where. Those details don't matter to me. Two of my sons are gone. I must concentrate on the one I can save. My future."

Ric embraced him and they walked out of the room as one.

"Oh my God," Damien whispered. He grabbed Will and, leaning over the arm of his chair, he pressed his face into Will's shoulder. "That poor man." Will had filled the boy in on much of their story, although he'd omitted many of the horrible details.

Will ran his fingers through Damien's hair. He'd been spending so much time with Elliot that he hadn't been grooming with much care. As he'd once predicted, it was silky soft without all that styling gel. "He's given up because he has to for his own mental well-being. We're not convinced Bran can't be turned."

He addressed the room at large. "We need eyes in the sky. I'll take the chopper out there and keep track of Bran's movements. We have enough people to block both ways out, so that's the plan, right?"

"It is," Val agreed. He projected a schematic on the screen at the far end. "Alex and I will take the bikes and cover the way to the Pike. Emil and Logan will be in the Escalade, waiting in the woods to block him from behind."

Duncan took up the debriefing. "MacLerie and I will take the other direction, with Anderson and Harry as back-up."

Will grimaced. "I'll radio everyone as soon as I see what direction he's going in. If we're lucky, he'll assume my chopper is only the media."

Damien's fingers tightened on his arm. "How will you know for sure it's him when he leaves?"

"The same way I kept tabs on him at the compound when you were there, with heat-vision goggles. The body temperature of a hybrid is different than that of a human."

"Except you'll be busy flying. You need a wingman."

Will realized what the boy was saying. "No. I'll be fine."

"He's not wrong," Val said.

"No!" Will repeated. "I'll manage. You've done enough, baby." He inwardly cringed at the endearment. He wasn't that sure of his position with the human.

"With Elliot heading back to Pennsylvania to live with his cousin, I'm not needed here anymore. I want to help." When Will opened his mouth, Damien jumped in. "I'll be safe up there with you." He looked at him with such trust and certainty that it robbed Will of his breath for a moment.

"Nowhere is perfectly safe. Bran could shoot at the helicopter."

"You'll make sure he doesn't touch us. I'm not a child, Will. And I'm tougher than I look."

Alex clapped his hands once. "Well, that settles that. You should get going, Will. Dusk is on its way."

Will stood, pulling Damien up with him. He gave in to the urge he'd had for a while and kissed him — nothing long, no tongue, just a show of his affection. To his delight, Damien not only didn't pull away, he repeated the gesture the moment Will ended it.

"We'll be fine," Damien said. "I trust you and you need to learn that I can handle myself. I will not be a burden to you. And I want to be a part of bringing this fucker down."

Will cupped his chin. "You have no idea how ugly this can get. We *are* monsters."

Damien smacked him on the arm. "Don't say that! Maybe he is, but you aren't. No one in this room is."

Will was incredulous. "You should hate me."

"Well, too bad because, like I've said, I love you."

Chapter Ten

Will was always happiest in the air. There was no doubt about that. And having his new love sitting beside him as he raced above the trees was an unexpected and delightful bonus. He kept stealing glances to make sure Damien was okay. He appeared to be not only fine, but excited about their adventure. Val had shown him how to use the goggles. He'd used them already to get a sense of how they'd work while looking down from the air. So, he was ready once they arrived at the camp.

There was no more media now that the congressman had been arrested and his wife had gone into seclusion. The camp was all but deserted, its unhappy inhabitants having apparently fled.

As Will circled the compound, Damien peered down. "There are still some of the humans left," he said over the mic. "Poor bastards might not have a place to go. We should do something to help kids like that. People like Father Ted—the priest this asshole's brother killed, according to Emil—knew how at-risk these kids are.

They need more than food, though. Do you think I could talk Alex into contributing to a new foundation or something to set up an anti-conversion camp?"

Will grinned. "I'm sure he would, but I'm happy to give you whatever amount you need, baby."

Damien chuckled. "I bet it would take a million dollars or more. I'd have to ask Emil to help me run the numbers."

"No problem. I can swing that."

"Yeah, right."

"Damien, I have something like a hundred million dollars. I've got it covered."

Shoving the goggles up his head, Damien spun in Will's direction. "The fuck you do!"

"We've been on this planet a very long time."

"Holy fuck." Shaking his head, Damien returned to his observation.

Will made a slow tour of the compound.

"There!" Damien pointed. "He's getting in a car."

Will turned his bird to follow Damien's direction. "He's going through the gates and heading toward the Pike."

"Then we've got him." Will wasn't worried about not being noticed by Bran now. He dropped down as low as he dared and followed.

Will could see for himself. Bran had left in a nondescript black sedan. He called it in over the radio to the others. "He's all yours, Captain."

From his perch in the sky, he saw the take-down unfold. Emil and Logan let him get ahead by about a quarter of a mile before pulling out from their hiding spot and tailing him. Will trailed behind them. He knew they were locked and loaded, and from what he'd seen of the former marine, she wouldn't hesitate to take out Bran. Part of him wanted it to end like that. Part of him hoped Dafydd was wrong about his son and that Annika would change him into an asset instead of an enemy.

Beside him, Damien peered at the road without the benefit of the goggles. He didn't need them now. He looked pretty chill, considering what was happening. Over the roar of the chopper blades, he could hear the boy's heartbeat, only slightly faster than normal. Maybe Damien was better suited to this sort of thing than he was. His own body practically vibrated with tension, reminding him that he was a reluctant warrior, at best.

Because there was only one way that led to the Mass Pike, Emil didn't have to worry about sticking too close to the asshole. So, neither did Will. They'd gone only a couple miles before they reached the point where the ambush had been set up in a wooded area with no houses nearby. Around a bend, the road straightened. He could see not only Bran's vehicle but way ahead of it. Two motorcycles, the biggest available, idled across the road, blocking the way. Dark figures with impenetrable visors down over their helmets sat astride them — Alex and Val.

Seconds later, Bran slammed on his brakes and tried to back up while also turning around. Emil also braked and jerking his Escalade, planted it perpendicular to Bran's car. Now that the fight was on, Will became calm and focused. The fucker was trapped. And just in case he thought he could get out and flee into the woods — which was exactly what he tried to do — Will lowered his chopper more and started circling the area, sending the trees into a frenzy of movement. Bran shielded his eyes from the whipping wind and looked up. The moment of distraction was all the others needed as they came running from behind their vehicles. Alex and Val drove their bikes to bracket him while Emil and Logan pointed their guns. The rest came screeching up from behind.

Bran looked wildly from side-to-side, ready to run through any hole. Finding none, he did the only sensible thing he could. He stopped and put up his hands. Will pulled away to reduce the wind and give the others room. Bran put up no fight as MacLerie shoved him to the ground, stripped him of his weapons and hogtied him for the journey back to the club.

"Woot!" Damien pumped his fist. "We got the fucker." He grinned like a madman at Will. "Can we go home now?"

Home. Will's heart swelled with the simplicity of the concept, that he and Damien shared a home. Will should have felt both relief and happiness. And yet, instead, a sense of dread sat heavily in his gut.

* * * *

"I'm going to state for the record one more time that I really don't think your being here is a good idea."

Damien squeezed Will's hand. "I'm sorry. I'm not trying to add to your stress. But it's important to me that I be a part of this. Bran did a lot of harm, and I need to see this through or frankly I'm going to have this scary fucker's face haunting my dreams. Nightmares," he amended. "Definitely nightmares."

He let go of Will's hand, reluctantly. "Don't worry about me. Concentrate on Annika. I'll be fine. I'll stand way back behind the wall of alien bodies."

Will's troubled eyes met his. "Please do. He may be disarmed and chained, but he's still dangerous."

"You worry too much, Father Willem," Annika said from his other side. "Damien and I will both be perfectly safe."

Will blew out a breath. "Right."

"You doubt this?" she continued. "Then you doubt yourself and the others. I do not. Nothing and no one will harm me with my hive standing guard."

Will closed his eyes briefly. "You humble me, and I will not fail you."

"Certainly not," Annika affirmed in a refined tone that, as usual, reminded him of some character straight out of Dickens. Or maybe Jane Austen, given that Annika was decked out in a floor-length dress with a narrow skirt that shimmered in pale blue and was trimmed with lace, a narrow ribbon tied under her breasts.

Wait, what? When had that happened? Puberty had come to town like a cyclone, apparently while he'd been playing spy at the conversion camp. It had to be part of her alien nature, and seeing her sudden maturity was more startling to him than Will's fangs had been. At least images of vampires were something he was used to, even if it was all fantasy. Seeing a child that he'd a mere two weeks ago made smiley-face pancakes for showing the first real signs of womanhood unnerved him. A fierce protective instinct stole over him, more powerful than what he'd felt when he'd found Elliot lying in his own blood.

I would die for her. I would kill *for her.* Glancing at the alien men around him, he understood, really and truly understood, some of what they must be feeling.

Damien made good on his promise, too, not wanting to be a distraction from Will's central duty. He dropped back from his side as they entered a room at the bottom of the stairs leading to the basement. He'd always been curious about what secrets lay here. He couldn't believe he'd once joked about someone being kept chained, and yet that was exactly the situation. Of course, there were now two. Despite his reassurance to Will, Damien's palms were sweating. So far, he hadn't seen much of Will's alien nature—or that of the other men. Sure, they were heavily armed and totally bad-ass, but nothing some humans might fit right in to. He had a feeling, though, that what he was about to witness would be otherworldly.

He entered the room next to Emil. He trusted the chef to the same degree as he did Will. Emil had saved his life, while Will had given him a wonderful future. His eyes popped at the array of weaponry they passed on their way to what had been described as cells. His first thought was that there was no way it was legal to keep this kind of stuff. Then he mentally rolled his eyes, as if these aliens had ever worried about human law, unless it suited their purpose. To think that for a thousand years, they'd been waging a war within their own kind. The information made him want to rethink everything he'd learned about recent human history.

Not that this was a time for reflection or a meltdown, for that matter, which he realized he was in danger of having, because this was too freaking much. Except he wasn't going to do that to Will after kicking up a fuss about participating. He was going to stand next to Emil and try to look like part of Annika's Pretorian Guard. At the far end of the room were three doors with small, square reinforced windows showing bright lights through two of them. A face appeared in one, startling Damien.

"It's okay," Emil said in a low voice. "He's been effectively neutered. He only wants a look at Annika."

"That's creepy."

"No, it's not sexual. She's our Queen, our touchstone, you know."

Then the man at the window was forgotten as Val opened the second door and stood aside. Everyone was quiet, ranging around the room in a semi-circle, except for Alex, who stepped forward to address its occupant. It was the man Damien knew as Bran, although that seemed overly familiar when he really thought of him as 'that fucker'. He rose from his built-in bed, wearing only his pants. He'd been stripped of everything else. Will had mentioned that he would have been naked but for Annika coming to meet him. He didn't like the idea of his young daughter seeing the guy completely unclothed. That made sense to Damien. So did the fact that a metal ring was around the guy's neck, tethering him to the wall.

"You've proven smarter than your brother," Alex said. "Surrendering instead of fighting means you stand some chance of living."

Bran's face remained passive. He said nothing, merely stood there with his legs braced, staring at them all. With his sunglasses gone, he had that dead look that Damien had seen once. It sent a chill down his spine as it had the first time, despite the phalanx of equally scary fuckers on Damien's side. Suddenly the idea of Annika getting anywhere near him seemed like a stupendously bad idea. Someone needed to get her the hell out of there. He took a half-step forward before he realized what he was doing.

Emil stopped him. "I promised Will I would keep you safe."

"When?"

"When you weren't listening. Plus, you also promised him moments ago."

"I know, but I'm worried about Annika getting anywhere near that freak."

"He won't lay hands on her." Emil's tone brooked no disagreement. It was absolute, which served to alleviate Damien's worry.

Alex moved to present a space for Annika to step forward. Will was right behind her. Damien could tell by the set of his shoulders how tense he was. Totally Defcon One stuff, and who could blame him. Queen or not, this was his little girl. Damien was a bit fuzzy on the *how* of it, but he knew she was a product of his relationship with his previous lover, Luuk. There were so many questions he needed to ask. *Later.*

Annika was fearless. With her back straight, she slowly approached the open cell. Each step was done with her usual, ethereal grace. How could Bran, the fucker, not drop to his knees and pledge his undying devotion to her? She must have been looking right at the prisoner, given the set of her head. If she was nervous, there was no indication of it. There was no visible tension anywhere in her body and her hands hung loosely by her sides.

Damien stood on his toes and leaned to the left to get a better view. Damn, his boyfriend was big, despite being the 'runt' of the alien litter. *Boyfriend?* Yeah, that fit, even if they had more than the usual amount of issues to deal with. He saw Bran showing some emotion finally, his eyes going wide. Then he pulled his leash to its limit with a single big step, coming up short from the confinement. He stared at Annika as she came almost within reach. Will's hands on her shoulders stopped her.

No one said anything. It seemed as if they all barely breathed. Damien wasn't sure exactly what they were waiting for, some acknowledgment by Bran that Annika was in charge. That's all he knew. There'd been no time to ask for more specifics. He wondered how they could even trust that whatever Bran did was genuine, as opposed to a ruse. *They must know what they're doing.*

It happened in the next instant. Bran slowly slid to his knees. "Is this what's been missing my whole life?" His voice was softer than Damien would have thought. There was a lilt to it, much like Dafydd's accent. He raised his hands in some kind of beseechment.

An almost imperceptible shift occurred in the room. Not quite relief, but there was a slight drop in the tension.

Annika took another step forward, Will sticking to her back. "You are welcome in the hive." The girl's voice was clear and calm. It even made Damien feel good.

A pounding caught everyone's attention. "My Queen!" The guy in the first cell had his face pressed against the glass. It was almost comical. Damien couldn't look at him, for fear he might burst out laughing. That was definitely not the thing to do at this pucker party.

And that's when it happened. With everyone's attention on that guy, Bran lunged, reaching his hands for Annika. There was more slack in his tether than had been apparent. Damien yelled out a warning and leaped forward. Will was already ahead of him. Grabbing Annika by the shoulders, Will tossed her to

Damien. He caught the girl and staggered with her back into Emil's waiting arms. He turned her away just as Will flew at Bran. Damien kept his head turned in Will's direction, worried about him as much as he was about Annika. Will roared before sinking his fangs into Bran's throat.

It was the spray of blood that forced Damien to close his eyes. He turned away and clasped Annika's head, holding her tight against his chest, his hands over her ears so that she couldn't hear as much of the horrible noises coming from behind him. There was nothing human about it, and he understood why Will hadn't wanted him to come. And yet, he would not regret it, because in what must had been one of the worst moments of his life, Will had trusted Damien with the safety of his child.

"Get them out of here." *Will.* His voice was like a rusty nail going down a chalkboard. It wasn't human, which was the point of all this, of course.

Damien tried to turn to him, again, but Emil held him close, much as Damien had with Annika. MacLerie also stepped in behind him, blocking Damien's view. He tried to break free and go to his man. How horrible he must be feeling. The men sandwiching him were immovable forces, though. He grunted in frustration.

"No," Annika said, clutching his arm. "He doesn't want us to see him like that." Her voice was surprisingly calm, considering a madman had just tried to— God, he didn't know what. Nothing good, that was for sure. Something fatal, almost certainly. Jesus, how was she not shaking? He fucking was.

Damien kept trying to break free, even as he was being herded out of the room. "Like *what*? See him *how?*" he clarified because Jesus, he wanted to be there for Will.

She brought their little scrum to a halt with no effort at all and stared up at him with her bright blue eyes. "A monster."

Damien shook his head. "He's not."

"Of course, he isn't. But you're going to have to convince him of it."

With that, they continued on their way, out the door and up the stairs. Music from the club blared and it all seemed so unbelievably normal, given the bizarreness of what had occurred in the basement. He felt schizophrenic, the duality of the life he'd been living—was going to keep living so long as Will didn't get stuck too far up in his ass about their relationship—sending him off-kilter. An entire alien drama had been playing out around him for at least the last year while he had led a pedestrian human existence. He'd had no clue. Billions of people hadn't. He'd gone down the rabbit hole now and nothing was ever going to be the same again. He was almost dizzy from it all. And the enormity of everything that had happened for the last week or so hit him like a freight train, making him reel even more.

He needed to do something to banish the horror of it, to ground him again. He would see Annika safely to her home, because that had been Will's unspoken request, even knowing that Damien made a poor guard, compared to the others. Then he was going to do the one thing he knew would soothe his soul and remind him of who and what he was, at least until he could be with Will again. Because his life was about to change forever—and with his full, if not pants-shitting, approval.

He was going to give up a lot, such his relative innocence about what was really going on in his world. One thing, however, would never change for him. He knew what he was destined to do, what he was good at and someone had once said that an army couldn't march on an empty stomach. He was a crappy fighter but an excellent cook. This was how he could contribute. He had seduced Will with his food long before entering his bed or by playing spy. At least, he thought he had. There was no one he dared ask about what their kind needed after wreaking whatever terrible vengeance Will was on Bran. He knew his man, though, what he liked.

The only question in his mind was whether to bake a cake or a pie.

* * * *

Will stood under the showerhead with the water temperature just this side of boiling. It was uncomfortable, but he needed to wash every trace of blood and gore off him, which naturally was nothing more than ash dusting his skin. It had left him within a minute under the spray. The water swirling around the drain ran clear. In his mind, however, he saw the 'before' pieces of Bran flying out of his mouth and spraying around the room. It coated his throat—or at least it felt as if it did—despite numerous passes of drinking and gargling. His body was as clean as it was going to get.

He needed more, to cleanse himself of the lingering stench that was Bran and what he'd dared to do. It was all emotional and symbolic now. He knew that. This extended foray into Harry's lab-based shower was helping him get his shit back together. He couldn't go see Annika or Damien until he'd reined in the monster and returned to being merely her father, his lover and a man who had only wanted to see the stars up close.

There was a knock on the opaque door. "How are you doing in there, Willem?"

Emil. Will wrenched the tap off and shoved the door open. Emil jumped out of the way as Will leaned out, dripping on the tile floor. "What's wrong? Where are Annika and Damien?" Whatever calm he'd managed to achieve was swept aside by instant and, yes, irrational fear.

Emil put his hands palm up. "Whoa. Sorry, dude. I didn't mean to frighten you. They're both fine. Annika is out walking Babette with MacLerie, Brenin and Demi acting as chaperones slash guards. Not that there is any reason to suspect she's at risk with Bran gone, but we figured you'd appreciate the extra security."

"I do, thank you." Putting his own kind aside, humans already posed a danger to his precious girl child.

Emil scratched his ear. "And Damien is baking in the family kitchen."

Will's lungs started working again. "Baking?" That was probably the least important fact that Emil had given him, yet it was the one that he latched on to. If Damien was making food, that either meant he was fine or so freaked out that he was desperate for a distraction. "What?" As if that mattered, but the word came out of his mouth anyway.

Emil shrugged. "I didn't ask, but given the amount of flour flying around, it might be a wedding cake."

Will snorted, which is probably what his friend intended. "Thanks for the update. Would you?" He gestured toward a rack of towels."

Emil grabbed one and handed it over. "Here." He stood watching Will dry off then said, "I think they're both worried about you. At least, Damien is."

"I'm fine," Will said briskly.

"I didn't say *I* was worried about you. It's the boy you have to convince."

"Yeah, I know." He stopped and stared Emil in the eye. "On a scale of one to ten, how freaked out was he about what happened down here?"

Emil grimaced. "I'd be tempted to say it was an eleven, except that would be too much of a cliché."

Will's heart sank at the information. *Shit, can I ever get Damien comfortable with me again?* Everything had happened so fast, from learning about his true nature to seeing it in action. How much shock and awe could a human accept at this point?

"And before you start writing the obituary for your relationship, the freak-out was over concern for you, not about what you were doing."

"Yeah, right."

"Seriously. Will, Damien was fighting me and MacLerie to get back *to* you, not away."

"That can't be true." He couldn't believe it. There was only so much disappointment he could take in this unexpected life he was living.

Emil put up his hands again. "You don't have to take my word for it. Ask Annika. She's the one who convinced him that the best thing was for him to do what you'd trusted him to — getting her and himself out of there."

Will opened his mouth to argue the point. Emil overrode him. "Better yet, ask Damien. You'll see. That boy loves you, Will, and one thing I've learned loving and living with a human myself is that they are stronger than you think. They're young and maybe appear frivolous and pleasure-seeking, but don't underestimate them. When it matters most, they are loyal and formidable allies. Talk to him," he emphasized before turning to leave.

"Oh, and I brought you clothes." He pointed to a pile on the counter. "Harry burned your old ones."

"And Bran?" Will couldn't help but ask.

"Val used the industrial vacuum. He's the Boston sewer system's problem now." Emil flashed a grin. "Take your time. Make sure that when you go to Damien, you're in the proper frame of mind. Better yet, talk to him. Tell him how you feel. I find Jase really likes it when I do that. I bet Damien will appreciate you sharing your feelings with him, too."

With that, he left. Will stood for long minutes, fighting the urge to get under the punishing spray again. Then he took Emil's advice, dressed and went in search of the one thing, the one person, who could make him feel a whole lot better.

* * * *

In the end, Damien made both a pie and a cake. And he did it in the family kitchen, because when Will came looking for him — and he had to believe he would — Damien wanted a private space for them to speak freely about what had happened. He also worried that somehow he'd let slip something that he shouldn't in front of the other club staff. Since learning the truth about the Stelalux family, he hadn't been around anyone other than those in the know. He wasn't sure he was ready to live this double life. Maybe the other boys could give him pointers. Quinn, Mackie and the rest of them seemed to move from one world to the next without effort. God, he'd been hanging with all of them in their personal living space, no less, for a while without realizing that something was up.

No, that wasn't true. He'd known they were different. Their size alone had set them apart and their unusual eyes, even their sexuality. So many gay men in one family defied statistics. Their wealth and natural power had always made him worry, a little bit, that they were into illegal activities. He'd hated whenever those thoughts had entered his mind. It had seemed like a betrayal of everything good and kind that Emil, in particular, had done for him. His instincts had been right, although no amount of imagination would have led him to the truth.

There was so much he still didn't know. As soon as Will arrived, he was going to sit him down, give him a big slice of pie, a bigger piece of cake and pick his alien brain. If they were going to make this thing between them work, Damien needed to know the score. What was expected of him? Should he kneel before Annika, kiss Alex's ring? Did Alex even wear a ring? He hadn't noticed. He thought he could do both those things, although they would rub his democratic soul wrong. Did he have to promise to obey Will, like Mackie had Val? He snorted. Nope, that was definitely not going to happen. Sure, he loved alpha males as much as the next boy but…

The big one, though. The super-humongous one was the hardest. "Do I have to let him suck my blood?"

"No. That is a choice you make, and I will never pressure you to do so."

Damien jumped. He hadn't heard Will approach. The guy was two feet away from him, wearing a different T-shirt and jeans from earlier in the day. His hair was wet, a testament to how he must have showered somewhere before returning home. Damien's mind shied away from imagining what he'd had to wash off.

Putting down the knife and plate in his hand, he asked, "Are you okay?"

"That is what I intended to ask." He jammed his hands into his front pockets and rocked back on his heels. "Matters downstairs ended rather badly, as I had feared. I didn't want you to witness what you did, but I am glad you were able to take Annika in hand. It eased my mind."

Damien didn't hesitate. He went to him and wrapped his arms around Will's waist. "I didn't see much of anything, although I can imagine what you had to do. I'm sorry. It must have been horrible, your fear for your daughter, then the need to, um, do what you did."

Will embraced him in a bear hug that squeezed the breath out of him for a few seconds. "It was upsetting, the part about Annika. I feel stupid at allowing myself to be distracted." He kissed the top of Damien's head. "Thank you for being more vigilant."

Damien smiled against Will's hard chest. "I didn't do anything. You guys are mega-fast and totally on-point always." He was pleased at the compliment, nevertheless. He wanted to feel useful. He wanted to *be* useful.

"We managed to miss that Bran had retained some slack in his chain. And he was quite convincing in his acceptance of our Queen." Will's chest shook on a deep breath. "Who knew he was such a good actor. He must have inherited that from Dafydd. Dracul was never that effective at hiding his true intentions."

"You were ready anyway."

"I'd hoped to be wrong, but I went into that room knowing that I would kill him. It was my right, too, when he went for my child. Not even Val would have insisted on taking that privilege away from me."

"It was terrible, though, right?"

"Not for me. Not entirely," he amended. He pulled away in order to look Damien in the eye. "This is part of my nature, to do what is necessary without much regret." He sighed. "Although, truth be told, I am not a natural warrior. I prefer flying."

Damien chuckled. "You're wonderful at that. Will you take me in your helicopter again some time?"

"Certainly. And in my plane."

"Do you have a rocket, too?" he teased.

"Not anymore."

"Huh?"

"I was a pilot for our ship. Please don't take the crash as any indication of my skills."

Beneath the joke, Damien saw insecurity, so he put his plan into action.

Releasing his hold, he backed up. "Sit." He pointed to one of the stools across the counter. "I've been baking."

"So I see." Will dutifully did as Damien asked. "Chocolate cream pie and" — he sniffed — "lemon cake. My favorites."

Damien winked. "I know." He placed the generous portions in front of his man and watched as he scarfed it all down. It was a good thing his alien man's diet wasn't restricted to only blood.

"What's it like?" When Will paused in his eating and glanced up, he explained, "Having my blood sucked? Would it...hurt?"

Will put his fork on his plate and grabbed his hand. "First, you must believe me when I say that I will never put you under any pressure to do that."

"I know. But if I wanted you to?"

"You might benefit from asking one of the other boys. I don't know what it feels like for a human." He rubbed his thumb along the back of Damien's hand. "The strike does hurt, except it's almost like a spark, jump-starting your pleasure. At least, that's how it feels to me. Then, as your blood is pulled through your veins, it's like your dick's being massaged."

"So, it's all sexual?"

"Mostly, yes."

"And does it make you come harder?"

Will's eyes sparkled. "Yes."

Damien barked out a laugh. "Fucking A, Willem. Why didn't you lead with that? Come on."

He dragged his man upstairs.

Will didn't give any resistance as Damien dragged him to the suite. He let his lover pull him into a hungry kiss at the top. They slammed against the wall, arms tangled and pelvis-to-pelvis. Hard cock met hard cock, grinding and humping. Their breaths mingled as each of them vied for the chance to swallow the other whole. Human though he was, Damien was no delicate creature. *Or shy, for that matter*, Will thought as the boy, *holy fuck*, stuck his hand down the front of Will's jeans.

When did he unsnap my fly?

It didn't matter. All Will cared about was that after the brutal event earlier in the day, this mutual claiming and affirmation of his relationship with this human was a balm. And this was with Damien fully informed about who he was taking to bed—well, almost fully informed. There was one more thing that Damien deserved to learn before committing himself to Will. He prayed it wouldn't be the deal-breaker.

At the moment, far from shying away from the reality, Damien was embracing it. God, he was going to let Will suck his blood. Will wouldn't have tried to broach the subject for a long time, hoping that if he kept putting himself in Damien's orbit, giving him his body however the boy wanted, that maybe—maybe—he would one day trust him with this one thing in particular that terrified humans.

Damien's piercing rubbed Will's tongue as he fucked his mouth. It made him mad for the chance to feel that thing along his dick. He broke off the kiss, to make the suggestion.

"Suck me!"

Damien grinned and nipped at Will's lower lip. "Right here?"

The idea had merit. No one they lived with would give a damn, but Annika could come walking along at any minute. And speaking of which… "Shit, we can't stumble into my bedroom like this. My daughter may be maturing right before our eyes, but not even my people are that casual about sex in front of our children."

Damien shook his head. "She's still out walking Babette in Boston Common with Demi and Brenin. MacLerie is with them, in case muscle is needed."

Will paused, his intense need to get inside Damien sidetracked by his more pressing duty. "Is she all right? I haven't seen her since… You know. Harry has a shower in his lab and Emil brought me clothes. I needed time to make myself more civilized."

"She's fine," Damien quickly reassured him. And there was sincerity in his eyes, making it easy to believe him. "Better than me, in some respects. Nothing seems to faze her."

Relieved, he said, "She's the Queen. It's kind of their thing to remain calm when the rest of us are losing our shit. It's hard to think of her in those terms, though."

"If you're concerned she'll be freaked out about our being in your room, we could go to my apartment."

Will raised his eyebrows and he cupped Damien's ass and tug it in close. He groaned because, *God*, it felt so good. "You have an apartment?"

Damien laughed. "Were did you think I lived?"

"I don't know." Will frowned. "I guess I've always thought of you as being in the kitchen and nowhere else—except my bed," he added with a squeeze.

Damien gasped. "Yeah, well, if you're going to keep that up, we'll never make it all the way to my place. Right now," he added with a moan, "I'm doubting we'll make it to your room."

"No worries." Will used his grip on Damien's ass to lift him off the floor.

Damien whooped, much as he had in the chopper when they'd captured Bran. But that misery wasn't something Will would think about. It had no place in his mind compared to the sheer pleasure he was going to enjoy once he got Damien into bed. He used his natural speed to tear down the hall, through the suite and into his room. He jumped the last few feet to land on the bed, rolling onto his back to take the brunt of the fall.

They laughed even as they grappled to take off their clothing. This was something extra, the ability to enjoy each other's company as well as their bodies. They hadn't gotten very far before Damien remembered Will's earlier entreaty. The boy escaped the kiss Will had him locked in before licking his way down his chest and onto, *oh yes*, his cock.

Damien swirled that extra special tongue of his around the head, stimulating the bundle of nerves located underneath. Will's eyes crossed and he fisted the bedding so that he didn't pull Damien's hair out by the roots. Because God, it was too much. Then Damien sucked the shaft into his warm, wet mouth and *inhaled* him.

"Shit! I'm going to come."

Damien wrapped his hand around the base of Will's cock and clamped it like a vise. The cum that had started climbing up his dick slammed back into his balls. Will wanted to launch up and take control, knew that he could do that with no effort at all. He forced the urge back the same way Damien's fist kept his cum prisoner. He made himself lie there as Damien worked his dick with his mouth, tongue, lips and lungs. The rapidly contrasting changes in sensations was driving him mad. He had to settle for moaning and rocking his head, then he morphed into pleading.

Damien pulled off his cock with an audible pop. "What? What do you want, Willem?"

He opened his eyes to slits, looked at his lover's lips, puffy from the lavish attention. "I want my cock inside you."

Damien's eyes lit up. "Two minds but with a single thought." He made to roll over to the head of the bed and stopped. "Do we need condoms?"

Will shook his head. "No. I can't infect you with anything because I can't catch any of your human illnesses."

"Best. Answer. *Ever*." With only one leg actually free from his jeans and shorts, Damien swung it over Will's lap. "Let's keep our eyes open. I want to watch you watch me."

Damien didn't wait for a reply. Lifting Will's shaft straight, he wiggled so that he lined the tip with his hole. Then with his gaze fixed on Will's, he slowly lowered himself. The tip had just breached the puckered ring when Will thought of something important.

"Lube." He tried to rise.

Damien shoved him back with surprising speed. "My saliva will have to do. I want to feel the burn, baby. Besides, you always feel so cool, so without the latex in the way, your skin will ease the sting."

Will wanted to explain about his body temperature, but that kind of tutorial wasn't on the menu at the moment. The next thing, Damien had seated Will balls-deep in his amazingly tight and welcoming ass. He did things with his channel to fucking milk Will's dick and his hole clenched in a way the encouraged him to come instead of stopping him. It was hard to keep his eyes open, but he did it because Damien wanted him to, and pleasing his boy was the most important thing at the moment.

"They get darker. Your pupils. I thought I'd noticed it before." He shook his head. "They're black, aren't they?"

Will nodded.

"Do they change into other colors?"

Yes, when I was ripping off hunks of Bran's flesh and spitting them out, they were as red as the blood coating my face.

He didn't say any of that, naturally. "Faster. Harder."

"Yes, sir." Damien picked up speed, placing his palms on Will's chest for leverage.

Will began a counter rhythm, bucking up to meet Damien's ass. He reached between his arms to take hold of his boy's leaking cock that bounced between them. He wasn't so far gone as to forget that pleasure was always a two-way street. He kept his grip firm, stroking the shaft with equal speed as the drilling Damien was giving himself. The boy's pre-cum slicked the way, easing Will's worries that they were going too fast and hard for a human.

That's when Damien rocketed matters into orbit.

He tilted his head, exposing his neck, and said, "Do it. Bite me. Is that the right way to say it? It sounds kind of snarky."

Will couldn't help grinning. He stopped jerking his boy for a second as he asked, "Are you sure?"

"Now," came the breathless reply.

Will hesitated only a moment more before giving into his heart's desire. He grabbed Damien by both arms and tumbled him over, careful to keep their bodies connected. Now he lay between the boy's splayed legs. He rolled his hips to seat his dick as far as it would go. The pulse at the base of Damien's throat called to him. He inhaled deeply, smelling that sweetness, and for the first time, knowing that soon he would be able to taste it.

"I want this more than my next breath," he confessed.

"Now, Will." Damien stretched his neck as much as he could, the cords bulging, his vein right there for the taking. But, and this was the best part, he kept his eyes open. He wasn't afraid of this. He wasn't afraid of *him*.

Will let his fangs descend, took one last lungful of Damien's scent and struck. They both convulsed, Will shooting his cum deep inside his boy and human semen hitting his chest. Yet it was the taste, salty and warm and yes, somehow sweet, all at the same time that consumed him. The flavor burst onto his tongue, filled his mouth, slid down his throat. He moaned and thrust his cock hard. Damien convulsed, his legs wrapped around Will's hips. His heels kicked Will's ass. So he thrust again and again and once more they were riding that incredible wave of orgasm.

And all the while, Will pulled at Damien's vein, afraid he'd be unable to stop.

Chapter Eleven

"Are you sure you're all right?"

Damien snuggled closer to Will's side. "You have got to stop asking me that." He stretched his recently bitten neck in order to press a simple kiss on Will's mouth. They were both swollen and sore, so he was careful. "I'm fine," he added as he settled down.

"You are amazing."

"I'm not going to argue the point, but why do you say that now? Was it the undercover work—or any of the...you know, rest of it?" There was no sense in dwelling on the ugly side of the day. The end had been awesome, and that was all Will chose to focus on. Except...

"Are *you* all right?" his boy asked.

Will tightened his grip around Damien's shoulders. "I feel that we've had this conversation before."

"Yeah, but I'm worried, you know?" Confession time. He'd said this before, but he needed to make it stick without any doubt. "I love you, Will."

The guy didn't say anything for long seconds, enough to make Damien start to squirm. Will's hold kept him in place.

"I love you, as well. Truly. It's amazing. I didn't think I could find this again with another human. I didn't think I'd let myself. The pain of losing him…"

Damien wiggled to get on top of him and rained kisses on his face and neck. "I can't promise nothing will ever happen to me, and you can't make it to me about yourself. You're not indestructible."

"No. I can make you stronger, healthier, longer-lived, if you are willing."

"I would need to drink your blood, right?"

Will furrowed his brows. "How do you know?"

"I ran into the boys while I was taking care of Elliot, and I asked. I figured you wouldn't mind."

"I don't. I just worry that all of this will reach a tipping point in which something about me and my kind will freak you out so badly that you'll run away screaming."

"Not going to happen. I don't scare easily. I lived by my wits on the street from the time I was seventeen, until Emil swept me off them and gave me a better way of life."

Now Will's eyes started to morph into more of a red. "I hate that… What you had to endure."

He reared up. "Hey, easy. Easy, baby. I'm fine and it led me to you, so how can I hate that part of my life?"

The color change stopped and Will relaxed beneath him. "You need to know something else about what my blood can do to you. There is one change you might not like, something that tests a human's love for my kind."

That's when he stopped talking. Will lay there with his eyes closed, tracing lazy circles on his lower back.

There was some tension in Will's brow and his breathing wasn't as relaxed as it had been moments ago. It was clear that whatever Will had to tell him, he believed that despite everything they'd said to each other, pledged, vowed, confessed, it would be a deal-breaker. If that were true, then he'd take the blood-drinking off the table. Except...

"I want to be with you as long as is inhumanly possible. What could your blood possibly do to me that would override that desire?"

Will took a deep breath and let it out slowly. "It's a matter of survival. Our kind always finds a way to continue. No females? No problem. We create them." Will stopped again, frustrating the hell out of him.

So he thought and considered what would be the logical continuation of what Will had been saying.

The light came on, a ridiculous leap of explanation that was so far-fetched that he almost didn't say it. As it was, he tested if what he was thinking was right, using an indirect path.

"Mackie's pregnant, isn't he?"

Will's eyes popped open and he lifted his hand to run his fingers through Damien's hair. "You are very smart, indeed."

Excited to have got it right, he pushed to a sitting position, straddling Will's torso. "Lucien gave birth to Demi?" When Will nodded, he added softly, "And Luuk birthed Annika."

Will froze.

Damien peered at him intently. "You have to tell me everything, Will. I deserve the truth and I can handle it. Who gave birth to Annika?"

"I did."

The answer wasn't unexpected. He'd worked it out already, the same as he had about the others. It seemed impossible that males could become fertile females, as well. The idea that someone who epitomized masculinity had done so, in particular blew his mind.

He splayed his fingers over Will's abdomen. "You have a uterus here?"

Will nodded.

Oh God, do I have questions, weird ones. "Do you ovulate every month? You know, have a period?"

Will barked out a laugh. "No. That is not part of our biology, so I don't have to deal with that. I have nothing but respect for human women. It is amazing what they've accomplished over the centuries, despite what nature and males throw at them."

Damien smiled. "Okay, that means we can have sex pretty much every day."

"I would like to think so."

There was only one more question to ask. "How did she get out? C-section?" That seemed obvious, now that he thought about it.

In way of an answer, Will rolled them onto their sides. "No. The human boys we change give birth that way. My body had a more natural process. It's how I was able to keep it from the others."

"First, why didn't you want them to know?"

"It's complicated. Alex was our captain and he has kept us together and fought the vicious ambitions of Dracul. He took on a role that would never have happened on our home world. He would have been a valued drone, and under extreme circumstances, a temporary leader until some young drone changed and produced the next queen. He has held the mantle of power for a very long time. I suppose I did him the disservice of worrying he couldn't step aside."

"Oh, baby" — Damien kissed him — "you must have been so scared, especially after losing Luuk. Alone in your fear and your duty."

"You understand. My beautiful boy." He kissed Damien, taking longer, deepening it, sending Damien's tired dick into motion. Will's was already hard and needy between them.

He broke away. "Wait, before you fuck me into the mattress again, I still don't get how Annika came out."

Will lifted his leg and took one of Damien's hands at the same time. He guided his fingers to a spot between Will's balls and his hole. The flesh there was slightly ridged, as if it had been cut or damaged at some point.

"Here?" Will nodded. "But not a C-section?"

"No. My body created the necessary channel for her to be delivered, then closed up again."

"Wow. So, um, not a third place to fuck you, huh?"

Will threw back his head and laughed. He rolled Damien over. "It doesn't freak you out?"

"Do my piercings? Or my tattoos?"

Will licked a stripe up one of Damien's neck tats. "Not in the least. They are part of what makes you the boy I love. I especially love the ornament in your tongue."

"Then stop worrying about my reactions to your characteristics. I think once I accepted the whole alien-vampire thing, the rest was anticlimactic."

"Please be sure. Very sure. Because it's not only about my biology or how you could end up fathering another Queen. We are still at war. We had hoped that because Petru and Merlin were brought into line by Annika, that all of the others would be, too. Bran has made it clear it won't be that easy."

"I'm ready to fight alongside you. I'm willing to die for you." It sounded cheesy to his ears, and yet the strength of the emotion behind it made it very real.

"That will never happen. I won't let it. More of us are arriving shortly. We won't be short of warriors. And when this is done, you and I will build whatever family we want."

"Good. I'm on board with that. In the meantime, let me reintroduce you to my tongue piercing."

* * * *

For the first time in their relationship, Mackie led. Taking Val by the hand, they went to the medical suite that Harry had built-out in the new building. It had everything they could ever need, including an operating theater. He'd been here briefly when poor Elliot had been in residence for a few days, mostly to lend moral support to Damien. Mackie hadn't been and still wasn't quite brave enough to look too closely at the room where Harry would cut the baby out of him. In several months, he'd be in there, whether he wanted to be or not. He trusted that Harry would perform the C-section successfully, that all would end well, yet the idea of it scared him. It was a part of this pregnancy he didn't look forward to. Even the throwing up was preferable.

His stomach had settled somewhat, as if getting over its 'mad' at his unexpected situation. It wasn't exactly happy, but he'd found a formula that worked to keep food down. The fatigue wasn't as great, either. He hoped that he'd defied expectations and had moved on from something that Val and Harry had expected to last months.

As much as Mackie was uncomfortable being in the medical space, Val practically vibrated with his displeasure. If he'd had his way, they wouldn't be there until absolutely necessary. But Mackie had a plan to make his husband less frightened of their situation and, hopefully, if the Gods were smiling on them, enthusiastic about it. Having a baby was supposed to be exciting, something joyful, even when plagued by morning sickness. So far, Val had only experienced the bad parts—the vomiting, and shit, the dying—which Mackie absolutely wasn't going to do.

That wasn't going to be enough for Val, the original Mr. Doom and Gloom. It was Mackie's job to turn that perpetual frown upside down. He didn't want to spend the next several months simply enduring the pregnancy and reassuring Val that it would turn out fine. He wanted to start experiencing the happiness of child-bearing right now. He knew that was easy for him because he could feel the effects of it all, while Val knew it only in academic terms. It was time to use modern medicine to bring Val further into the event, like other twenty-first century fathers.

Unfortunately, he'd had to use a bit of subterfuge to get his husband there. He'd stated it in health terms, as in 'we need to see how the baby is doing in order to be sure everything is all right'. Harry, bless him, had backed the idea. And it was a good one, but Mackie suspected Harry only wanted to play with his new toys.

Mackie steered the reluctant Val to the cheery room opposite the one Elliot had spent time in. This one held all kinds of equipment. Harry was already waiting for them and greeted them warmly.

"Come in, gentlemen. This is going to be exceptionally fun for all of us. I haven't had a chance to use this ultrasound before. I thought I was being precipitous in buying it. I'm very glad to have been proven wrong."

Mackie was excited and concerned at the same time. Now that they were here, he was afraid the plan wouldn't work. What if seeing their baby, healthy and secure where he needed to be in Mackie's body, didn't ease Val's worries? There was nothing to be done, however, except soldier on and put his trademark Mackie spin on things.

"I can't wait," he replied. "This is so exciting, isn't it, Val?"

Val merely grunted. "It will be good to see that everything is as it should be."

"And fun to see our baby."

"Fetus," Val corrected.

"*Baby*," Mackie insisted. Maybe it was easier for Val to think of their child in clinical terms, but that wasn't how Mackie wanted it to be. "Do I need to take my pants off?" he asked Harry.

"No, no. Hop up here and push down the waistband. You do have a full bladder, yes?"

"Yes," Mackie confirmed. "I am extremely uncomfortable, so I must have drank enough."

"I'm sorry it's necessary in the early stage. Once your womb is larger, the amniotic fluid will do the job of the water. Val, please stand on the other side."

They did as told, Mackie grabbing Val's hand, because he wanted that connection and the reassurance. He might be doing this for a particular purpose, but it didn't change the fact that he was nervous. *Please, let everything be okay.*

Once Mackie's softly rounded belly was bare, Harry squeezed gel on it. "I know it's a bit cold."

"It's fine," Mackie quickly assured him before turning his head to look at the screen.

Harry, bless him, wasted no time. Pressing the wand on the spot where Mackie's miraculous womb was supposed to be, he turned on the machine.

At first everything was shades of gray and the noises sounded like a person's ears after getting water in them. Mackie squinted but couldn't make anything out. Then something happened that caught his breath. He gasped and turned his face to look at Val.

"Do you hear that?"

Val blinked a few times as he watched the screen. He switched his gaze to Mackie. "Yeah, I do. Sure, I do. Holy fuck, Doc, is that a heartbeat?"

Harry grinned from ear-to-ear. "It is indeed. And if you look here"—he pointed at the screen—"that fluttering is the heart. And see?" He traced around parts of the image that were darker than the rest. "That's him."

At some point, Val had put his hand on Mackie's shoulder. He squeezed it now, and Mackie squeezed Val's hand in return, the only outlet for his excitement. "Oh, Val, it's his little head. And is that a tail?" He glared at his husband. "Did you put a lizard in me or something?"

Harry chuckled. "That is perfectly normal development for both our species. It's early days, Mackie. Give the poor boy a chance to grow."

Mackie blinked back tears. "It's definitely a boy, then?"

"Oh, yes."

"Annika said it was."

"Did she really?" Harry asked. "Well, she would know, I suppose." He pulled the wand up and wiped the goop off Mackie. "Everything looks perfect. Your pregnancy is progressing exactly as expected." He patted Mackie's hand. "I will deliver your son in due time and you shall both be fine. This is my promise to you, to both of you," he added, looking at Val.

"Thanks, Doc." Val's voice was thick, and the obvious emotion in it gave Mackie hope. It had been Val's aloofness that had scared him the most.

His plan had been a success, for both of them. Everything was more real now. He gave a watery laugh, his emotions starting to run amuck. "I guess there's no denying I'm really pregnant."

Val raised one eyebrow. "The endless vomiting wasn't sufficient proof?"

Mackie frowned. "It could have been food poisoning or a stomach virus."

"Yeah, right." He got serious. "How are you feeling? Do you need blood?"

"I'm fine, Val. I think the worst has passed."

"I hate to be the bearer of bad news, but it can come in waves. Poor Lucien could go a whole week before the sickness came back."

"Thanks for the pep-talk, Doc," Val practically growled. "Don't listen to him. You're doing great." There was a pause, then, "I love you, and I love that you're carrying our child. You're so fucking brave, Mackie."

"Throwing up is hardly a portrait in courage. But I appreciate the sentiment."

Val bent to kiss him, nothing too passionate. It was more than they'd done in days. He would take what he could get.

Harry pushed a few buttons on the machine and handed a picture to Mackie. "There you go. We'll do one of these every couple of weeks, just to reassure us all." With a pointed look at Val, he left.

Val huffed out a breath before bending to kiss Mackie again in the sweetest, gentlest way possible. This one had a little more oomph to it. "Thanks, baby, for pushing me into doing this. It has helped. And I'm sorry I've been such a cold ass these last couple of weeks. I was scared."

"Oh, Val, I knew that. I just hated that you shut me out," he admitted. "It hurt my feelings, and I was worried that I was losing you. And," he added with the meanest frown he could manage, "I really hate that you went out and put yourself at risk all those nights."

Val kissed him for a third time. *Wow, we're on a roll.* "It wasn't that many and I was never in any real danger."

"Nevertheless," he intoned. "Demi said that Trey was apoplectic about the whole thing. Plus, you took risks and could have ended up on the losing end. You are not invisible, Val."

Val put his hand up. "I'm done with that and have apologized profusely to both Duncan and Paz. It won't happen again, because I've found a new way of letting off steam—beating the crap out of Willem."

Mackie raised his eyebrows. "Really? That's not how I heard it went down."

"I drew first blood, but okay, so it's a fifty-fifty thing about who comes out on top. The point is, it's a healthy way to work out my natural aggression."

Mackie gave his husband what he hoped was a coquettish look. "I can think of a better way."

Val furrowed his brows, then shook his head. "No. No way. We can't play while you're pregnant."

"We can if we're careful." When Val opened his mouth again, Mackie jumped in to elaborate. "I cleared it with Harry. No beatings, natch, but a little bondage isn't going to hurt me or our son. And, Val, I've missed our playing so much.

"Please?" He wasn't above begging. "Tie me up, Val. Those complicated Shibari knots you use. I don't want to be able to move one muscle. I want you to drench me in your cum, then you can jerk me off while I suck your blood. Or, I don't have to come. That's your call, totally, Master. Please, sir, remind me that I'm your boy."

Without saying another word, Val scooped him up and carried him out. Instead of heading to their bedroom, however, he strode to their playroom.

Yes!

* * * *

Mornings had become surreal. Will and Annika still came down for a wonderful breakfast prepared by Damien, only now the family chef had started his day waking in Will's bed. They'd slipped into the routine without much fuss the day after the Bran debacle. Will had worried when he'd sat his daughter down to explain that he and Damien were a couple and that Will had invited him to live with them. She, naturally, was ahead of them.

"Certainly, Father Willem. Papa," she'd corrected. "For he shall be Father Damien from this point on, and I do miss having someone to call Papa. I always knew you'd be together. It was obvious that is where you both belong."

"You understand that I will always love Luuk. He was my first love, but Damien must be my second and last one. I intend to spend the rest of my life with him, and he has graciously agreed to do the same."

"And will you give me sister queens?"

Will had dropped his gaze because he didn't have a clear answer for her. "We have discussed it as a possibility. It's too soon for any decisions to be made. Matters aren't yet resolved with Dracul."

"They will be soon."

"Do you know something the rest of us don't?"

Rather than answering, she'd kissed him sweetly on the cheek and had skipped off with Babette at her heels.

Seeing Damien toiling in the kitchen as he and Annika descended the main stairs did funny things to Will. Part of him didn't want his lover, his partner, to act like a servant. The other loved the sight of him in such a domestic setting. Despite the rest of the family swarming to be fed, it was as if Damien did all of this just for Will and Annika. And he was a tremendous chef. Plus, it made him happy to do it. He was whistling as he pulled quiche out of the oven.

"Good morning, Father Damien." Annika raced to her usual seat at the counter.

Will followed at a more leisurely pace, his eyes on Damien, looking for any sign that Annika's labeling him her 'father' bothered him. He'd said it didn't, yet it seemed premature for a young man to enter such sudden parenthood. Except his face lit up at Annika's arrival. He poured her a glass of chocolate milk and handed her a fat muffin of some sort.

There were more smiles where that came from. Damien flashed one at him as his boy handed him his mug of coffee. Will responded with a kiss, nothing more than a peck, but better than any hit of caffeine. The morning was bright and happy and gave Will an unexpected sense of optimism, until he caught sight of Alex flying down the stairs. Val was right behind him, while Quinn and Mackie trailed at a more sedate pace.

None of them looked happy.

"What is it?" Will's barked-out question caught everyone else's attention.

Neither Alex nor Val said anything. The grim factor was off the charts, and if either of them retained molars after all of their teeth-grinding, it would be a minor miracle.

"What's going on?" Damien asked, as he set his latest dish on the range and took off his oven mitts.

Will put his arm around his shoulder and went to stand beside Annika. "Nothing good, baby."

"I would not say that, Papa. This is the beginning of the end, and we must pass through it for the new beginning to start."

"That was quite a mouthful, honey." Damien grinned at her.

"It will all work out. You'll see."

Damien nudged Will. "She's kind of reassuring, especially because Alex and Val look like World War III has started."

"I expect it rather has," Will responded, then immediately gave him a reassuring side hug.

Alex had the remote and was bringing what looked like his email onto the smart TV. "I received a message early this morning."

A video came on screen and the image immediately froze Will's blood. He instinctively pulled both Damien and Annika closer to him.

"Is that—" Damien started to ask.

"Yeah."

"Dracul," Annika clarified unnecessarily. "He isn't nearly as impressive as I'd pictured."

"He isn't looking his best." *Christ.* Not only had Petru been right all along and the fucker was alive, but the trip he'd taken into the cistern had also left him as hideous on the outside as he was on the inside."

Dracul's marred face still managed to convey a disdainful expression. "Greetings, Captain."

"God, he hasn't lost any of his unbearable smugness," Will observed.

"Indeed," Alex replied. "Notice the pause for dramatic effect."

"You've watched this already?"

"Several times," Val confirmed. "It's not getting any better."

"Congratulations on the neutralization of both my older sons. You've saved me the trouble of rectifying my past mistakes."

"How does he even know that?" Damien asked quietly.

"No idea," Will replied. It was disturbing that Dracul still had his eyes and ears in the world. He shouldn't have been capable of knowing any such thing. Perhaps he'd merely assumed that when Bran's very public showing had abruptly stopped, that it had meant his death.

Dracul continued in his oily voice. "Our numbers have dwindled considerably, have they not? And with no clear winner as of yet." He paused. "I trust you aren't surprised that I live still. Tell that fucking highlander that his sword wasn't as mighty as he thought. I hope he's enjoying my leftovers, though."

MacLerie growled and took a step toward the TV, as if he intended to rip it off its pedestal and chew it to pieces.

Brenin stopped him with a hand on his chest. "It's only words. He can't hurt me anymore."

"So, I've been lying low, as you'll have surmised, recuperating, regrouping, and I'm ready"—Dracul flashed his fangs—"to finish this. Are you?" He leaned forward. "Don't worry. You don't have to bother finding me. I'll be coming for you."

The screen went black.

Will liked to think he spoke for them all when he said, "Egotistical motherfucker."

Turning off the TV, Alex agreed, "Yes. The consistency is almost comforting. Well, at least we know where we stand. It's convenient, actually, for him to do the traveling."

"Are we really going to just sit here with our thumbs up our asses waiting for him to what? Attack?" Val demanded.

"In a way, yes," Alex replied. "We don't know where to find him, so it always made sense for this whole fucking mess to end here. And we'll be ready. When are the others arriving?" he asked Val.

"This weekend. They're congregating at Christos' in Greece and he's flying them in."

"He's another pilot?" Damien asked Will quietly.

"Eh." Will waggled his hand.

"Then we'll be as ready as we can be," Alex declared.

No one said anything for a good, long while.

It was Annika who broke the silence. "May I have chocolate chip pancakes for breakfast, Father Damien?"

They all turned and stared at her. She smiled brightly back at them.

"Why the hell not?" Will replied. "If we're going to fight for the survival of the world, we may as well have chocolate chip pancakes."

"Exactly," Annika agreed—and who was going to gainsay the Queen?

Epilogue

Annika had picked her favorite dress, the blue velvet with the lace-trimmed sweetheart neckline and the full skirt. It was perhaps a bit childish, but she knew it highlighted the color of her eyes. How she looked mattered in particular, given that she was about to meet the rest of her hive. Mackie had braided her hair in the perfect Elsa style. She felt beautiful and, for some reason, that was important today of all days. No, not some reason. She knew why. She was meeting the last of her drones and she wanted them to see her at her best for this first meeting.

Her fathers stood beside her in the middle of the living room, both looking quite fetching in black pants and shirts, like matching book-ends. She couldn't wait for them to make her a sister. With their similar coloring, they would create a queen far more traditional than she. That would be good. She wanted her hive to be happy and settled, whatever that took. It was sweet the way her fathers both acted as if she were in need of protection. That day would come eventually but not now. The males arriving from the garage at any moment would pledge their devotion to her. She would know if they were sincere or not, just as she had with the hybrid, Bran. And as with that male, any traitors would reveal themselves. They wouldn't be capable of hiding it for long. Then her fathers would, as they'd already done, shield her from harm.

Father Damien leaned closer to her. "I bet you really feel like Elsa now, huh?"

She tried to frown at him but knew she missed the mark. Even after such a short time, she had grown very fond of him. They were often silly together, and better yet, Father Damien had the ability to get Papa to join in. Since they'd become a couple, happiness had entered into Papa's life in ways that she could never provide. She would be eternally grateful that the human had not only accepted their alien culture, but he'd also embraced it.

"Do you think I'd freak everyone out if I broke into *Let It Go*?"

"That depends on how well you can sing it, sweetheart."

"Papa! Was that a joke?" He winked at her. "Father Damien has made his mark, I see. I like it," she added with her own wink.

Oh, this is what they'd lacked all these years — simple joy and the ability to find it even in the worst of circumstances.

"They have arrived," the captain said to the room at large. Everyone was milling about, as if unable to keep still. Only she and her fathers appeared calm. "Val is bringing them in now." That stopped everyone in their tracks. They all concentrated on the elevator doors leading from the garage, and a minute later, they opened.

They came in trailing the warrior—Val, three males, two human mates and two hybrids. They were loaded with bags, a testament to how they were prepared to stay for however long it took. Annika sincerely hoped that it wouldn't take long. She was not a Queen who would require her hive to stick close to her. When it was done and her plan for Earth was in motion, these men could make their home anywhere they wanted. It would be helpful, in fact, that they had already spread out and established roots in various places. They and their families were the seeds of her hive.

One of the humans and his offspring had lovely dark skin, demonstrating that the blending of their species would produce interesting beings who were perhaps better than either of them separately. This was her hope for the future.

They all approached and formed a semi-circle in front of her, the humans and the hybrids being guided by their males. As one, they dropped their bags, then went onto their knees, hands clasped in front of them, heads bowed. It was all perfectly respectful and sent a thrill through her. The boy with the skin like milk chocolate sneaked a peek at her, mischief in his eyes. She wanted to look stern, yet she couldn't help smiling.

These hybrids would make excellent consorts when the time came. And it would, sooner than anyone knew.

Want to see more from this author? Here's a taster for you to enjoy!

Alien Slave Masters: The Undercover Pet
Samantha Cayto

Excerpt

Ben Miller went from having goosebumps to beads of sweat in less than a minute. Naked and leashed, he stumbled out of the small cargo ship along with Rone, Frey and Preen and into a steaming jungle that reminded him of every sci-fi vid he'd ever seen—the kind where bugs as big as houses barged from nowhere to crush you to death and suck your juices. For once, he wasn't focused on the very real danger that Travians presented. Instead, he swiveled his head anxiously to peer through the tall vegetation surrounding the rebels' primitive settlement.

The heat and humidity were oppressive, making it hard to breathe. The weird sounds bombarding him sent a shudder through his body. He felt under attack by millions of insects and other horrors, even though nothing had actually touched him yet. Everything about the planet was inhospitable to a non-insect species, human and Travian alike. Now Ben understood why the rebels had chosen this place to host their base of operations. For beings that naturally preferred cool, clean and orderly, this place would be that last one they'd want to live on. It was the perfect hideout.

Rone's jerk on Ben's leash caused him to stumble, a reminder that he was walking too slowly for his alien master. Frey grabbed his arm to help him keep his footing, giving him a tight smile in the way of an apology. Ben returned the look, letting Frey know that he understood how Rone had to keep up appearances. The whole mission depended on the rebels believing that Rone was a merciless privateer who was delivering a gift, along with more weapons.

He picked up his faltering feet and hunched in on himself, presenting the picture of a cowed and frightened human. It wasn't hard to do, given that at least the second part was true. He was scared spitless of what was to come. If all went as planned, he would soon find himself the possession of the mysterious rebel leader's right-hand male. Dane had already gained a reputation of being a brutal killer. It hadn't been hard for Rone to ferret out the male's name. It was whispered about the far-flung stations of the Travian Empire by vicious aliens that didn't spook easily. Dane, however, terrified even the most ruthless of them. It was said that the male had single-handedly turned on the entire crew of a military cargo ship, slaughtered them then delivered his prize directly to the Leader.

While no one seemed to know the identity of the Leader, and indeed simply called him that—Leader—Dane was well-known. He'd finagled his way to the Leader's side and represented the best way to get into the inner sanctum of the rebellion. If the plan succeeded, Ben would soon be in Dane's bloodthirsty hands. Frey had tried to warn Ben what he might face and provided advice about ways to cope with being a pet. But all the 'lessons' had done was convince him that his life would soon become almost unbearable. There was no real way to prepare for it. His fear had manifested as a large clump lodged tightly in his chest. Instead of trying to banish it, he embraced it. If he was to succeed in his mission, Dane needed to dismiss him as nothing of consequence and not worthy of monitoring.

As they approached the open-sided structure, one of the Travian guards intercepted them. Like the others lounging around staring at them, this guy was practically naked. The only thing he wore besides tall boots was a black loincloth that existed, as near as Ben could tell, as something to rest the weapons belt on around his hips. Seeing all that pale, heavily muscled skin on display, as well as the sizable bulge behind the cloth, gave Ben a small flutter in the pit of his stomach. He supposed it was a good thing that even in his terror, a glimmer of sexual interest shone through. His gay orientation made him the perfect choice for this desperate mission—that and his kick-ass engineering skills. If anyone was going to be able to extract the information they needed from the rebels' computer systems, it was him.

The guard planted his feet, forcing Rone to either stop or plow into him. "What are you doing, privateer? You're not allowed inside."

Being a high-caste male, Rone didn't get intimidated easily. Although Ben barely knew the guy, he could tell by the set of his shoulders that he was relaxed and unimpressed by the show of force. He stood with one hip cocked, the three leashes dangling from one hand. His 'pets', Ben, Frey and the odd little creature, Preen, came to a stop behind him. Ben mimicked Frey's posture, keeping his head down and his hands clasped behind his back. Preen, as usual, marched to a different beat and simply squatted on the hard-packed dirt.

"I wish to speak with Dane." Rone's tone implied boredom, as if the guard was wasting his time.

"No one sees Dane, nor is he interested in what the likes of you have to say." He tossed his head in the direction of Rone's ship. "Go back. You'll get your credits once the cargo is unloaded." The guard turned to walk away.

"Are you so willing to risk the male's wrath?"

That got the guard's attention. He hesitated long enough for Rone to clarify his intent. With a quick jerk of the leash, he had Ben careening forward. The only reason he didn't face plant was because Rone grabbed him by the hair and held him up. Ben had been growing it out for the last few months as this bold plan was being hatched by both humans and Travians far above his pay grade. So, Rone had no trouble fisting enough strands to keep him upright. The grip brought tears to Ben's eyes.

"I have a gift for him." Rone shook Ben's head a little. "A pretty human pet."

In a perverse way, Ben took a measure of pride that he'd been chosen for this mission because of his looks as much as for his skill. While his dark-brown hair and eyes didn't hold Frey's pale, exotic beauty, they were still much different from the unrelentingly black hair and eyes natural to Travians. Plus, Ben's hair, even long, curled enough to make a nice contrast to the straightness of the aliens'.

He kept his gaze downward as the guard silently scrutinized him. The urge to cover his groin with his hands was strong. He made an aborted attempt at it, only to have his hands batted away by Rone hard enough to make him give a small cry of pain. That short show of fear, discomfort and Rone's heartless mastery were all to the good. This was why he'd volunteered for the mission. He'd been seen as the perfect choice. As a soldier — mostly in name only — and a virgin to boot, he wouldn't have to act so much as react to the terrifying situation he was thrust into as a captive. He'd had no training about how to survive as a prisoner and no experience parading around naked in front of anyone outside of a shower.

Dax had argued strongly against picking him, which had made Ben more determined to do it. It also eased his hurt over how the man he loved — Dax — didn't love him back. Dax didn't trust him, apparently, to succeed, either. Ben would show him, and maybe make the man proud. Wen, Dax's alien lover, had counseled Ben about how Travian males viewed younger ones. They liked submission and the mean ones liked instilling fear in their boys. Trusting the advice that his former rival, now friend, had given him, he let the shudder that ran through his body show. And he made only a half-hearted attempt to blink back the tears threatening to leak out.

The guard reached out a hand, making Ben flinch. The alien only managed to skim his chest before Rone yanked him back. "It is for Dane and no other. Even I haven't touched it. But, if you don't think he'll want the pet, I'll be happy to keep it for my own pleasure."

To make his point more clearly, Rone dragged Ben close to his side and cupped Ben's cock and balls with his free hand. Ben barked out a quick cry of distress and jerked away from the hold. At least he tried to. Rone's grip on both Ben's hair and junk tightened, keeping him in place.

He sobbed out a pathetic, "Please," then forced himself to stay still and silent except for his heaving breath. The humidity made it hard for him to seem as if he were getting enough air into his lungs.

"Well?" Rone demanded.

A few seconds ticked by until the guard relented. "Very well. Follow me."

Rone immediately relaxed his grip on Ben's hair and released Ben's cock and balls. The guy even took a second to furtively pat Ben's head before tugging him forward with the leash. They quickly passed an array of guards into the relatively coolness of the open structure.

The rebels had been clever about clearing as little of the jungle as necessary in order for small ships to land and to provide basic living quarters and storage facilities. They could have erected a climate-controlled haven for themselves, yet they had been sufficiently disciplined to forego comfort and convenience to keep their base as unnoticeable from space as possible. Still, a ceiling and walls made from a concrete-like material managed to drop the overall temperature. It also created a dim environment for Ben's human eyes. He squinted to see what lay ahead.

After passing through a small and easily defensible entry room, they arrived at a long corridor. They tramped silently down it and into a much larger, almost cavernous space. At the far end sat a dais with a single high-backed chair — a throne, to Ben's way of thinking. Of course, the Leader must sit there when addressing his males. *Shit*. Ego and ambition seemed to be traits that humans and Travians shared. Although guards ringed the space, the throne was empty at the moment. The only other occupants were a male lounging to one side of the dais on a much smaller chair than the throne. Another Travian kneeled between the male's legs.

Ben squinted to get a better view of the scene as he was yanked along. He couldn't be sure until he got closer, but yeah, the seated male was getting an enthusiastic-appearing blow job. The boy doing the sucking had a cascade of intricate braids down his hunched, slender back. The larger male, likely Dane, had one hand on the boy's head, although it was hard to tell whether that was for convenience or guidance. In his other hand was a tall glass of something. As they approached, Dane shifted his gaze from his boy to their group. He took a lazy sip of his drink while keeping his eyes on them. If he was getting any pleasure from the blow job, his expression didn't show it until the last moment.

Just as the guard and Rone came to a stop, Dane's lips parted on a silent exhalation. He pulled the boy away from his crotch with that hold on the hair then—surprisingly to Ben—shoved his glass to the boy's mouth. The boy accepted the offer before turning around and resting against his master's thigh. The alien had the same kind of elven beauty that Frey had but with Travian coloring. Like Ben and Frey, he was completely naked, except for his collar. No, not only that. A delicate gold chain ran from the collar to rings pierced into his nipples then down his flat, hairless stomach to one hanging loosely around his hips. Yet more chain connected to a series of rings surrounding his long, thin dick and held in place by a piercing through his glans. The adornment was both startling and surprisingly erotic.

The boy flicked his gaze over them, eventually resting it on Ben and giving him a thorough inspection. Frey, who had stopped right behind Rone and next to Ben, gasped softly. Rone jerked on all the leashes briefly, silencing him. Ben gave Rone a sideways glance while resisting the temptation to check out Frey. He didn't understand why he'd reacted as he had. It hardly mattered. It was showtime. If Dane didn't accept him, the whole mission would go to shit.

"What is this?" Dane's icy tone caused the temperature to drop about ten degrees.

The guard answered with obvious trepidation. "Apologies, sire, for the interruption. This male says he has a gift for you."

"Indeed?" Dane's stare was the kind that could turn someone to stone—or at least make them piss themselves.

Rone, though, had ice water running through his veins, as near as Ben could tell. With a jerk, he sent Ben to his knees in front of Dane. "If it pleases you, sire. I would like to show my appreciation for your business by gifting you with this exotic pet. As you can see, it is a human and an untouched one, at that. I would expect it to give you much pleasure, as my own does. I humbly ask you to do me the honor of accepting it."

Mother! Of all the obstacles Dane had expected to encounter on this mission, having a new pet thrust upon him hadn't made the cut. Of course, all the rebels and the scum they dealt with like this privateer tried to curry favor with him. Everyone wanted to advance, to get closer to the Leader, and Dane had succeeded in planting himself right in the middle of that path. He was used to deflecting bribes of various sorts and more personal favors being offered. This, however, was something entirely new and different—a fetching human boy kneeled at his feet, quivering with fear.

His fingers tightened involuntarily, eliciting a mew of pain from Kath. Dane immediately loosened his grip.

Kidnapping a fuck boy and forcing him to be his pet had helped create and maintain his carefully constructed persona of a vicious, murderous traitor to his people. And while he had to treat him harshly in public, he also tried not to be too gratuitous about it. He changed his hold to a petting motion—condescending, yet not painful. That was the most he could do for the boy at this point. Later, when this damnable rebellion had been crushed for good, he would do what he could to make up this period in the boy's life. Perhaps he could even find him a position that didn't involve selling his body to strange males.

He lounged against his chair and affected the bored attitude that served him well among these cutthroats. They saw him as confident, which led to them being less so. It gave him an edge that he desperately needed with the whole group, especially the Leader, most importantly. His relaxed air, along with a few personal challenges that ended in bloody death, had eased his way to the Leader's side. He only needed a little more time and he was sure he could raid the Leader's personal files and gain the definitive list of who within Travian society belonged to this heinous movement.

"An excellent effort to gain my favor, privateer. But as you can see, I already have a pet." Dane tugged gently on Kath's hair so that the boy's face lifted for inspection.

The privateer tipped his head in acknowledgement. "Very pretty, sir, and I expect highly trained. Too trained, perhaps." Reaching down, he mimicked Dane by yanking the human's head back by his long, curly hair. "This creature has a more exotic allure, don't you agree? And I can assure you from personal experience with my pet that human bodies are delightfully tighter than any Travian's."

"I would expect so," Dane murmured, racking his brain for a good reason to refuse the offering. "How did you acquire these creatures?" Now, he was just stalling for time.

Rone nodded toward the fair-haired boy behind him. "That one I won off a male too stupid to keep it. This one," he added with another yank of the kneeling boy's hair, "I captured when I raided a human cargo ship. These inferior beings sometimes possess goods of interest to our people. It was easy enough to overpower and slaughter them, and I hoped to find something of value to your cause. Unfortunately, this boy was all that was worthy of your attention. It was difficult not to take for my own pleasure, but I thought you'd appreciate unsullied goods."

Clever male... He was trying to remind Dane of his own supposed feat of mutiny in which he'd murdered his captain and crew to deliver weapons to the rebels. That setup had been carefully orchestrated by the Supreme Council.

"Humans have nothing of use to us or our cause, privateer." He let derision drip from his tongue. "I expect I could find some pleasure in this thing you offer me, but I'm quite satisfied with what I have."

He pushed Kath's face back into his crotch and willed his dick to stiffen again. These public shows of sex seemed to cement his control over the rank and file even more, dumb males that they were. The fuck boy immediately started lapping at Dane's cock and balls to encourage his erection.

The privateer inhaled deeply and inclined his head. "Very well. I am disappointed that I couldn't serve you better. I'll leave the human as a fuck toy for the others."

The head guard, Abell, who'd stood quietly to one side after bringing the privateer and his exotic menagerie in, huffed in amusement. "On behalf of my males and I, we accept the gift."

Right. It must have taken the span of a heartbeat for Rone to take Abell's measure. The male wasn't very smart and somewhat lazy in his ambition. The idea that he would share the human with others was a laughable lie. He'd hoard the human pet for himself then parade his exotic prize in front of him and the Leader. The privateer was cleverer than most of his ilk. He clearly knew that Dane would never tolerate a subordinate having something better than what he did. And an untrained human pet was something to covet more than a trained fuck boy.

Shit!

When Abell moved to take possession of the boy's leash, Dane stopped him with a word. "No." He kept his tone calm and his voice low, having found that being understated was more impressive than being overtly aggressive.

Abell stopped in his tracks and shot Dane an eyeful of pure hatred before wisely banking his reaction.

"I have changed my mind. Your thoughtful gift is gladly accepted." He shoved Kath away and flicked down the kilt he'd taken to wearing in the oppressive heat to cover his only half-hard dick. "Go get him."

Kath stood with the supple grace of his kind. The body chain Dane forced him to wear tinkled with every step. Every pair of Travian eyes tracked the boy's sensuous movements as he approached the privateer. No surprise. Kath was a beautiful boy. In the proper garments, he would make a convincing female. Dane had recognized the value of using him as an ornament the moment he'd seen him in the seedy victual establishment on an outer station.

The boy had a certain pride to him, as well. Even naked and adorned like the slut he was, he glided across the floor with enviable confidence as if the guards' attention was beneath his notice. He stopped in front of the privateer and held out his hand.

"Sire?" Kath's silky voice was like a caress up Dane's cock. He bet every male had the same reaction.

Kath dared to shoot Rone a silent *what the fuck?* from under his lashes as he demurely waited for the male to hand him over the end of the human's leash.

Rone gave him a subtle reply by the twitching of his eyebrows. The male was obviously surprised to see him there. Kath understood that, of course. Dane had snatched him so fast from his station that he hadn't had time to convey the sudden, yet useful, change in his status. At least now Rone would be able to confirm to their superiors that not only was Kath still alive, he had become well-placed to discover the full roster of traitorous males in their midst.

That didn't explain what Rone was up to. He'd obviously been working on getting closer to the rebel base by slowly taking over Kuren's old privateering territory—or at least that was what Kath had heard. Bringing a human boy as an offering to get in his good graces made sense if Rone were truly the vicious privateer he pretended to be. Dane had quickly become the most direct path to the reclusive Leader. Kath knew, however, that Rone wasn't such a male. His treatment of his own pets, both the beautiful human boy and the lavender creature squatting by his feet, belied that idea. *So, what exactly is the plan here?*

Sign up for our newsletter and find out about all our romance book releases, eBook sales and promotions, sneak peeks and FREE romance books!

About the Author

Samantha Cayto is a Boston-area native who practices as a business lawyer by day while writing erotic romance at night—the steamier the better. She likes to push the envelope when it comes to writing about passion and is delighted other women agree that guy-on-guy sex is the hottest ever.

She lives a typical suburban life with her husband, three kids and four dogs. Her children don't understand why they can't read what she writes, but her husband is always willing to lend her a hand—and anything else—when she needs to choreograph a scene.

Samantha loves to hear from readers. You can find her contact information, website details and author profile page at https://www.pride-publishing.com

Lightning Source UK Ltd.
Milton Keynes UK
UKHW010736170920
370067UK00001B/43